A MESSAGE FROM CHICKEN HOUSE

M. A. Griffin's heart-in-the-mouth thriller is about the brave kids who fight back against a government plot to make prison permanent. In a world that feels like tomorrow – a world of school, friends and first love shadowed by adult corruption – it's only the teenagers who can expose the truth. And the government scheme they uncover is far more sinister than anyone could have guessed . . . Sound familiar? Let's hope not!

BARRY CUNNINGHAM
Publisher
Chicken House

LIFERS

M.A. GRIFFIN

Chicken House

2 Palmer Street, Frome, Somerset BA11 1DS
www.chickenhousebooks.com

Text © M. A. Griffin 2016

First published in Great Britain in 2016
Chicken House
2 Palmer Street
Frome, Somerset BA11 1DS
United Kingdom
www.chickenhousebooks.com

Cover and interior design by Helen Crawford-White
Typeset by Dorchester Typesetting Group Ltd
Printed and bound in Great Britain by CPI Group (UK) Ltd, Croydon CR0 4YY

The paper used in this Chicken House book is made from wood grown in sustainable forests.

1 3 5 7 9 10 8 6 4 2

British Library Cataloguing in Publication data available.

PB ISBN 978-1-910002-25-4
eISBN 978-1-910002-26-1

For Jake, Maya, Eva, Aggie and Amelia

1

It must have been quiet for him to hear the rattling.

That's what the noise first seemed to be: a sound like the clatter of dice in a plastic cup.

It was coming from the darkness at the far end of Back Half Moon Street. Preston pushed himself upright against a rusting roll-top bin and peered into the gloom. Now it was a stuttering *chit-chit* sound; something about it immediately wrong.

It made the space between Preston's shoulder blades go cold, his back straighten and his stomach tighten.

Preston realized his legs were struggling for strength. It was hard to see what might be down there — it was 2 a.m. and ink-black. Above him the outline of a fire escape. At his feet, a blown can skittered. The alley curved left and he made his way towards the bend. The building stopped a few paces ahead of him and a space with a high metal railing around it emerged from deep shadow. Sirens wailed somewhere in the distance but faded into silence.

Chitter-chit-chit.

Preston felt panic rising in his chest. *Christ. A beast at the end of the alley.* Fighting his fear, he edged forwards and peered beyond the fencing. Over the railings was a drop and beyond that a sunken garden, high-walled, spread out around the back of the main building. The windows were shuttered and dark. There were a couple of low outbuildings – both rendered white – and a security barrier and office, lights out. Down in the sunken area, a black Lexus was parked.

He'd never seen this place before.

Fourteen years tracing the shape of Manchester, and he'd never followed the left-hand curve of Back Half Moon. But why would you? Thousands of commuters, bankers, buskers and shoppers would pass by the mouth of the alley every day without ever thinking anything of interest lay beyond.

He'd never night-walked before, either.

Everything was different at night, like turning over a stone and seeing something weird and alien underneath. Watching something that was usually ignored, usually . . . unwatched.

The sound; the *chitter-chit* sound was still down there in the dark somewhere. Preston studied the alleyway ahead of him, letting the memory of Alice brighten the darkness, only to remember she was gone. It had been over forty-eight hours since she'd disappeared, and it was all his fault. He *had* to find her.

Preston gave the buildings beyond the high fence a final furtive check. Then he shinned up and over it, lowering himself down the other side. It's what Alice would have done – he felt sure of it.

The sunken garden was further down than he had thought. He let himself drop and landed in a crouch. He looked up. Over three metres to the top of the fence; he wouldn't be getting out the way he'd come in. He spent a moment praying he wasn't permanently trapped on the wrong side with a terrible creature.

His eyes adjusted to the gloom. There was the Lexus, three empty parking spaces around it. There were clipped hedges, a pool and an urn, steel planters with elegantly shaped trees in them. There were lights inlaid along the paths, half-lit, like eyes. This wasn't a house. It was corporate. The windows were for offices, or labs, Preston thought. *What is this place – pharmaceuticals?* He made his way forwards. The sound was louder.

The back of the building was four storeys of white render and steel, windows of mirrored glass. On the top floor, a light was on – a surprise in the early hours of a Monday morning – and Preston could see the silhouette of piled files, papers and a glowing desk lamp bent over as if in prayer. Someone was up there, working late. Small polished signs studded the outside of the building at shoulder height, like those brass plaques beside the doors of solicitors' offices. As he drew closer he saw each displayed an acronym – M.I.S.T.

His heart gave a jump. *Mist.* He'd seen that in Alice's notebook.

She'd been here.

The sound, eerie and unnerving, was getting louder. Preston padded down a gravel path, rain falling, the green fans of uplit garden ferns glistening. He turned back to take another look around.

Then he saw it.

A flight of sunken steps dropped to a doorway set at cellar level, a steel fire door with one of those bars across it that made it look like it was for escape only. The door was propped open, and inside was dark, but it wasn't inside that Preston was looking at.

Preston was looking at the kid in the goggles.

Two steps up from the door, hunched in a crouch on his heels, was a boy dressed in black. It was his teeth Preston could hear, clattering in his mouth. He was suffering some sort of fit, shuddering there in the foetal position as if a current was being fed through him. His feet shifted and jerked in a way that looked as if some invisible force was needling him from all sides and he was recoiling from a thousand fearsome pin-pricks. His chin was pressed against his chest.

Preston dropped to a crouch and felt his blood ice up. He didn't doubt for a second he was seeing something unnatural. This wasn't some sort of epileptic fit; it was something more controlled. Then there was the sound coming from the kid's mouth, the machine-gun rhythm of his teeth. The sound he'd heard in the alley.

Preston staggered backwards, half-running until he felt himself thump against the perimeter of the sunken garden. He lost his footing and sat down hard. He wanted to look away, but he found he couldn't; he had to watch as the kid twisted and shuddered.

It was slowing now. A moment later, he was still, curled up on his side. His teeth had stopped. Preston tried to swallow, but his throat had filled with sand. His heart felt close to bursting. *Had the kid passed out? Or had Preston just watched someone die?*

The fire door clanged in its frame, making an empty steel echo. It had stopped raining, Preston realized. He put his face in his hands for a moment, shook his head clear and looked at the kid again. He remembered reading that insomniacs often suffered hallucinations.

That was it, he thought – he was going mad. Some kind of reaction to everything that had happened. First Mum leaving. Dad losing it. Now Alice going missing.

He pressed his palms into the gravel at his feet and felt the sharp stones sting his skin. It didn't feel like a dream or some sort of nervous breakdown. The kid – probably dead, Preston guessed – was still there, curled up like a newborn. Preston rose to standing, using the wall for balance, testing his legs. A wave of sickness climbed his body, then faded. He waited for a moment then he made his way forwards, his trainers crunching on the gravel. His pace slowed as he reached the top of the steps leading down to the fire door, clammy fear running a finger down his back. The boy didn't seem to be breathing.

He looked weird. His final fit had thrown the goggles from his face. Preston checked the building. The light was still on in the top-floor office, but no one was watching. He stooped and picked the goggles up. They were still warm from the kid's skin. They were like no goggles he'd ever seen before, the lenses enlarged to the size of saucers. Preston wasn't about to hold them to his face – a crazy kind of terror prevented him – but if he had, they'd have covered most of his forehead and both cheeks, almost reaching his top lip. The frames were made of something odd: black and soft and pliable but not rubber. And the lenses were weirdly thick and heavy. When Preston gingerly held them up, it was clear they were close to impossible to see through, the kind of things you might imagine an astronomer wearing to stare into the boiling heart of a star. He dropped them on the steps next to the curled up boy, suddenly desperate to be away and clear of the building, back down Half Moon and out on to Deansgate, where there were bars and bookshops and takeaways and maybe some people at a taxi rank being normal. He should check if the kid was breathing, he knew he should. But the boy and the goggles were horrible.

Preston made his way back to the perimeter wall. 'I'm not going mad,' he said in a whisper, wiping his palms against his jeans. The clouds broke for a moment and the moon appeared. This was better. The world, which had slipped its axis and gone lunatic for a moment, seemed normal again. He was in an empty car park with a black Lexus in it, not on another planet. 'I'm not going mad.' He leant against the cool brickwork and wiped the rain from his face with the sleeve of his coat. 'I'm not going mad,' said Preston one last time, just to be clear.

And that was when he heard the voice.

'Kid.'

It was a cracked voice, deep and urgent, and it was coming from somewhere in the darkness above him. Preston looked, trying to trace it.

'Kid,' it said again, and this time the voice had softened, as if it was taking pity. Preston realized he had a hand across his mouth to stop himself screaming with fear. His heart was bucking so hard he felt it was about to punch him open.

Then a face appeared at the railings above him; a man with shoulder-length hair and a dark military cap. He was up and over the fence swiftly and dropped to join Preston, wincing as he straightened up.

He too was dressed in black: close-fitting combat trousers, heavy boots, big gloves with padded silver fingers, a bag strapped diagonally across his chest. His face was deeply lined and his rough skin dusted in grey stubble. He was well over forty, Preston figured – but broad and strong. He scowled. 'This is no place for a schoolkid,' the man said. He had a scratchy northern voice. 'You need to go.'

Preston was too taken aback to answer.

The man regarded him carefully. He seemed troubled. He looked across to the open fire door, the small bundle of darkness that was the boy, and checked the light in the high office window, his face tight. He tore back a Velcro panel in the left arm of his jacket and pulled out a little radio.

'We have a situation here,' he said into it. There was the crunch of static and chopped-up garble. The man struck his radio sharply with an open gloved hand and swore. 'Say again,' he said. He didn't talk like a cop, Preston thought; there was a scruffy roughness about him. Security guards didn't look like this either – they were usually broader guys with bad tattoos and beer on their breath.

His radio fizzed again and this time the man heard whatever answer he'd been expecting. 'Exactly,' he said, and turned to Preston, pocketing the radio once more.

'Whatever you've seen, kid – I'm going to need you to forget it.'

Preston found himself stammering. 'What? I haven't seen anything.'

The man regarded him, one eyebrow raised. 'You sure?'

Preston nodded, a little too eagerly, he knew. 'Seriously.' It sounded as hollow as a homework excuse. 'I've not seen anything. I was looking for a friend.' That bit, at least, was true. 'I was following her. I thought she'd come down here.'

The man nodded. 'Well. You'll need to be getting home.' And then he held out a palm, as if to shake. 'Here,' he said. It seemed an odd gesture, a stranger in a black bodysuit in a city-centre car park with an outstretched glove. Why did Preston take it? He didn't know. Pressure. Fear. Stupidity. The handshake was firm and the man released a little smile of – what – relief? Something stung Preston in the centre of the hand, like a wasp between their palms. He winced.

'Sorry, kid.' The man shrugged. Then he said, 'Sleeptight.'

Preston examined his palm. There was a little bead of blood there. His head swam and for a mad moment he thought his hand had a little eye in its centre like the one in Alice's notebook. But it didn't; he was just bleeding. 'I haven't slept yet,' he said absently. 'Not since Alice.'

Then Preston found his jaw didn't work any more. His perspective tipped and he fell over, conscious that the man was still watching him even as he felt the gravel against his cheek. He tried to say something and it came out a garbled grunt, like the radio. He felt himself cough. Then his eyes shut themselves and he slept.

2

Preston woke late. He'd slept in his clothes. His knees were bruised and a low pain throbbed as he shifted position. For a while he lay still, staring at the ceiling of his room, a headache probing the backs of his eyes.

He needed painkillers. He reached for a glass of water by his bed and felt his phone in his pocket as he shifted position. He dug it out, his fingers clumsy. It took him three goes to get his passcode right.

There was a text message waiting for him and he hit the icon, blinking the sleep from his eyes. When he saw it, Preston felt a blur of heat in his chest. *My God. It was from Alice.* For a second, he couldn't breathe. He opened the text.

Sorry, it said. *Going in.*

That was it. Three days of silence. Three words. He stared at it, put the phone down, then picked it up and stared again. It had come last night, just after three in the morning. A matter of hours ago.

'Press.' He discarded the phone hurriedly and struggled up on to his elbows. His dad was at the door. 'You were late last night,' his father said. 'I heard you come in but I was in bed.'

Preston licked his lips – they were cracked – and smiled. 'Sorry, Dad,' he said, reaching for the first lie that came to him. 'I was at Mace's place. Lost track of time.'

PC Faulkner straightened his back, took his cap off and ran a hand over his scalp. He was wearing full uniform. He'd lost weight since his wife had gone and it looked too large for him. The ironed shirt with the top button done up meant a big job: maybe a briefing or major deployment rota. The line – *I was in bed* – meant he'd drunk so much he couldn't remember anything. Preston couldn't either. They watched each other briefly, neither able to speak, neither recalling much of the night before. *We need our old lives back*, Preston thought.

'It's your interview this morning,' his father said, examining the cuffs of his jacket unhappily. 'At the station, remember? With the DCI. I'll take you.'

Preston swung his legs out of bed. This was the one he'd been dreading, the interview with Detective Chief Inspector Sinclair that Mace had helped him script. It was going to be mostly lies. 'I'll just be a minute,' he said. He needed to check the text again.

But his dad stayed in the doorway. He spoke haltingly. 'Just tell the truth, pal,' he said. 'I wouldn't want you getting in any trouble . . .'

Preston nodded. 'The DCI's your boss. I get it.'

'And I'm sorry about Alice. I really am.'

For a second, Preston wondered if his dad somehow knew

about the text. He rubbed his eyes, and waved his father away. 'Yeah,' he said. 'I know.'

Preston sat in the interview room, his head throbbing.

He had a sour taste in his mouth. His hand hurt, too. He winced, looking at it under the table. There was a bruise the size of a small coin right in the centre of his palm, as if he'd been pierced by a splinter. He picked at the scab and it bled freshly. The wound was small and clean. Was it a sting? He couldn't remember. 'We're here to talk about Alice Wilde,' said DCI Sinclair. She didn't look at Preston as she spoke, just tapped the end of her pencil against the desk and lifted the corner of the folder she'd set down. Preston shifted in his seat, rubbed his palms together. He'd never been in an interrogation room before.

Of course he knew they were here to talk about Alice. He'd been practising. So he said, 'I know.'

Sinclair looked at him. She was a middle-aged woman with a tired face, dark eyes and tousled grey-black hair. She rubbed her chin with the thumb of her left hand. 'Mr Faulkner,' she said after an extended blink. 'This isn't a game. It isn't TV. I suggest you co-operate.'

Preston felt himself blush. He hadn't meant it as a wise-crack. He didn't want to disgrace his dad. But ever since Alice had gone missing, he'd had trouble thinking straight – especially after last night. Especially after the message out of nowhere. Sinclair switched a digital recorder on and spoke into it: the date, the time. Then she pushed a photograph across the table, pinned it with an index finger and spun it. 'Showing Preston Faulkner a recent photograph of Alice Wilde,' Sinclair said. Preston looked into Alice's face and felt

11

his body loosen with fear.

He knew the picture, of course; it was that one of them both that Mace had taken in December. There was a little wink of coloured light in the background from the Christmas tree on St Ann's Square. Alice was pure Alice – wide warm smile, freckled nose, big brown eyes, hair pulled back and tied, woolly hat with ear-flaps, badge front and centre, the one that said 'Get Happy!'

The picture had been cut down the middle, Preston sliced off. He could just see the shoulder of his winter coat. He'd sat next to her and they'd eaten hot dogs from the markets. Late-night shopping; maybe the Thursday before school broke up – Alice pushing her bike across St Ann's Square, Mace listing the worst Christmas number ones, then singing snatches of each in turn, his mock-choirboy voice making them laugh. Preston felt tears starting to come and had to look away. Crying hadn't been part of the plan. *Grip it*, he told himself.

'When did you last see Alice Wilde?' asked Sinclair. Preston swallowed hard and bit a fingernail. *Breathe*, he told himself. *Get it right. Remember what Mace said: the best lies are the ones closest to the truth.*

'Couple of days ago,' he said. 'Friday. The fourteenth.' He'd told this story a few times now, but only to himself in the bathroom mirror. Any inconsistencies, and Sinclair would be on to them, probing and tugging until it all unravelled. Then she'd be outside telling Dad his kid was a liar and Faulkner senior wouldn't be able to show his face in the station again. Having his son interviewed by his boss while he paced up and down outside in his uniform must feel pretty bad as it was, Preston figured.

12

And then there was Alice. He couldn't let her down either – he'd made her a promise. It's just that he hadn't ever dreamt it would come to this.

'Tell me about your final meeting,' said Sinclair, her gaze cold and steady.

This was it. Preston took a shaky breath and started. 'It was Friday night,' he said. 'Start of half-term. Maybe six thirty. Alice came round after school.'

'She often do that?' Sinclair said.

Preston nodded.

'Describe her behaviour that evening please, Mr Faulkner.'

Easy: she'd been weird. All wrong. He'd tried to get it out of her, but she didn't want to talk. Instead, she'd skipped through some tunes, half-watched Netflix; restless, walked to the window and back, looked down at the rush-hour traffic. Preston had kept pushing. They'd known each other since they were three – that's what you get from living across the corridor in the same block; Alice and her mum in 23, Preston and his dad in 25 – you get to know a person so well you know when they are hiding something. And Alice hadn't been right for ages. Weeks. Since she hooked up with Ryan, in fact.

Then, just as she had to go home for tea, there was the crazy promise she made him keep. The pleading eyes. She'd held his hands in hers, tight around the knuckles until his fingers went white; she was intense. Scared.

'Alice was fine that night,' said Preston, and he raised a smile – the same empty one he'd given the visiting community officer when he'd asked all this stuff yesterday. 'We listened to some music, we watched a bit of TV. She talked about her homework. She was looking forward to the holiday. We both were. Then she went.'

Sinclair's face went empty. She didn't like what she was hearing, but she was trying to keep it out of her voice and eyes. This cop was cleverer than the community support guys, though, Preston was sure of that. She was going to see through this. 'I need you to think hard,' she said. 'This could be important. Did Alice have anything unusual to say to you? Any –' she paused, looking for an appropriate phrase – 'last words?'

Yeah, three of them. They came this morning.

'Press,' she said that previous Friday evening, holding his hands too tight. She stood close to him. Their feet were almost touching at the toes. 'I need you to listen. What if I went night-walking and didn't come back?'

And since those ten words, Preston hadn't slept. Instead he'd been fighting his bedsheets through the empty hours when the city outside dreamt, and hearing Alice ask him, 'What if I went night-walking and didn't come back?' over and over again. He'd known better than to laugh when she first said it. She'd been doing that thing with her lips – pushing them tight together in a thin line – that she did before exams when she was thinking things out.

Plus, it was the closest their faces had been since for ever. Since they'd been really small, since way back, when close faces didn't mean anything. He could see her pupils dilate, feel her breath on his lips. She smelt of science, period five, the day before October half-term. It was her last year of high school.

'What do you mean?' Night-walking, he was thinking, and a dark half-understanding was starting to grow, a sense that

things weren't the same between them any more.

'Say I went away,' Alice said. 'Exploring.'

He thought of her on her bike – the beat-up BMX she wheeled round town at weekends. 'Exploring what?'

Alice shrugged. 'The unwatched life,' she said. She was all riddles that night, as if she was speaking a script. 'You'd come and find me, wouldn't you?' She was close to whispering. It sounded like a threat.

'Yeah.' There'd been next to no hesitation in Preston's answer. 'I'd find you,' he said. And he'd meant it.

'Mr Faulkner,' Sinclair said slowly. 'My question.'

Preston felt the heat in the memory fade. He didn't like being referred to as Faulkner. *PC Faulkner* – that was Dad, not him. 'She didn't say anything unusual,' he said. 'Just "see you tomorrow" or something like that. I mean, I can't remember exactly, but . . .' he trailed off. Mace had warned him against over-talking.

'And you're sure about that?'

'Yes. I'm sure.'

'Because you don't sound it.' Sinclair leant back in her chair. Her suit jacket was creased at the crooks of her elbows. Her white blouse was crumpled. The light above them had started an exasperated buzz.

'I am,' said Preston. This time he made sure his voice was firm.

Sinclair gave a little grunt and returned her attention to the folder, leafing thoughtfully. 'And there's been no contact since then?'

'None.' She'd spot the lie, surely. Preston felt his phone pressing against his thigh, front-right pocket of his jeans.

15

Sorry. Going in. It felt warm, as if it was overheating. What if the DCI asked him to place it on the desk? He tried not to squirm. 'None,' he said again.

'She didn't call or text – and make you promise not to mention it?' Sinclair's pause was perfectly timed. She smiled. 'To the police, for example.'

Preston bit his tongue. *Friday night* he thought. *She means Friday night.*

She'd shouldered her school bag and made for the door. Still wound up tight and frightened, but at the same time with that shine in her face that came when she had purpose. 'One more thing, Press,' she'd said. 'Will you promise me something?'

He'd still not clocked how serious this was getting – that would come later, in the long, stripped-back hours of sleeplessness, listening to sirens and students out on the streets below the high-rise. 'Sure. Anything.'

'If the cops come, don't tell them about this.'

He had laughed. There was no hint of levity in her expression, though. Her eyes were big and serious, her neat fingers tight around the strap of her bag. His face had fallen then. 'Course,' he'd stuttered. 'I won't let you down.'

Two hours later, he would let her down in ways he couldn't have possibly imagined, ways that would wake him up and torture him at night.

'No,' Preston lied. 'She never even mentioned police – why would she?'

Sinclair had found the sheet of paper she wanted. She raised it, bent it towards herself and studied it. 'We're just about done here,' she said, looking up, sustaining that empty smile. Stupidly, Preston smiled back. The heat of the relief had tipped him off guard. 'Before I get you back to your father, though, I wonder whether you can tell us anything about this, Mr Faulkner?'

Sinclair placed the sheet of paper on the table between them.

Preston felt his heart give a start of recognition. He felt his mouth open slightly, his eyes widen. Sinclair had got him. Whatever he'd promised Alice, he'd given himself away in the closing moments of the interview.

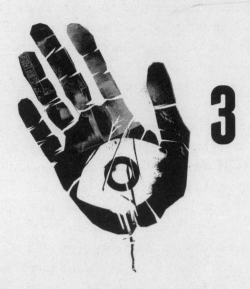

3

The picture was a graphic of a hand, open-palmed with its fingers unfolding. There was an eye in its palm. And underneath was the part the DCI wanted him to see. Sinclair would know he recognized the writing there.

The Jupiter Hand, the text said. And underneath, a version of those weird words Alice had chosen when they'd last met: *Watchers of the unwatched life.*

The light flickered and buzzed. *Unwatched. Weird choice of word.* The room seemed to dip into darkness, as if a shadow had shouldered the moon out for a moment. Preston rubbed his eyes.

'Familiar?' Sinclair asked. Her hand was poised, pencil at the ready.

She wanted answers.

He'd first seen the hand and the eye that previous autumn. DCI Sinclair's question brought it all rushing back. In a weird way, it might have been the last time they'd been happy together, that day way back, Alice and Mace and him. Properly, stupidly, carelessly happy, as they used to be at junior school.

They'd been walking across the playing fields, back from the shops, the grass half-mud, the rain coming down in fine sheets. They'd got cans of pop and gummy bears, heavy wet coats and cold hands, and they were heading for the warmth of the computer rooms.

The three of them had logged on, a desktop each, side-by-side. There'd been a handful of other students around that day: a kid finishing a Textiles project; two girls giggling at a bunch of online videos. Mace had tried stealing Alice's sweets, but ended up yanking a book from her bag instead. With Alice, there was always a book. This one had been a big, battered novel with Post-its fringing key pages, a bearded guy in a prison cell on the cover.

'What's that?' Preston had said.

Alice had looked up from her screen, distracted. 'The Count of Monte Cristo,' she'd said. 'Guy called Dantès gets framed for a crime. Banged up in this weird nightmare prison on an island off the south coast of France. Classic. Way too complicated for your tiny brains, boys.' Mace had riffled through it, started reading sections in a silly voice. 'Elliot Mason,' Alice had declared flatly, 'sometimes I genuinely wish we'd never met.' She'd pulled up a website and had been spending the last few minutes silently studying it.

Mace was still skimming with a grin. 'You know what the CIA were fond of doing with American prisoners?'

Preston and Alice had groaned as one. 'I'm sure you're going to tell us,' Preston had said.

'I'm one hundred and twenty per cent serious, brotherman. Mind control experiments. They ran for over twenty years, starting in the fifties. Seriously . . .'

Preston had got pretty adept at switching off when Mace got like this, and he'd found himself reading Alice's screen over her shoulder instead. 'Urban explorers?' he'd said, studying the site. 'Urbex? What's that?'

Alice had raised her chin from her hand and indicated the screen. 'The real world's interesting enough if you look at it the right way. Lift your eyes,' she'd said. Then she'd repeated it – kind of implored it, really, 'Lift your eyes, Press.'

'What are we looking at?' he said.

Alice had scrolled down then, leaning back from the screen so they could see. It was a community site: posts with text and pictures from loads of members. The pictures looked like a collection of interiors – abandoned buildings, stairwells, lift shafts, rooftops. Then they changed into cityscapes at night, shot from tall buildings. Then one from the gantry of a crane. One from the teetering summit of a skyscraper.

Alice had grinned at them and her eyes had danced brightly. 'Urban explorers look at the world in a different way,' she'd said, her voice dropping to a whisper. 'They go looking for the secret parts of cities.'

'Where is that?' Mace had said, pressing a sticky index finger against the screen. Alice had shrugged, scrolled up and down a little more.

'Any of Manchester?'

'Oh yeah, plenty.' Alice had taken them back to the home page then. And there'd been a series of tabs giving access to the posts in complex categories. Preston still remembered the list: Cranes. Hospitals and asylums. Tower blocks. Sewers and cellars.

He gave a whistle. 'Nice one.'

Alice was filtering the entries according to place now. She found Manchester and brought up the posts. At the top of the list was a post – some guy calling himself Urbex808 had put it up – composed of a series of pictures taken from the telecom tower – the city a blanket of golden lights beneath the glow of a smoky autumn evening, the sun still blurring the edges of the skyline. There was no doubt, Preston thought; it was daring and impressive stuff. The telecom tower was seriously high.

Mace had nearly choked on his gummy bears. 'Christ!' he'd said. 'How did they get up there?'

Alice gave a satisfied smile. 'See?' she'd said, turning the screen so they could all look. 'Everything looks different if you know where to go. Nothing's boring. Our problem is – we forget how to look. We forget to lift our eyes.'

There'd been a silence then, and Alice had retraced her clicks, back to the home page. It was strangely designed – all gothic black decorations. At the top of the screen was the site's unusual title: The Jupiter Hand. And to the right of the text, the image Sinclair was to show him months later: the open-palmed hand with its curling fingers, the eye nestled in the centre of the palm like a dark coin. Underneath the picture was the phrase, 'Watchers of the unwatched life'. It had struck Preston as stupid and funny and a bit self-important sounding at the time. He'd grinned at it as he read – whoever these guys are, they really fancy themselves, he thought.

But he didn't think that now. That image, that weird phrase, made him cold and uneasy. There was something sinister lurking under it. Something dangerous.

'How did you find this?' he'd said.

'Ryan,' Alice had said. She'd shrugged, pulled off her hat and

21

ruffled her hair.

She hadn't elaborated.

That reluctance to speak, Preston thought in the back of the car as his dad drove him home from the police station, had been something to do with Ryan. Even way back then, before they'd started to drift apart, she'd been seeing Ryan. She hadn't told them; she'd kept it secret – they wouldn't find out about it till much nearer Christmas – but she'd been with him.

He was the one who had got her into this stuff.

4

His dad dropped him back at the flats, lingering in the lobby with the squad car on double yellows outside while Preston waited for the lift.

'I'd better go,' his father said, raising a weary hand, palm out – a signal that seemed to mean both stop and goodbye both at once. 'I'm on nights after this, remember,' he added, 'running around after politicians. There's that big New Conservative conference the day after tomorrow.' He replaced his cap.

Preston tried summoning a smile. 'Have a good day, Dad.'

Upstairs in the flat, he shut the door of his room behind him. For a few moments he stared at his things, feeling somehow detached from his surroundings. His books looked odd: a bunch of photography manuals, a load of travel writing from Mum – the stuff that always got her enthusiastic – a bunch of comics. The pile of magazines at the foot of his desk seemed somehow childish. So did the skateboard and the cycle helmet with its stupid stickers. If he'd ever had a younger brother, Preston thought, this is what his room would've looked like. It was like a bedroom borrowed from another boy. He sat on the bed and wiped his face.

No wonder Alice preferred hanging out with Ryan. Sharing secret plans with him. Scribbling in her notebook.

Preston blinked his head clear. *Her notebook.* It came back to him as if it had been waiting for this moment to reveal itself.

Wednesday morning, the previous week; he and Alice and Mace sharing greasy hash browns from a paper plate in the school canteen before the start of lessons.

Alice was up at the counter getting hot chocolate and her school bag was on the table in front of them, her copy of The Count of Monte Cristo *sitting open on the table with Post-its marking the pages she liked.*

Mace was goofing around. 'Oooh!' he'd said, going through Alice's stuff with a grin. 'A diary!' And then he was pulling out a notebook from the back of Alice's bag: proper grown-up notebook with a loop of elastic to hold a pen against it. 'Dear Diary,' Mace had begun, adopting a feminine squeak. He unsnapped the elastic loop. 'Today I realized the true emptiness of my life. Hanging out with two Year Tens with only a brain cell to share between them has finally driven me to despair . . .' Preston had laughed through the performance. Mace was right; the two of them often said that if they'd never shared the same tower block, there was no way Alice would've ever come near them: two lads a year younger and a whole lifetime less cool.

Then Mace had opened the notebook and instead of

continuing his performance, his face had hardened into something sombre. 'What's this?' he'd said, placing the notebook open on the table between them. Preston had checked for Alice then, feeling a little fist of guilt against his stomach. She was queuing for her drink. They shouldn't be looking at her stuff like this. Preston had leant forward.

There were maps. Pages and pages of little hand-drawn pencil maps. Manchester streets, routes, sections of the city circled.

'Put it back, Mace,' said Preston.

Mace had pulled a face. 'Pirate treasure!'

Some of the maps were coloured; felt-tip lines in red and blue and black. One or two had been crossed out entirely, scribbled through and replaced by new versions. One page had the word mist *written across it, and a loop of felt-tip around it. Even at the time Preston had thought it was strange, tucked away at the end of Back Half Moon Street. And on another page, Alice had drawn an open hand with an eye in its palm. The one that Sinclair had shown him. The one on the website. This wasn't homework or revision or stuff for exams. The two of them had known, instinctively somehow, that the contents of the notebook were a private matter, a secret project.

Alice was coming over now, walking slowly, tired. 'Put it back,' Preston had said, and they'd fumbled it between them for a moment, so that she saw before they could slip it back in her bag.

The weird thing? She'd been really angry. She'd scooped up her stuff, spilt her hot chocolate. 'Jesus! I can't believe you guys sometimes,' she had hissed. There had been the start of tears at the edges of her eyes. She looked weary and burdened. 'You're pathetic!' she'd said, louder than she should, and stormed out. A couple of kids from the year above whooped and cheered at that, delighted by the dramatic distraction. Preston had felt himself twist with embarrassment. What an idiot he'd been. That book meant something to Alice. He'd messed it all up just by looking at it.

'There's nothing to see here!' Mace was chorusing to the canteen in his American cop voice. He'd turned back to his friend and wiped his nose. 'Did I ever tell you about the Lazeria map?' Then, without waiting for an answer, he plunged into a wide-eyed account. 'Under the North Pole – it's been proved, this has – I'm one hundred and thirty per cent serious, brother-man – there's a three hundred-metre-deep canyon into which meltwater drains. The earth under Alaska is actually hollow, and the United States government . . .'

Preston had put his head in his hands. 'Mace,' he'd said wearily.

Mace had faltered for a second or two, then brightened. 'What about the Ellwood kid, then?' he persisted. 'A genuine Manchester mystery.'

Preston sighed. Mace had tried this tale before as well. 'It's yesterday's news now,' he'd said then, swatting it aside. 'Just another missing person case. Leave it.'

Mace had given an indignant choke on his breakfast. 'Just another missing person? Not when it's a politician's kid that does the vanishing. It's unsolved is what I'm saying.'

The two of them had fallen silent then and eaten hash browns together for a moment, sharing the last of the hot chocolate. Then Mace had said, 'We really pissed her off, didn't we?' his face empty of its usual mischievous glow.

The memory felt suffocating. A squall of rain drummed at his window, but Preston opened it and gulped at the air. Cars

26

were hissing through the puddles, past Victoria station towards the outline of Strangeways in the distance. Somewhere below, a neighbour's radio was tuned to the news.

'Greater Manchester Police have issued a recent photo of missing Manchester schoolgirl Alice Wilde,' it said, 'and have appealed for witnesses who may have seen the sixteen-year-old girl between nine and ten o'clock on Friday evening. One witness claims to have seen the girl on Deansgate . . .' There was a scratch of white noise as the station was changed, then eighties music. Preston felt his heart lurch and then sink.

Alice on Deansgate, Friday night. Just hours after she'd left the room he was standing in now, swinging her school bag over her shoulder, wound-up tight as if she was waiting for something to start. 'Will you promise me something? If the cops come, don't tell them about this.'

Preston looked at his marked hand.

What if I went night-walking and didn't come back?

There was something he couldn't quite remember, he knew – it was hiding in his head somewhere. Something that had happened to him.

Teeth like dice in a plastic cup, he thought. Lift your eyes. Goggles like saucers. Sleeptight.

'And I woke up in my clothes,' finished Preston with an empty shrug.

He'd told Elliot Mason everything he could remember. The two of them were drinking chocolate milk and kicking about in Mace's bedroom, waiting for the night. Mace's parents' flat was out on the edge of the Green Quarter behind the cinemas and casino: a galley kitchen, three bedrooms and a TV room. A balcony with pot plants and a view of

Strangeways. The place was small and warm and smelt of cooking. It was Monday evening, a cold and drizzly end to a grey day. Mace's mum was making them something for tea. Later, they were going for a night-walk – together.

Mace's folder of theories was out. He'd been regrouping the material. There was a pile of UFO-related stuff, Preston could see – Area 51 and the Roswell incident prominent amongst them.

'But you remember being in the centre of town, yeah? Walking in the rain. Back Half Moon, you said? M.I.S.T.?'

Preston shrugged. 'Yeah.' In truth, his memory had been coming back in parts during most of the day. Back Half Moon Street, the fire escape and the kink in the alleyway ahead that took it round a corner into darkness. The high fence. Shattered teeth rattling in a plastic cup.

Mace grinned. 'That's what I thought. Look at this,' he said, closing his bedroom door more firmly and carefully than usual. 'This is secret societies and groups.' He knelt on the floor, leafing through a collection of printed documents.

'Please,' Preston said with a wry smile, placing his palms together in mock prayer. 'Don't give me the Illuminati lecture again, right?'

Mace stuck two fingers up and flashed a grin. 'I've been looking into M.I.S.T.,' he said, clearing his throat. 'And there's very little information out there.'

Preston sat on the floor, his back to the radiator. 'Go on,' he said. 'Surprise me.'

'It's an acronym: the Manchester Institute of Science and Technology. M.I.S.T. It specializes in –' here he checked his notes, flicking back and forth amongst the scribble – 'Ah! "Technological prototyping and development for criminal justice", it says here.'

Preston remembered the light on in the high window. 'Criminal justice – like DNA testing, or something?'

'Could be,' said Mace. 'I thought of that. But I can't find anything specific on their website.' Mace's laptop was open on the floor amongst the research material. He rattled the space bar until it sprang into life. Preston scrolled up and down, clicked his way through a couple of pages. The M.I.S.T. website was as bland and unhelpful as a company could be without appearing secretive: an impenetrable mission statement that finished with an italicized slogan, *Making our cities safer;* an 'Executive Board Members' section that amounted to a list of hyperlinked names that meant nothing; a series of photographs of laboratories with happy-looking white-coated staff. Even the 'Contact Us' section was sparse: a single telephone number and email address.

'Is this a front?' Preston found himself asking.

Mace clapped his hands together. 'The sceptic is convinced!'

'Nowhere near. It's a crappy website. Thousands of companies have those.'

Mace raised a finger. 'There's something else.' There was an edge to his friend's voice. He leant over the laptop and brought up another tab. Preston recognized it immediately: satellite images of the city.

From above, Manchester looked like a dropped plate. As if it was held together by masking tape and glue, as if two cities playing chicken had crashed into each other, crushing the Irwell between them. An instantly recognizable chaos unlike any of the places Mum had written articles from. There she was, back in his mind suddenly – smiling, leaning against a fountain somewhere or looking out over a Mediterranean bay. Preston hid his eyes a moment, pressing a palm across them. *Grip it.*

He shrugged. 'And?' he said, swallowing hard.

Mace zoomed in.

As the city drew closer it crystallized. There was the broad stroke of Deansgate, the bland hull of the shopping centre, the big wheel in Exchange Square, the gun shops up on Shudehill. The Midland, where the New Conservative politicians would gather, and Manchester Central, the big convention centre; the streets and squares and postal districts packed tightly in around the Irwell and the Ship Canal – all present and correct.

'I don't get it. What am I looking at?'

Mace said quietly, 'Here,' and tapped the screen with the tip of his pen. Preston recognized Half Moon Street – the section circled in Alice's notebook. Then he realized why Mace had fallen so strangely silent.

'Oh my God,' he said. 'That's not possible.'

But it was. He was seeing it with his own eyes.

The screen displayed Half Moon Street all right – but it was a stunted little alleyway that petered out at the edge of an empty lot. No bend left into the darkness, no high fence, no sunken garden or gated car park, no labs. Just a derelict patch of waste ground.

'Could this be out of date?' he tried, peering at the screen for an explanation. By way of answer, Mace had pointed at Chetham's and Victoria station, both recently reconstructed. Building work had finished only a matter of months ago, but there they were, fresh and new. And yet, a kilometre up Deansgate, there was a hole where M.I.S.T. should be. 'But that's impossible,' Preston found himself fruitlessly repeating. 'How can you do that?'

Mace, for once, was short of suggestions. 'GPS was developed in the States in the nineties,' he said with a shrug. 'It's relatively old tech. But there's a European equivalent – the Galileo Positioning System. It's possible that we might be using that to feed historical data into search engines to keep things concealed.'

'So – we're seeing Half Moon Street ten years ago?'

'Five or ten, something like that. Basically, images could be overlaid so that we see the past, not the present.'

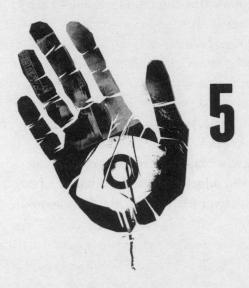

5

Staying over at Mace's place was a phrase that had been used to conceal all sorts of things over the last few years. Trying to sneak into a club on South King Street? Staying over at Mace's place. Going to watch Gilligan's crappy punk band and having a secret cider with Quinn afterwards? Staying over at Mace's place. But staying over at Mace's place had never been cover for breaking into a government building. And that, surely, was what M.I.S.T. was, Preston thought as he gazed up at the fire escape towards the roof at the side of Back Half Moon.

Who else could arrange for satellite images to be doctored or removed?

'Christ,' exclaimed Mace, looking back over his shoulder. 'I've never noticed this street before. It's like Narnia.'

'Weird, isn't it?' Preston said, thinking, *the unwatched life.* 'The fence I told you about is just round this corner.'

Mace fumbled for his phone, tapped an app open and started speaking. 'A Monday night in October,' he said, his voice low. 'Approaching twenty-three hundred hours. Light rain. This is Back Half Moon Street, off Deansgate, Manchester.'

'Mace. What the hell?'

Mace pulled up. He indicated the phone. 'Voice memo.'

'I figured that. What for?'

'Brotherman,' said Elliot Mason with mock patience, 'we're on the edge of a major discovery here. I want it captured. Do you mind?' he held the phone up, raised an eyebrow, and spoke into it. 'Cloud cover light. Visibility good. The alleyway is crowded with bins and detritus . . .'

'Detritus?' Preston laughed. 'Who are you, David Attenborough?' He stopped suddenly and the words dried in his mouth. There was something happening in the sunken garden.

It was still huddled down below them in a cloak of darkness below the white face of the M.I.S.T. building, punctuated by a succession of half-illuminated floor lights. But this time there were people in the space. Preston sought the cover of the alley wall and pressed himself against it.

Mace drew up at his shoulder. 'What?'

Preston nodded down into the dark space below. His memory was returning clearer than ever. 'Last night,' he whispered, 'I saw a boy here. He had goggles on.' Preston found his breath came out at a tremble.

Mace regarded him seriously. 'So who are these guys?' He squinted. 'Three men,' he said into his phone. 'Two dressed in dark colours.'

Those two looked similar to the man with the wasp in his

gloves. They were checking the steps. The other one seemed to be a lab technician, white coat over a light-blue shirt, dark tie, white hair and a wide nose. Preston couldn't be sure but they looked to him to be in the exact spot he'd seen the kid with the goggles.

'They're checking the place where I saw the dead kid I told you about,' Preston said, and as he did so, more memories returned. The chattering teeth of the boy, the curve of his shuddering shoulders. *This is no place for a schoolkid.* 'I have to find out what's going on,' he said, almost to himself. Preston shuffled forwards to the fence and crouched. He was pretty sure he couldn't be seen.

Behind him from the safety of the alleyway, Mace hesitated for a moment, kicking his trainers at the corner of a puddle. 'Damn it,' he said eventually, and crept forward to join his friend.

Preston stayed low and pressed his face against the rain-streaked struts of the fencing. The conversation seemed to be drawing to a close. One of the men was already inside; the man in the lab coat still held the fire door open. Preston wondered what rooms might be beyond the door. *Labs? Storage facilities?*

Mace tapped a couple of tabs of chewing gum into his palm and threw his head back, pressing his cupped hand against his mouth. Preston glared him into silence. Mace chewed, raised both hands – *calm down* – and crept close. 'Did I ever tell you about . . .' he began.

'Jesus, will you give it a rest?' Preston hissed. The man at the top of the stairs had his eyes fixed on the skyline of the buildings up above their heads. If he dropped his gaze to the mouth of the alley and they were seen, they'd have some explaining to do.

'Those guys down there are putting in some serious late shifts,' Mace whispered, 'keeping their jobs pretty damn secret, don't you think?' He held out his phone, switched on his camera. 'I'm going to get some footage.'

They both watched the sentinel figure of the man in the lab coat for a second. He seemed to be concluding a conversation with the other figure and beckoning him inside. There were low lights on within the building. The figures had moved indoors, but the fire door was still wide open. Preston caught a glimpse of something inside before it swung shut. Something metallic. Something big.

'Got it!' Mace said, drawing back into the alley.

'Got what?'

'I'll show you. Let me slow it down.' They huddled around the screen of Mace's phone. The picture was poor. It wobbled and in the foreground the bars of the fence kept blocking the view. The fire door pixelated and blurred.

'See?' Mace said, jabbing an index finger against the screen. 'Machinery.'

Whatever it was, it was the full height of the room, a squat gunmetal-coloured chamber with huge industrial-looking iron joists bracing it. It reminded Preston of one of those haulage crates you see on long trains. There was a glimpse of banks of computers, just beyond it, before the door swung shut.

'What is that?'

'I don't like the look of it, brotherman,' Mace said. 'There's kit just like this holed up in the Nevada desert. I'm one hundred and thirty per cent serious. The American military is—'

'We have to check it out,' Preston said, 'Whatever it is.' Alice's message wouldn't leave his mind. *Sorry. Going in.* He'd tried to reply to it twice since the interview with DCI Sinclair. But the messages wouldn't deliver. Preston couldn't figure out why. Or what she meant. Going in where? He squinted at Mace's jittering footage again. There was definitely something beyond that door.

'Are you crazy?' Mace was saying. 'If we go down there, they'll see us for sure.'

'Maybe there's another way.' Preston said. *Lift your eyes*, he thought. Over the rooftops, clouds eddied and rolled, city lights turning their bellies yellow. Further up, a plane scored a straight line of vapour across the night. Before all that, though, was the fire escape.

Preston studied it. 'Follow me,' he said.

6

At the top of the fire escape there was a chest-high wall, beyond which was the flat roof of the M.I.S.T. building. Mace panted and chewed gum as he joined his friend after their climb, looking out along Deansgate towards the Beetham Tower. He had his phone out again, covering times, dates, cloud cover. 'The city skyline is dominated by creaking steel rigging,' he was saying, looking out across it, misty-eyed. 'Manchester. City of cranes and rain. Cranes lifting towers floor by floor out of the ground across Castlefield, through Spinningfields and out into Old Trafford and Gorse Hill. Cranes beyond the goods warehouses and the conference centre in Barbirolli Square. Stands of cranes over Salford . . .'

'Can we get a move on?'

Mace scowled. 'My colleague Preston Faulkner also present,' he said.

The air was chill and fresh up on the roof, and the noises of the night echoed: the high-pitched hum of electric trams, the wail of cop cars and ambulances, the shriek of Deansgate drinking girls pitching in and out of taxis. Up beyond the pollution, stars glittered like diamonds in dust.

'How is this going to work, exactly?'

Preston paused, assessing their options. The roof was windy and wet, but walled. There was a doorway, again with a security strip, across the other side of the roof. Something caught his eye, and he padded across to the door.

Even in the darkness, the tag was visible. Preston leant in close. It had been sprayed on to the brickwork using a stencil – an open hand with long twisting fingers and an eye in the centre of the palm. The Jupiter Hand. Preston traced the image with the tip of his fingers. This meant Ryan's crew. And where Ryan went, Alice did.

Ryan. Maybe he was at the heart of all this.

After the notebook incident. A half-decent game of footy had broken out on the back pitch – a rarity – and Preston was watching it, hands in pockets, waiting for Mace to bring him some crisps from the canteen.

Ryan was at his shoulder without him noticing. When he spoke, Preston had jumped. 'Shitty thing to do,' he'd said, 'looking through other people's stuff.'

Preston hadn't known what to say. He'd been angry. It was none of Ryan's damn business. What gave him the right to pass comment on the way they conducted their friendship? He'd only been going out with her for a couple of months. They'd known her for years, grown up with her. He'd boiled in silence for a moment, glaring at Ryan's floppy hair, his earring, then he'd said something childish.

'Hey,' Ryan had said, mock impressed. He'd blown his fringe out of his eyes and folded his arms. 'Big man. Stop, you're scaring me.'

Preston had squirmed with embarrassment, but tried not to show it. He hated that tears seemed to come to his eyes at times like this. 'Well, if you hadn't stolen my closest friend . . .' he'd said, but then stopped himself.

Ryan had grinned. 'Stolen your friend? Jesus, Faulkner, you're such a kid.' He shook his head, watching the football. He'd smelt of cigarettes. 'Go get dead,' he'd said.

The worst thing? Preston had bottled it. Rather than give as good as he got, he'd turned and left so Ryan couldn't see him looking defeated. In the canteen, Mace had forgotten his crisps.

'They were here. Alice was here,' Preston said, as Mace joined him beside the tag. He swallowed back the bitterness of the memory and turned away from the wall. The roof was punctuated by glass pyramids designed to let as much light into the upper floor rooms as possible. Some of them were huge plates of impenetrable glass caked in the grime of the city. Others had opening windows installed. There was a chance they could force one.

'We need to get in,' he said, 'and find out what's going on.'

'Are you sure about this?'

'Course I'm sure.' Where Ryan went, Alice did. This was the way forward, he was sure. *Going in* meant this place.

'We get trapped in there, we're 404.'

Preston shook his head – 404 was geek-speak for lost or knackered. Whenever Mace was away from a computer or an internet connection, he tended to get antsy. 'Listen, Mace,' he said. 'Alice was up here. I know it.'

'Jesus,' said Mace, swearing through his teeth. He looked scared. 'Everything's about bloody Alice. She's gone, Press. You're not going to swoop into a room and rescue her, you know. She's gone!'

Preston put his hands on his hips, breathed out. 'What, so we give up?'

'What else can we do?' Mace said. 'This is crazy. There are guys in that building –' he thrust his finger at the floor – 'who might kill us.'

Preston rolled his eyes. 'Please!' he hissed. 'Not the New World Order or government cover-ups again.'

'I shouldn't have let you talk me into this.' Mace was pacing now, biting his fingernails. 'Bloody Alice,' he said again. 'You should forget about her.'

'I swear I'll punch your lights out if you say that again.' Preston was surprised at the vehemence of his feeling. His hands trembled as he squeezed them into fists. He hadn't fought with Mace for months. Well, weeks.

'Come on then, big man,' Mace said, striding towards him and thrusting his chest out.

Preston hit him in the mouth.

Mace doubled over. 'Christ!' he said in a high voice, holding his face as if it was coming apart in his hands. 'That was big-time unnecessary!'

Preston looked out across the city, trying not to yell out. He had to admit something. He couldn't hold it in any longer.

'Big-time unnecessary!' Mace repeated, pointing to his split lip.

'You don't understand,' Preston said. He swallowed hard. It needed saying. 'This is all my fault.'

It'd happened on Friday night, just after Alice had gone. She'd left her phone behind by accident. Then Dad had got on to him to do the washing-up and sort out a takeaway and pretty soon it was close to bedtime and he hadn't taken it back.

Just before ten, Preston was getting ready for bed, slinging his clothes into the laundry basket, putting the atlas back, tidying his stuff, when he saw the phone again. A sleek black one – a real grown-up's phone. Just like Alice to have it, Preston was thinking as he toyed with it.

Then its screen had lit up and it had vibrated.

At first, Preston had put it face down on his bedside table and watched it spin slowly as it rattled – Alice's texts were nothing to do with him; he'd learnt his lesson after the embarrassment with the secret notebook – but eventually he couldn't resist. He picked up the phone and turned it over.

A text was on the screen. From Ryan. I need help, it said. Come get me no kidding.

Preston had stared at it. It didn't look like a joke. It was for real. And it meant Ryan was in some sort of trouble.

For a second, Preston was ready to call Alice's mum and dad and tell them. She was his oldest friend, after all. But then something happened. His phone was in his jeans pocket, tangled up at the foot of his bed. He didn't go and get it. He didn't call her. He stood in his boxer shorts looking at the text message on Alice's phone, thinking about her and Ryan and he felt something cold and hard knot up inside him.

He clicked Reply. Go get dead, he typed.

For a moment, his thumb hovered and he didn't breathe.

Then he had hit Send.

The shame had come quickly. The heat of it made him sweat.

He deleted the outgoing message. Not that it would make any difference – it was sent now – but Alice shouldn't see it, he thought. But then she'd see Ryan's initial text when he gave the phone back. Preston deleted that one as well. Christ – things were getting worse. He'd have to slip it through her letterbox to avoid handing it over in person.

He'd stopped. Stupidly, he wiped the phone clean as if it was a crime scene weapon and put it down.

He'd watched it, waiting for the outraged vibrate of a response.

No reply came.

Instead, he'd imagined that he could see someone in his room – the outline of a faceless figure. Betrayal, a thin, dark spectre rattling its chains at the foot of his bed.

'Jesus,' said Mace, wiping the blood from his mouth. 'You really did that?'

Preston didn't say anything. Telling the story had drained him.

'So . . . you think Ryan was in proper danger?'

'Could have been,' Preston said quietly. In a way, it was a relief to have said it at last.

'And now Alice has gone looking for him?'

Preston shut his eyes. *This was why it was all his fault.* 'Maybe.'

'But Ryan thinks she told him to get dead.' Preston's heart sank. He nodded. 'Damn, Press. What were you thinking?'

Preston took a long, uncertain breath. 'Sorry.'

'It's not me you need to be apologizing to . . .' Mace began, his voice rising, and for a second, it looked as if there was another fight on the cards.

Then a light went on.

Instinctively, both boys dropped to their knees. A nearby pyramid of glass was illuminated. Someone was moving about below them. The boys stared at each other. Mace spat blood and wiped his lip with the sleeve of his coat. Preston crawled carefully towards one of the windows, glad of the distraction. If there was one way he was going to fix this mess, it was by finding Alice. Confessing.

Below was a corridor lined with security-protected doors with keypads. Labs and offices. Preston drew back quickly. There was a figure in the space below. Some sort of security guard, by the look of his uniform. He had a walkie-talkie slung at his hip, and a gun, and he walked with his feet facing outwards. A moment or two later, the lights went out. Preston could hear him clattering down a set of stairs nearby.

What sort of building had twenty-four-hour armed security? And keypads at each door?

Mace had crawled over to watch with him. 'A guy with a gun!' he said through his split lip.

Preston stood up and brushed the gravel from his jeans. 'But no alarms or movement sensors or anything, right?' He thought about Alice again. He had to fix this. 'So we can at least have a look around.'

7

It took twenty minutes to force the window. They used their front-door keys, working them under the frame, twisting them carefully, levering them up in unison, swearing and cursing, trying again until finally they could get their fingers under and yank the buckled window hard. The drop from their rooftop perch was a big one, and it was hard to land quietly. Once inside, Preston beckoned.

Mace shook his head. 'I can record my observations from up here,' he hissed. 'A guy on the roof might be useful.'

'Don't go anywhere.'

Mace scowled in response, lowering the window. It needed a good shove before it closed properly.

Preston was in a warm, whirring building, servers and processors pumping out heat as they flickered and hummed. He swiped his phone torch on, and followed its glow towards an open space ahead. It was a reception area for the top floor, one wall entirely glass, looking down over the car park and gardens. Green sofas were arranged around a coffee table with travel magazines. Further back was a sleek desk area with a laptop and intercom, a couple of desk-top phones blinking with messages, and a little pile of business cards. Preston cupped the light of his torch, wondering if someone below might look up and see it bobbing. The desk drawers were locked. Next to the phone was an ID card on a lanyard, cast aside by its owner. Preston pocketed it.

Suddenly, further down the corridor, a door opened. Preston was seized by a cold fear and ducked down beneath the desk. He crushed himself into a ball in front of the chair, closed his eyes like a child and held his breath, his body pulsing like a drum. *This is it. I'm 404 for sure.*

'Yes, it's a secure line,' a voice said. 'Go ahead.' Footsteps padded. 'Unscheduled?' There was a period of silence. 'Yes. Yes.' Now, an exasperated sigh. 'There is a protocol . . .' There was a longer pause here, then the voice spoke again. It was a male voice; not a security guard, Preston reckoned. 'I'm aware that's what we stated in the service-level agreement, Minister, but I hardly think . . .' Another pause, then, 'Very well.'

Preston waited. Where was the speaker now? Staring out of the windows? Preston tried to make some sense of what he'd heard. The conversation had been brief, confusing – but *protocol, agreement, Minister* – they surely meant only one thing, didn't they? Government. The company's website had mentioned *technological prototyping and development for criminal justice.* So a government link might make sense; DNA testing, he'd first thought. Did the UK have a complete DNA database? Was that what the pinprick in the centre of his palm was about? By the hum of the building and the temperature of its corridors, there was certainly enough kit to power something huge. Preston bit his lip.

'It's me.' It was the man again, very close. He was leaning on the polished top of the reception desk just over Preston's head. The lurch of terror seized him bodily. 'We have an issue,' the voice said. 'Armstrong's on his way. He wants to observe the next delivery.' This time, the man was so close that Preston could almost hear the other speaker's response. 'Under an hour.' Pause. 'No, it's more than that. He wants to see the valve.' Further silence. 'Yes, he has the latest figures. And the spending review's due to be announced. It doesn't look good. Yes. Yes. We need this one to go smoothly. Right.' There was the unmistakable clatter of a phone skimmed on to a surface after a call. Preston could hear the man taking deep, slow breaths. 'Bloody hell,' he said to himself. Preston listened as he paced, wishing he'd leave. But he didn't. The crouch beneath the desk was agonizing. Seconds dragged into minutes. Sometimes Preston would guess he'd gone – and be on the verge of standing up and rubbing his calves – then the guy would shift position again and Preston would freeze. He was at the window, Preston guessed, watching for the visitors.

In his pocket, he felt his phone vibrate.

He hooked it out and checked the time. It was just after 11 p.m.

Gates open cars coming in, Mace had texted.

That would make sense. This was the visitor the earlier speaker had been expecting, then. What name had been used? Armstrong? Mercifully, the man moved too – in response to the arrival, Preston guessed – setting off down the corridor. There was the beep and hiss of glass-panelled security doors, and the descending echo of his footsteps as he went downstairs.

Preston moved out from the desk, legs aching, checking the glow of the rooms further down the corridor, where a few men in white coats appeared to be moving between labs and offices, working.

He made his way across their line of sight and out to the floor-to-ceiling glass windows, where he crouched against the arm of the sofa, getting as low as possible, staying back from the glass, craning his neck to see what he could.

He was directly above the sunken garden. He couldn't make out the fire door where the kid had died, but he could see the low glow of uplighters along the path edges, the raised barrier at the security entrance and the delegation of vehicles pulling in. Three black Mercedes with what looked like smoked glass. They pulled up. The back doors of the third opened and a man got out from each side. They both wore knee-length smart coats over dark suits and carried briefcases. One had a hat and carried an umbrella.

They crossed the car park and were met by two men in white coats striding out of the building towards them. There was a cordial shaking of hands – the kind of handshakes, Preston figured, that were firm and steely enough to indicate a display of strength. Everything about the meeting suggested it wasn't a welcome one. Preston's phone buzzed and glowed and he pressed its screen against his coat to hide the light. A text from the roof.

Government, it said.

The figures waited a moment, a huddle of four, talking with their heads bowed close together. Preston tried to work out which one was Armstrong, and which was the person who had made the call at the desk up on the top floor. Then a fifth figure emerged to meet them, and Preston recognized him immediately. It was the man he had seen the previous night, the one with the black boots and shoulder bag and the wasp-sting handshake. He was gloveless this time. He turned to indicate the building and grounds around him, pointed to the gates and fence, faced the uppermost office and lab windows and swept an arm out. Preston froze against the sofa. He was low enough not to be seen, he was sure. Plus the room was dark. Glass reflects. Nevertheless, his heart gave a kick of anxiety. The man continued speaking. Whoever he was, he seemed to be an employee of M.I.S.T., and a prominent one at that. After a moment more, the five of them turned and began to walk inside. Preston could just hear the *poc-poc-poc* of an umbrella in the foyer as they stepped inside. Once they'd vanished, the car headlights came on, and with a hiss, the vehicles reversed through the puddles and made their way back out through the security barrier.

What now?, said a text from Mace a few moments after the car park had fallen into stillness. Preston thought. What had the man on the phone said? That someone wanted to observe the next delivery? To see the valve? If they stuck around for a bit, there might be a chance they could see what that was. And that might begin to loosen the knot he was trying to untangle. It could lead him to Alice.

There was a windowless door behind the desk area. Preston pushed at it. Locked. He checked the frame, saw a magnetic reader, and touched the ID card to it. There was a click. He pushed the door open a couple of centimetres. Some sort of service stairwell, unheated and dusty. He slipped through. The air was cold enough to make his breath come in clouds.

Going in, he texted Mace, thinking, *hell of a way to spend a Monday night.* Then he jammed his phone in the pocket of his jeans and made his way downwards, moving as quickly as he dared. The building had four floors, he knew, and the thing he was looking for – *the machinery*, Mace had called it – was in the basement.

Wall-mounted service lights gave the stairwell a grey glow. The area wasn't used often; there were fire extinguishers and a couple of pallet trucks for deliveries, nothing else. Every floor had a locked door and a magnetic card reader.

By the time Preston reached the basement level he was struggling to calm his nerves. He thought of Alice's little book of maps and sketches. Had she been here, in these corridors, or was this all a colossal mistake? He fumbled with the ID card on its string and took a steadying breath. He'd find out, one way or another.

The basement door clicked. He pushed at it, and it opened.

8

It was dark beyond – dark, quiet and very hot.

Preston pushed his way through and heard the door swing shut and the lock engage behind him. There was a huge room with a brushed concrete floor and banks of computer servers, all flickering. He broke into a sweat and unbuttoned his coat as he took it in. The place was the length of a football pitch and the entirety of the back wall was lined with tech, all whirring and blinking. The capability must be immense, Preston thought – it was like some subterranean supercomputer, stretching on into the darkness as far as he could see, the kind of thing that he imagined might power the national grid. Cables snaked across the floor, connecting subsections of the computers like arteries; black plastic down-pipes on the walls spilt wires. The whole building was plugged into this vast basement machine. *Christ,* Preston thought, *for all I know, the whole damn city could be plugged into this.*

And then there was the thing at the end of the room.

It was the hulking outline of the machinery Mace had filmed on his phone. It was the size of a bus. A dark, iron bus – a house, even – supported by metal struts on a poured-concrete base. It seemed to have a mouth at its front end, steps rising to a strange sort of entrance. You could, Preston reckoned, go inside it, as if it was some sort of zero-gravity training chamber for spacewalking, or maybe a sealed quarantine pod for doctors to treat high-security patients. The words of the man upstairs came back to him suddenly. *Armstrong's on his way. He wants to observe the next delivery. He wants to see the valve.*

It was the weirdest thing he'd ever seen. It made his shoulders and back go cold with fear, despite the clammy air. It made him want to leave. He'd seen enough.

He turned to go. His hands were shaking as he fumbled the card against the magnetic reader. His legs felt weak. Whatever it was – the valve – it didn't belong in a basement in Manchester. It didn't belong anywhere. Something about its squat silhouette, its open jaw, the shape and feel of it, made him want to get as far away from it as he could. He was about to slip through the door when it happened.

The room was suddenly doused in light: bright light dropping in flat, broad blades from the high windows. Outside in the car park a vehicle had pulled up, its engine a deep growl. This wasn't a sleek Mercedes. It sounded bigger, a truck maybe. There was the slam of doors, the low buzz of voices.

The next thing Preston knew, there was the sound of the fire door lock turning, and the heavy door was being hauled open, outwards. Cold air flooded the room. *Jesus.* Preston squinted at the half-dark that lurked in the corners of the open space. He needed somewhere to hide, and fast. If he sneaked out now, he'd be spotted for sure. So he ran, quick and low and terrified, and pressed himself into the shadows of the basement wall. It was an exterior wall, cold; nets of spiderweb fogged the brickwork and clung to his shoulders. The shadows hid him pretty well.

A group of figures had moved into the basement. One was powering up a laptop on a low table up near the mouth of the valve, the other walking its outside, checking connections, inspecting cables and switches, pulling levers, powering it up. The big, hulking container came alive with a low rumble, breathing stickily. A figure entered, a man in a suit and a long raincoat carrying a briefcase. His polished brogues clicked as he walked. This was one of the figures he'd seen through the window from the top floor – the visitor. Some sort of government inspector, if Mace was to be believed. Armstrong, they'd called him.

He wants to observe the next delivery, Preston thought. *He wants to see the valve.*

This had to be linked, somehow, with the discussion at the fire door, the boy with the goggles. The noise of the valve was unsettling now: a strange and rising hum. Preston cursed himself for thinking such a crazy thought, but the machine sounded as if it were breathing, like the thing was an iron lung or a metal heart even, wheezing as it expanded and contracted.

One of the figures was stooping over the laptop, punching at the keys, the blue-green light of the little screen throwing his face into sharp relief. Two other figures had appeared at the door. They were armed policemen in bulletproof jackets and black uniforms. The man in the suit had stationed himself with his back to Preston, briefcase on the floor beside him, fingers interlaced behind his back. Outside, the van – it had the sliding-door sound of a van – was being unloaded.

Then the scene became stranger still. Preston held his breath. A line of figures had established themselves at the entrance. Each member of the queue was a kid – a boy – each one stooped and tired-looking, each one in cuffs, wrists twisted together, hands behind his back. Some looked older, as if they were maybe seventeen, their silhouettes fuller. But others looked to be his age and one in particular was crying, his shoulders jumping oddly as he wept.

And all of them had dark, distorted faces. Plastic faces, it looked like. It took Preston a moment to realize what he was seeing. His pulse was thumping painfully as he watched, swallowing the desire to scream or run.

They were wearing the big, weird goggles with lenses the size of saucers.

And they were being checked off as they came in. The man at the laptop had a handheld scanner. The red light of the laser flickered as he checked off a tag on their cuffs. A list was updating on the laptop screen. When the first kid in line had been scanned, a man took him by the arm and led him to the machine. The handcuffed boy walked uncertainly – Preston remembered how thick the lenses of the goggles were, how dark they made everything – stumbling on one of the steps up to the mouth of the valve. The figure at his elbow paused and said something. The kid in the goggles dipped his head to hear, nodded, and moved forward into the jaws of the box.

They were putting them in the valve.

The queue moved forwards. Preston felt sweat prickle his shoulders and neck. There was something very wrong here –

a line of teenaged boys, handcuffed like prisoners, blinded by black goggles, being scanned and led into a metal freight container. Preston wondered what would happen when it was full. It didn't look as if it could be dragged out of the basement and shipped somewhere. The whole set-up looked much more permanent: the concrete base with what looked like rubberized pads, the cables feeding in and out of the machine, the energy source – it all suggested a storage container designed never to leave the basement.

A valve, the M.I.S.T. guy had called it. Preston bit his fingernail, trying to remember what a valve was. What did a valve do? It was more than a box or chamber, it had moving parts, like for a system of pipes and liquids. Didn't it respond to pressure and regulate flow, like a tap?

Preston watched, cold with fear and horror, as fifteen boys were scanned and led up the steps. The youngest one – the skinny guy, cried all the way. The last one, a taller, fuller figure, raised his head as he went in, as if he were sending up a hopeless final prayer. The headlights of the van outside brightened again; the engine was running and someone was slamming its back doors closed.

Then the heavy metal door of the valve shut firmly behind the last of the handcuffed figures. The man with the laptop punched a couple of keys, waited for something, then powered down and closed the lid. The guy in the suit moved to talk to him; there was a brief discussion. Then the remaining figures – there were three – moved outside, still in conversation. They pulled the fire door shut behind them and Preston heard the keys turn to lock him in again. Voices dropped as they moved away, back towards reception.

Preston licked his dry lips and tried to swallow, his eyes

still on the valve. It was humming again. A wheezing creak emerged above the drone, then a clanging.

Preston pulled his phone out and squeezed it hard in his fist, willing his trembling fingers to work. He was patterned in gauzy web. A couple of spiders scuttled across his sleeves and he shook them free. *Meet me at the window*, he thumbed, and pressed Send. There was no way he was staying a moment longer than he had to.

There were fifteen kids trapped in a box in a basement in Manchester. This was something for the police.

He set off up the stairs, fast.

And as he went, he swore he could feel the basement room reach its fingers out towards him – as if the valve itself and its silent prisoners were following him upwards or calling him back, using up the last of their breath to do so.

9

On the top floor, all was quiet. At the third skylight, Preston paused, looking up. The little window he'd got in by was closed but not latched.

'Mace,' he hissed. He was feeling steadier now. Safer.

No answer. The expected face at the window – a bloody grin and a thumbs up – didn't appear. A few minutes passed. Preston began to eye the door at the end of the corridor. If the men in suits were visiting the top-floor labs, this is where they'd emerge, and he'd be caught out in the open.

'Mace!' he tried again. *Where's he gone now?* A few more minutes passed. Preston checked his phone again. Half past eleven. Ten minutes of silence since the text.

Then came the sound he'd been dreading. The rhythmic clatter of shoes on stairs. The delegation of scientists and government officials making their way up to the top-floor rooms. *Dammit.*

'Mace!' Preston called, his voice louder than it should have been. And then, his friend appeared, a pale and fearful face at the window like a head on a stamp. Preston felt a liquid rush of relief. 'Thank God,' he hissed. 'Someone's coming!'

Mace fumbled at the window and opened it. 'What?' he said.

'Get me out of here!'

Mace began to wriggle his shoulders through the gap and leant in, dropping an outstretched arm towards his friend. 'Gimme a second here . . .' he grunted. His coat, soaked in rainwater, restricted his movement and he grimaced.

'Speed it up, Mace!'

Preston threw a glance at the doorway. They were getting close now. Was that shadows he could see, playing across the walls through the glass door? One person, leading the group, was talking to the rest, though the words were indistinct. Preston looked in the other direction, up to the reception area. He was going to have to choose. He could make a dash for the desk – and be there safe and hidden in a matter of seconds, or he could risk escaping up and out of the window.

'Here,' Mace's hand was outstretched, his face tight and red with effort. Preston reached up. He could brush his friend's fingers. He jumped; grabbed. Mace's hand held his – just. Mace slithered further through the window as he took the weight. 'Bloody hell,' he managed, blowing hard. Then he began to pull.

It was slow.

Mace grunted, struggling with the weight. His lip was bleeding again. Preston could hear the steps clearly now, and with a horrible sinking fear, he recognized the change in timbre as they reached the corridor at the top of the stairs.

They'd be through the door in moments. He was hanging suspended in the corridor before them, his legs pedalling stupidly.

'We keep a bank of servers active twenty-four hours a day, so you'll notice a change of temperature as we enter these areas of the building...' a voice was saying on the other side of the door. Preston could hear an ID card being swiped. There was a monotone bleep – the card declined, *thank God* – and the user tried again. Mace gave an almighty pull and Preston felt himself rising faster now; he could taste fresh rain on the night air above him. There was another swipe of the card and this time it was accepted. The door opened, but his head was out now and Mace was on his back on the roof, gasping, and Preston was pulling himself, his fingers scrabbling for grip on the window's edge, his muscles burning as he hauled himself out into the night.

As soon as he was through, he lowered the window slowly and rested it on the frame, just in time to see a group of figures pass below. They didn't look up.

He hadn't been seen.

Preston collapsed, struggling for air, flooded with terror and relief in equal and horrible measure.

For a while, he looked at the night sky and breathed in great lungfuls of air, feeling the adrenalin buck and twist as it subsided; he watched the ragged clouds blown across the moon. Next to him, he could hear his friend gasping and spitting blood, then rolling on to his side.

'Let's not...' Mace said, still fighting for breath, '... try that again, eh?'

Preston grinned with relief. 'Agreed,' he said. He raised himself up on to his elbows, orientating himself again, thinking about the fire escape now – about the bus home, about a shower. Maybe, he thought, he might even sleep properly tonight; forget about the darkness of the basement room, the weird open mouth of the machine, the valve, and never come back. His snooping was over. There was no way he was getting himself mixed up in anything further. Now was the time to beat a speedy retreat; there'd be other ways of finding Alice. He could ...

There was someone climbing the fire escape.

A figure reached the top, checked the alley below him and clicked a torch on, sweeping the roof with its dancing beam.

For a second or two, Preston tried not to believe what he was seeing. The man was dressed in black, a flash of silver across his chest where a shoulder bag was slung. It was him. And he had a gun.

'Boys,' he said slowly, a torch in one hand, a gun raised in the other. 'Don't move.' He crossed towards them and they lay on their backs in the puddled rainwater, holding their breath again. Mace wiped the blood from his mouth and gave a long frustrated sigh.

'Dammit,' said Preston, lifting his eyes and squinting.

'You've been spying,' the man said, 'so you'll know we've got important visitors downstairs.' He slowed as he reached them and beckoned with the gun. The boys got groggily to their feet. 'So I made my excuses and left,' he continued. 'Figured you'd be up here.' His face was like a clenched fist; hard and angry. He pulled his radio from his belt. 'I'm bringing them in,' he said. There was a fizz and a voice said something. 'You two are coming with me,' the man said, half-whispering. He nodded towards the fire escape. The boys turned and set off. Mace put his hands in the air, holding them above his ears like someone doing sit-ups. 'Put your damn hands down, kid,' the man snapped. 'This isn't the movies.'

Down the fire escape they trudged, through the darkness of Back Half Moon, under an old industrial archway of rusting iron and across a cobbled yard where a black van was parked. This adjoining building was huge – four storeys high, an old textiles place – and it belonged to the same organization, Preston noticed; there was the same brass plaque with M.I.S.T. embossed on it. The man swiped a keycard in an electronic reader beside another metal door. It blinked green and he put his shoulder to it. It opened inwards with a scrape.

'I really need to get home,' Mace said as they hovered at the threshold. His voice trembled.

The man gave him a wide, sarcastic grin. 'Then you shouldn't have been up on our roof, kid. Inside.' The man held his gun up, displaying it as if Mace hadn't noticed it before and cocked his head towards the entrance.

'It's just that . . .'

'Shut it, Mace.' Preston gave his friend a scowl.

The man nodded. 'Wise words. In you go.'

Inside, there was a small room with a concrete floor, a wall of metal lockers and a lift with a sliding silver door. They rode up four floors in icy silence. Preston felt his spirits sink as they climbed. This was big-time trouble they were in now. If these guys were government security, he'd be finding himself back in police custody in a blink. *What the hell would Dad say?* It didn't even bear thinking about. Next to him, Mace was wide-eyed, equal parts terrified and fascinated.

*

The first thing Preston noticed as the lift door slid back was the size of the place. They were in a converted warehouse with a high roof spanned with steel joists and an exposed brick wall of grimy windows. It smelt of coffee and roll-ups and dust.. Ahead of him, there were three desks, each with glowing screens and keyboards, arranged together in the open-plan workspace. Electric fan heaters hummed. Two large wall-mounted plasma screens showed CNN and the BBC streaming twenty-four-hour news. A third screen looked as if it belonged in an airport or up at Piccadilly station – a display of dates, times and lengthy lists of figures that reminded Preston of the candidate numbers the exams officers handed out at school. There was a big map of the city pinned with coloured markers.

The central desks were unoccupied except for one where a black-skinned, round-faced woman in a jumpsuit, her hair tied back, typed. She looked up as they entered. 'Shade,' she said. She was American. 'Have you lost your mind?'

Shade took a breath. 'No choice, Esther. My batch of Sleeptight's knackered and the kid can't stay away.'

There was a chilly silence. Fan heaters whirred and tech hummed.

Then someone started talking. 'Large, open-plan room,' said a shaky voice. 'The space is dominated by a series of three desks . . .' *Mace and his damn voice memo.*

'What's he doing?' Esther said. She rose to standing, kicking her chair back. 'Kid!' she shouted. 'What the hell?'

Mace blanched. He fumbled with the phone. 'I'm pausing it,' he said. 'Sorry. I'm pausing it.'

Esther gave him an icy stare. Then she returned her gaze to her colleague. 'You *did* dose him, though, right?' She placed her palms over her eyes and rubbed. 'Jesus,' she said eventually. 'A couple of schoolkids here? What now?'

Preston tried to place the American accent. East coast, he reckoned. Washington or New York, maybe. He wiped the rain from his face, trying to organize his thoughts. Whirring servers, winking lights, a water cooler, a knackered sofa with side table and ashtray, laminated street maps, two-way radios and plasma TVs – some kind of surveillance operation?

Preston felt a familiar nudge: Mace, nodding towards a third desk. A tidy, orderly space with a photo frame and a pile of paper clips and Post-its. Esther and Shade weren't the complete team. There was a third person.

'Double dose,' Shade continued, not noticing. 'And he still came back.'

'That doesn't make sense,' said Esther, crossing to a table where a pile of medical blister packs were neatly stacked. She checked them carefully. 'Same as last time,' she said. 'We got a bum dose?'

Shade opened his hands out and shrugged in exasperation. 'Yep. Cost-cutting pen-pushers trying to save cash have landed us with this problem.' He indicated the two boys shivering shoulder-to-shoulder behind him as they adjusted to the warmth. 'They were snooping around.'

Esther plunged her hands into the pockets of her combat trousers and stared at her boots, kicking at the dust for a second, a frown creasing her forehead. 'What did they see?' she asked. Shade looked at her and shook his head in silent reply. Preston watched the two of them. This was bad news. Esther worked a knuckle against her eye, then blinked. 'Goddammit,' she spat.

Shade scratched his chin. 'It gets worse,' he said.

'Armstrong's here.'

'Tonight?' said Esther, straightening. 'He isn't due until the end of the week.'

Shade nodded. His jaw was tight, his eyes solemn. 'Wanted to see the delivery. Stood there and watched the . . .' paused, made an enigmatic face. 'You know.'

The valve, Preston thought. *The missing word is valve.*

Esther pinched the bridge of her nose. 'This means he's considering shutdown, right?' she said quietly, scanning the room. 'Before the conference. He's going to make it all vanish before anyone finds out.'

'Could be. A full inspection, I'd guess. Not just operations. He'll want to see security too. Shutdown's possible.'

Preston wondered what shutdown was, and why it was so bad.

'Where is he now, exactly?' Esther said.

Shade cocked his head. 'The labs.'

'He'll be coming over here.'

'Likely, yes.'

Esther opened her palms out. 'The files. The transit records. The dormant valves. He checks the paperwork and sees what we've been up to, we're finished.' She paced. 'Jesus! What do we do, Jonathan?'

Shade crossed the office space to a pair of filing cabinets, then threw his hands up in exasperation. 'We need to clear this stuff. We need to wipe the hard drives.'

'Then there's the other valves,' Esther said. 'If he realizes we've kept them open . . .'

'*Shit.*' Jonathan Shade clenched a fist and ground his teeth.

'And we've got a couple of trespassers too.' Esther gave Preston a calculating gaze. There was a long silence. Tension tremored in the space between them. Eventually, Esther said, 'Say I go and check the Castlefield valve, check Cooper Street, I call Frankie out at Blackstone Edge make sure the food valve's all good. Then I go over the dormant ones.'

Shade nodded, taking his jacket and gloves off and flexing his fingers. 'Right,' he said, direct and clear. 'I'll deal with this place. They'll have to help,' he said, jamming a finger in the boys' direction. 'It's the only way. I'll give 'em triple dose Sleeptight when we're done.'

Esther nodded, crossing the office and reaching for her jacket and keys. 'Agreed.'

Shade looked at the boys and gave one of his cold grins. 'Gentlemen,' he said, 'you are our new and unofficial night-wardens.' Then he rubbed his hands together. 'We've got work to do.'

10

Preston tried not to think of Dad. He'd be starting his night shift – which meant he'd have gone back to the flat to change his shirt and get something to eat, checked his son's bedroom and found it empty. And if that was the case, he'd be calling anytime now, frantic and furious. That's why Preston had switched his phone off. Mace, with laboured reluctance, had done the same.

Shade drove them hard. The first shift, through midnight and into the small hours, was back-breaking: box file after box file of paperwork needed moving into a small side room and stacking, to be locked away. The place was untidy and disorganized, that was for sure – cluttered with three or four years' worth of chaotic paperwork.

The three of them toiled wordlessly for the most part, and the boys understood their place. Shade was mute and remorseless, working with frantic energy, checking his watch regularly, eyeing the rolling news. Preston thought about everything the wardens had said. Phrases snagged in his head. He thought about *shutdown*. He thought about *dormant valves*, about *Frankie out at Blackstone Edge*, and whether that was the same moorland his dad had driven him across once. He thought about *transit records* and *if he sees what we've been up to . . .* This was a bigger operation than Preston could have guessed. And there was something here the wardens badly wanted to hide.

As the first two hours neared their close, Shade wiped his forehead and leant back against his desk for a break. They'd made good progress; a teetering pile of stacked boxes half-filled the stockroom. Preston and Mace watched the nightwarden warily and continued to work.

Shade ran a hand across the stubble on his chin. 'So listen,' he said in his gravelly voice, his bright eyes on Preston. 'What brought you to M.I.S.T.? You mentioned a friend?'

Preston nodded, still shuttling boxes. He was too tired to work out what story to tell. The truth would have to do. 'You'll have seen her in the news, I bet,' he said. Alice had only made it local so far, but as they'd worked, Preston hadn't been able to help gazing up at the BBC coverage on the wall-mounted TV, half-expecting to see her face. It was covering Manchester's preparations for the conference season, speculating about Armstrong's potential challenge for the leadership of the New Conservatives and latest round of spending cuts; economic correspondents in grey suits, their mouths moving wordlessly, the volume down. 'She's called Alice,' he continued. 'She's been missing for three days. It's in the papers.'

Shade grunted. 'Seen it. I'm sorry. I know how it feels.'

Preston clenched his teeth. He seriously doubted it. 'You do?'

Shade fell silent, staring. It took Preston a moment to work out what had his attention. It was the empty desk. 'Yeah,' Shade said eventually. 'I do.' The desk had been kept tidy, sure. But maybe it hadn't been used for a long time. Either way, there had been a third member of the team. And whoever they were, it sounded as if they too were missing.

Mace put down a box of papers. 'Mr Shade,' he said, a glint in his eye, 'do you know anything about the Ellwood kid? That was round here as well.'

Shade raised an eyebrow. His meaning was clear. Mace stooped for the box and carried on working. 'That was a few months ago, right?' Shade said slowly as the boys moved back and forth, finishing the last of the boxes. The filing cabinets were almost clear now. Shade was booting up, getting ready to start on the IT system. He spoke as he worked. 'The politician's kid that went missing. Nah, I don't. I spend – as you've gathered – a lot of time looking after the M.I.S.T. buildings. I don't get out much.'

Preston thought about the word in Alice's notebook. Maybe she'd planned to explore the compound, but hadn't had time. 'Are you a security guard, then?' he asked. It was a gamble. Shade might shut him out. But there was something about him, Preston figured, an adrenalin-fuelled panic and a deep fatigue, that had put him in the mood for talking.

Shade shrugged, tapping his keyboard. 'Sort of. Like I said, nightwarden.'

'What do you look after?' Mace asked, tucking the final box of papers away and blowing the hair from the eyes. 'Is it to do with the machine?'

Shade's eyes grew cold. He ran his tongue along his lips. His shoulders had dropped a little, as if he was closing up. One too many questions. 'I've got work to do, boys.'

'The valve, I heard them call it,' Preston said. 'I went down to the basement and I saw it. I saw them lead a whole line of boys into it.'

Shade stared at the screen before him. His fingers had stopped moving on the keyboard. 'The valve,' he said. His voice sounded as if it might break.

'What is it?'

Shade gave a bitter laugh, hit a key and pushed back on the castors of his chair. 'Complicated question,' he said after a pause. He was uneasy, exhausted – Preston could see it around his eyes. He steepled his fingers together, thinking about what to reveal, thinking – Preston guessed – about the triple dose of Sleeptight he'd administer at the end of all this. 'It's a Kepler valve,' he said eventually. 'And, yeah, I look after it.'

Preston and Mace looked at each other. Mace gave a shrug, his face flickering with awe and excitement. 'What's a Kepler valve?' Preston asked. When Shade didn't answer, he pressed on. 'It's as big as a bus. What does it do?'

'It's a prototype. I'd have got it smaller eventually.'

'*You* built it?' Mace said.

Shade nodded, lips pressed tightly together. 'I built lots of them. And now I spend my life chained to them. Keeping an eye on them in case they misbehave.'

Preston thought about the shuddering kid, the chatter of his teeth. Surely there was a connection; the valve and the boy. 'Does it kill people?' he asked quietly.

'Sometimes,' Shade said. His voice sounded hollow. 'But

mostly it's worse than that.'

He looked as if he might say something more, but then his eye was caught by the rolling news and he scoured the desks for the TV remote. When he found it, he boosted the volume.

On the screen, an overweight man with side-parted grey hair and a bulbous nose was talking. 'Armstrong,' said Shade bitterly, placing his hands on his hips.

Preston recognized him. He was one of the group he had seen hurrying across the car park in the rain, the one who was here to see the valve and begin an inspection. The footage on the TV screen had evidently been captured earlier in the day – Armstrong stood before the Houses of Parliament in a raincoat and a gaudy tie.

'I don't think I'm being particularly controversial when I say that our current prison system isn't working,' he was saying. He had an oily voice. His chin wobbled as he spoke. Across the bottom of the screen, his name appeared: *Christopher Armstrong, Justice Secretary.* 'Its ability to deter crime has been significantly weakened. Crowded and outdated accommodation is a major issue. Wandsworth, Wormwood, Armley, Strangeways – these Victorian prisons clearly aren't fit for purpose. Radical solutions are necessary if our prison system is to be the deterrent it was before the previous government dismantled it. We need to be tougher on the kind of crime that matters to the British public.'

A question was asked. Preston didn't catch it – Shade was jeering noisily at the screen.

Armstrong continued. 'No, that's not the case. Whichever way you look at it, crime is going down. A fifteen per cent decrease in robbery. A similar fall in domestic burglary. Our policies are working. Yes, we accept there is still a way to go. Yes, we have to make further savings. But today's figures are encouraging; they give us a clear indication that this government's tough stance on crime is working.'

The clip ended and a news anchor turned to a studio guest.

Preston found himself remembering the strapline on M.I.S.T.'s website. *Technological prototyping and development for criminal justice*, it had said. That's why Armstrong was here. The government's justice secretary here in Manchester – it had to be connected with M.I.S.T.

Preston thought about DNA databases again. Valves.

Shade cut the volume and tossed the controller on to his desk. 'We have to make further savings,' he said, repeating Armstrong's words. 'He can say one thing to the cameras, but it'll be another story tonight. Esther's right. He's closing us down. It's getting too dangerous, with the conference coming up.'

'Is shutdown bad?'

Shade closed his eyes, managed a nod. Preston watched him: a tired man, trapped by something – circumstances or science, maybe – beyond his control. He almost felt sorry for him. Then the radio hissed and crackled. Shade picked it up. 'Esther,' he said. 'That you? Go ahead.'

Esther sounded urgent. 'I'm coming in. We've got major trouble here. Clear a table.'

Shade blanched. 'What's happening? What's going on, Esther?'

'Clear a damn table!' she said. 'Stuff just got crazy.'

The radio fell silent.

'Jesus,' Shade said.

The next few minutes were frantic. Shade swept a pile of

blister packs to the floor and dragged the empty table into the centre of the workspace. Preston and Mace followed a series of barked commands, carrying the final armfuls of material as quickly as they could and piling it all up inside the cramped stockroom, clearing a space for whatever the hell was coming.

A matter of minutes later, the lift sprang into life and began its brief ascent. The three of them faced the lift doors, breathing hard. Preston felt something suddenly flood his body: fear and adrenalin shaken together. Mace stood ramrod straight, terrified.

'What's going on?' Preston whispered.

Mace let a shaky breath escape. 'Whatever it is, it's not good.'

The doors opened.

11

Esther was carrying a body in her arms. The body of
another boy.

'Coming through,' she said through gritted teeth.
Shade helped her to the table, taking the boy's legs. Esther
laid the body gently on its back on the table they had cleared.
It was covered in some sort of tarpaulin and was wet with
rain.

Shade said, 'Esther, what the hell—?'

'You're not going to believe this.' Esther wiped the sweat
from her brow.

Shade rubbed his eyes. 'If Armstrong comes in now, we're
finished.'

Preston found himself inching forwards, compelled to look.
The body was small, slight – a kid of maybe fifteen, he reckoned, though it was wrapped in such a way that the head and
face couldn't be seen. A pair of boots emerged from the end.

Esther cleared her throat. 'Castlefield valve, just after midnight,' she said, her story coming between steadying breaths. 'Swear to God – Castlefield valve. Beyond the warehouses and the canal basin. No one around, thank Christ. If I hadn't been doing a routine check of the tech I'd never have seen the kid arrive.'

Shade ground his teeth. 'No way.' He reached an unsteady hand out and touched the covered body at the knee. 'They shouldn't be coming through.'

'How many's that now? Six?' Esther said.

Shade touched the material again and blinked; Preston could have sworn he could see tears glazing his eyes.

Esther took hold of the edges of the tarp, the tips of her dark fingers flexing delicately. 'We need to get these boys out of here. They can't see this.'

'And put them where? We'll triple dose 'em afterwards. Come on.'

Preston couldn't tear his eyes away. Mace, at his shoulder, was the same. With a nod at Shade, Esther began to unwrap the body.

It was hard to look at what lay beneath, it being at once familiar and terrible. There was a dead boy there, and he'd evidently been wearing goggles – the same strange full-face goggles Preston had seen on the other kids, the ones that gave their wearer the big glittering eyes of a dead fly. They'd been pushed up askew over his blond hair to reveal his face. He was in his mid-teens.

Shade said, 'What have I done?' For a second, it was as if he'd forgotten how to stand up. He had to lean on the table.

Esther began picking away at the boy's neck, trying to find

a way in under the line of the shirt. Her fingers were shaking. 'We need an ID,' she said. The silence in the room settled like dust. After a moment, Esther hooked a fingernail around something metallic – it looked to Preston like the kind of dog tag worn by American soldiers – and pulled it free from the boy's clothes.

She read a series of numbers aloud from it.

Shade stirred, shaking off his silent sadness and moving to his desktop computer. He scrolled through a database, his hand unsteady on the mouse. Mace gave Preston a nudge and directed his gaze at the second of the two TV screens, the one with the lists of numbers. They were the same length as the one Esther had just read out. Identification codes, Preston realized.

Whoever the body was – there were more of them some-where, all listed on the screens above.

'Yeah,' Shade confirmed. 'One of ours. Went BTV five months ago.'

'BTV?' Preston said. The others looked at him.

'Beyond the valve,' Esther said. Shade glared at her. She cleared her throat and stuck her chin out, defiant. 'Well,' she said, looking back at him. 'They've seen it all now, haven't they? They may as well know.'

'Know what?'

The two nightwardens didn't reply. Shade's shoulders had rounded and dropped – he was eaten up by some dark feeling Preston couldn't understand.

Only Esther's gaze had softened. She re-tied her hair with long fingers. 'Jonathan,' she said gently, 'these boys are with us now. You've tried to lose them and they've come back. If the Castlefield breach is what we think it is, we've got enough trouble. Armstrong's here. Might be better if you just level with 'em.'

'Beyond the valve?' Preston repeated. 'What does that even mean?'

'It means,' Shade said firmly, 'through the valve. Into it.'

'Into that box?'

'There's a place –' Shade examined his fingertips, choosing his words carefully – 'inside the Kepler valves,' he said. 'Beyond them.'

Mace drew back, his face wrinkled in thought. 'Inside? Like a room?'

'Something like that.'

'And this boy's been in there?'

Esther nodded. 'Yeah,' she said. She gave them a hopeless smile. 'But the thing is this: once they've gone in, they shouldn't be able to get back out.'

'Then why go?' said Mace. 'You'd have to have some sort of death wish.'

Preston felt a sudden and swift gathering of sense. The M.I.S.T. buildings and their mysterious mission statement: *Technological prototyping and development for criminal justice.* Armstrong – the justice secretary. What had he said on TV? *Radical solutions are necessary if our prison system is to be the deterrent it was . . .*

This wasn't about DNA databases or criminal records. This was about punishment.

This was about prison.

'Oh my God,' he said. He'd gone cold. 'Who do you send beyond the valve?'

'The kid's bright,' Shade said, a dark twist of sarcasm in his voice. 'I'll give him that.' He licked his lips. 'Of course you don't *choose* to go into the valve if you can't get back. You get *sent* there. We send you there.'

Mace put a palm across his forehead. 'What? It's a *prison*?'

Shade gave a bitter laugh. He pushed his hands into his pockets and rocked back on his heels, his mirth dying. 'I wanted to change the world,' he said. 'Instead I invented a prison.'

Preston looked at the screen. The numbers – the lists and lists of six-figure numbers – were prisoners. *Kids.* There were dozens and dozens, close to a hundred, surely. He wiped the fatigue from his eyes. 'This is going to sound dumb,' he said, his head feeling oddly light, 'but how can all those people fit in a metal box in the basement of the building next door?'

There was a long and uneasy pause. It looked as if no one wanted to answer.

'It's not big enough,' Preston clarified pointlessly.

Esther tried a smile but gave up. She inflated her cheeks, let out a long breath. 'Kepler valves are bigger on the inside,' she said.

For a moment, Preston felt like laughing at the joke.

But the room was silent and the faces were cold and sober.

12

'**W**e were working on particle acceleration,' Shade said later. 'My brother and me.' He was drinking vending-machine coffee from a plastic cup. Esther was next to him on the sofa. Preston and Mace were warming themselves with drinks too. It was close to three o'clock, early Tuesday morning. 'Esther had come over from Penn State to help us bring the project in on time. There were two big Kepler valves over at the university back then, see – a team of fifteen physicists working with us on it. Then, one day, the whole financial system seized up – the stock markets crashed and our funding dried up. Investment in CERN was the only thing anyone could budget for; suddenly we were yesterday's news. Then, to top it all, the valves started misfiring and we didn't have a particle accelerator, we had . . .' Shade wiped his lips, shook his head at the memory. 'We had something else. We'd made something else.'

'What was it?' Preston said.

Shade smiled. 'An elevator. A shuttle. A teletransportation system. I dunno. Start asking details, kid, and we'll be here way past your bedtime with a flipchart and a magic marker. Skip it, unless you fancy four hours with a calculator talking Gödel spacetime. Some things are better left alone.' Shade faltered. He looked at the half-wrapped figure of the dead boy, then at the empty desk.

Preston turned and examined the desk too. He had to ask. 'Who does it belong to?'

When Shade spoke, his voice was just dry breath. 'My older brother.'

Esther looked up from her tea and wiped her eyes nervously. 'Want me to take them home?'

Shade shook himself, scrunching his plastic cup in a fist. 'Time for your Sleeptight, boys,' he said. He got up, began rubbing the life back into his limbs. 'Let's forget this whole damn night ever happened, eh?'

'Ah, come on,' Mace said. 'There's no need . . .'

He didn't get any further.

The intercom next to the lift doors buzzed. Shade's face fell. The room was still. The intercom buzzed again.

Shade made his way across to the lift, his steps slow and wary. He looked back at the assembled company, his expression uncertain.

Then he leant into the mic and pressed a button. 'Yeah?' he said.

'Jonathan Shade,' a voice said. It wasn't a question. Preston recognized it immediately and so did Shade – he grimaced like a man with a migraine. 'Christopher Armstrong. I and my associates would like to come up.'

Shade glared at his companions, his burning eyes issuing a fierce instruction that was immediately understood. Esther leapt from her seat and began bundling the body of the boy into the tarp and carrying it into the stockroom, breathing hard. Preston and Mace watched, fused still with fear.

'Lads,' hissed Shade. 'Disappear.'

Preston pulled Mace by the arm and they stumbled after Esther. Preston looked over his shoulder and watched, agog, as Shade gathered himself and pressed the intercom.

'Mr Armstrong. We've been expecting you,' he said. There was a hollow lightness in his voice. 'Come on up.' He pressed the door release and below them, Preston heard the door-lock click and buzz, and someone push it open. Armstrong and his colleagues would be up in the lift in a matter of moments.

Maybe this was shutdown.

Esther placed a hand on each of the boys' shoulders as they stood in the doorway to the small stockroom. Padded coats hung on a rack of pegs. Rows of boots stood to attention beneath them. There were three filing cabinets huddled along one wall, all the stacked documents and papers cleared from the workspace outside, and a bare light bulb. Dumped unceremoniously against the back wall, the wrapped body of the boy filled the air with a sharp metallic scent. 'Guys,' she said, bringing her face close to theirs. 'You need to stay in here. You come out only when we tell you, understand?'

Preston nodded. Esther was kind and calm. For a second, he thought of Mum. 'Got it.'

So Preston and Mace found themselves hiding in a room the size of a broom cupboard next to a dead body, watching through the crack between door and frame. It was hard to see.

Preston's legs cramped. Mace was craning his neck next to him, chewing gum. Armstrong had arrived, flanked by a pair of assistants who began unbundling laptops, wires, phones and modems. Frosty pleasantries had been exchanged.

Now, Christopher Armstrong was speaking. 'Your team's record isn't good, Shade,' he was saying, taking off his coat and brushing the rainwater from his suit. 'The recent breaches have been a disaster. If the press get hold of it, someone's head's going to roll. And it won't be mine, I assure you.'

Shade said something – it wasn't clear. Esther stood next to him, hands clasped behind her back, upright and professional.

Armstrong listened, tapping his teeth with a forefinger, then strode beyond them both. He was closer to the stockroom door now and Preston could pick out his words clearly. 'Be that as it may,' he said, straightening his tie, 'the prime minister is yet to be convinced this project represents value for money. The public purse is far from bottomless, Mr Shade. And you're over-budget again, I notice. Colleagues –' he was speaking to his assistants now, a black guy in a dark suit and close-cropped hair, and a blonde-haired young woman with dark-rimmed glasses and a briefcase – 'I want a look at the recent deployment data for Category A prisoners BTV. Check systems and processes are robust.'

And so the work began. The tension out there was almost visible – Preston and Mace watched as the government inspectors busied themselves. Christopher Armstrong was a powerful presence. When he spoke he was cold and abrupt. At times, he would lean over the shoulder of one of his colleagues and point something out with a scowl. Esther made him coffee which he didn't thank her for. He sipped, winced, and put it aside to get cold. Maybe half an hour passed.

'Who exactly are we dealing with here?' Mace hissed eventually. 'I don't like the look of this guy.'

'He's a politician,' Preston said. He fumbled for his phone. 'What do you expect? Let's see how he checks out on the net.' He powered it up, dreading a missed call from Dad. In a few moments, a simple search had generated thousands of hits: official government websites, newspaper opinion pieces, hatchet jobs and character assassinations, speeches and video clips. Preston clicked a local piece from the *Evening News*. *Westminster Politician Assists Police with Enquiries*, it was called. It was a few months old, and carried a picture of Armstrong taken climbing into a taxi late at night. 'Check this,' Preston whispered. Mace adjusted his squat, shifting closer, and the boys read. Much of it was about some sort of routine investigation following a traffic accident.

But then Mace said slowly, 'Oh my actual God.' Preston had seen it too.

Police investigating the death of Westminster aide Jacob Ellwood have asked prominent Westminster politician and Justice Secretary Christopher Armstrong to assist them in their enquiries.

'Ellwood,' Mace mouthed. Preston didn't need a reminder. The missing kid, the one Mace had been building theories around for the last few months, was called Ellwood. This dead guy – Jacob Ellwood – must have been the dad.

Mr Armstrong, a robust campaigner for prison reform and regular visitor to Manchester's Strangeways, was reported as being happy to assist. 'I will do anything I can do to help clarify the circumstances behind this

unexpected tragedy,' Armstrong has said. 'I have worked closely with Jacob Ellwood for many years and will miss him terribly as a colleague, strategist, and friend.'

'What about the missing kid?' Mace said, his voice a low hiss. 'Run another search.'

It took a couple of tries, but a combination of 'missing person', 'Manchester' and 'Ellwood' took them to the article they wanted.

Increasing numbers of Greater Manchester Police officers are being deployed in the search for Chloe Ellwood, the missing daughter of Westminster aide Jacob Ellwood who was killed in a traffic accident in central Manchester last month.

Mace was leaning in, his breath quickening. Whatever the hell this was, it felt important. They skimmed the rest.

Representatives of the media have speculated that Miss Ellwood's disappearance is linked to her father's death, and may be the result of a tragic suicide attempt. However, a police spokesperson has ruled out any conclusive judgement on Miss Ellwood's motives or intentions, and reiterated her family's message to return home.

'What does it mean?' Mace whispered. Preston ran a hand across his eyes, trying to think. There was some sort of connection here between Armstrong and this traffic accident, and then between the traffic accident and this missing kid Chloe Ellwood. All of that was on the one hand. And on the other was this crazy thing in the basement of M.I.S.T., a valve that worked as some sort of weird prototype prison. Armstrong was surely involved there as well, Preston figured. There was another thought, too. A dark one – a thought that chilled him with its doomed inevitability. That text he'd got from Alice – *Sorry. Going in.* She was going into the valve, Preston knew with a cold certainty. She was following Ryan through. Urban exploration – the notebook, the circled streets around Back Half Moon.

Preston minimized the internet search and opened his text messages. As if looking at that brief communication again might somehow deny his worst fears. He was tired. His fingers jumped. He fumbled the phone and it spilt out of his hands and clattered on the floor. *Dammit.* Outside in the workspace, one of Armstrong's assistants had heard it, he was sure – he could see the black guy in the suit look up from his laptop and rise to his feet. *Double dammit.*

'Shit. We're 404,' hissed Mace.

Preston looked up, followed his friend's gaze. The guy in the suit was crossing the floor of the workspace towards the door of the stockroom, and he walked in that slow slight crouch that suggested a man who knew he was about to find something he didn't want to. *Oh, hell.* Preston glanced at the body of the boy wrapped in a tarp and rolled up in the corner.

This was bad. This was very bad indeed.

He slipped the phone into his pocket.

The stockroom door opened.

The guy in the suit was there. He looked as if he'd been slapped. 'Bloody hell,' he said.

13

It was weird seeing Christopher Armstrong for real, close up. This was the guy on the posters up and down Deansgate, the face on the news – the politician with the cold eyes and thin lips, the man with the grey suit and dark tie who talked justice and rehabilitation. Armstrong puffed up, clenched his fists, watching as his assistant led the two teenage boys from their hiding place. Shade closed his eyes, looking for a second as if he were reeling off a silent curse. Esther stared at the ceiling. The ticker-tape roll of the TV news glowed silently.

Armstrong stared at Preston and Mace, running a careful hand across his balding scalp, deciding something. 'Just what in God's name is this?' he said evenly. After a silence in which no one seemed prepared to answer him, Armstrong spoke again. 'May I remind you, Mr Shade, that these premises are the property of Her Majesty's Government, and as such are subject to restricted access rights to members of the public!' He paused, sweat beading on his forehead, and loosened his tie. This time he shouted. Preston jumped at the force of it. 'Particularly to a pair of Manchester street rats!' Armstrong bawled.

'Street rats,' Preston said coldly. 'Nice.' He clenched his fists hard, staring at Armstrong. *Go get dead*, he thought suddenly, hotly. And with that thought rushed everything else that had been spinning through his head for the last few days – the text message that had sent Ryan to his death. Alice in his bedroom on Friday night, still in her school uniform, her toes nearly touching his. *Sorry. Going in.* The little notebook full of maps and colours – *mist* scrawled in the corner of a page. An open-palmed hand with an eye in the centre, watching the unwatched life. The Count of Monte Cristo. A dark squadron of boys trying to escape from the jaws of a box in a basement. *Technological prototyping and development for criminal justice. Radical solutions.* In Armstrong's world, that's what everyone else was – Ryan, Alice, Mace, the Kepler valve prisoners: all just street rats.

'Good God, man!' Armstrong said coldly. Shade's face had closed up. He'd plunged his hands into his pockets. 'How many regulations are you happy to break in one night? Safeguarding? Insurance? Official secrets? What the hell possessed you to think this was a good idea? Classified projects are classified precisely because they are highly sensitive.' Armstrong was jabbing a finger at the wardens. 'How do we handle this if it goes public? Have you thought about that?' Esther tried to speak, but a vicious glare was enough to silence her. 'Needless to say, it's an important week for the party. And yes, for me too,' Armstrong fumed. 'How much do the kids know? How long have they been here?' He paced, then threw his hands out. 'Don't answer. We'll just have to clean this mess up as quickly and quietly as we can. They'll need a heavy dose of Sleeptight. They'll need taking home tonight. And Mr Shade,' Armstrong said, raising a finger. 'Clear your desk. You too, Miss Klein. You no longer work here.' There was a wounded silence. Shade's face was expressionless. Esther put her hands over her eyes for a second or two, then composed herself. Armstrong started giving orders, snapping his brief-case shut. 'Ross, see to it that we run shutdown from tonight. Let's make sure we clear the tech before the end of the week.' Ross nodded, hurrying back to his position at his laptop and clearing up. 'Shade, I expect your badge and belongings boxed up and these boys dealt with. From tomorrow, you are no longer permitted on the premises.'

And that was it – in a few moments of icy silence, Armstrong had swept up his raincoat, disconnected his tablet, checked his phone and stalked out to the lift, his assist-ants in pursuit.

Preston didn't know where to look. Mace blinked, still shocked. Shade stared at his boots, his face hot and red; anger, shame, fear all written across it. Esther wiped her eyes.

'I'm so sorry,' Preston managed, and his voice was small and dry.

Later, they sat around the low table. It wasn't yet dawn, but it was close. The first commuter buses had grumbled beneath the windows, heading towards Piccadilly. Shade had started talking again an hour or so after Armstrong had left. To start with, he'd been all tight-lipped fury, and even when Esther had placed a consoling palm on his shoulder, he'd been coldly unresponsive. Eventually she'd managed to get him back, gently coaxing him into action.

Now, the two nightwardens were communicating, at least. Esther had dried her eyes and apologized to the boys and started to talk it through, to make some plans – going back to the States again, spending some time with her family.

Shade was slower to recover. For a long time he watched the steam rise from his coffee. Then he raised his head and looked at each of them – Esther first, then the boys. 'Sorry,' he said. 'It's my fault.' Esther put a hand over his.

Preston took his chance. 'I got a text message from Alice. I know she's in there,' he said. 'BTV. Just tell it me straight. How do I get her out?'

Shade shook his head. 'You can't,' he said. 'If Armstrong's running shutdown, no one's getting out.'

'What do you mean?'

'When the valves are closed down, there's no way back.' Shade crushed his plastic cup and binned it. 'Imagine a tap. Once the valve is shut, nothing comes back out. Whatever's already in there stays in the pipes.'

Mace said, 'Stays in? So they're trapped for ever?'

'Once Armstrong runs shutdown, they won't last long. No food and water.'

'So who . . .' Mace broke off, figuring it out. 'Who usually feeds them?'

'We do,' Esther said.

'So, let me get this straight,' said Preston. 'You guys go BTV to drop off supplies?'

Shade nodded. 'I've been so often now I can't remember how many times. To start with it's strange.' He shrugged. 'You'd be surprised how quickly you get used to it.'

Preston looked at Esther. 'You too?'

Esther nodded. 'It wasn't in the contract. But we've done it anyway. Kept it from Armstrong.'

Mace gave a whistle and shook his head, blinking. 'So you just ditch the stuff and then go?'

'Pretty much,' said Esther.

'How long has this been going on?' Preston asked.

Shade took a long breath, rubbing a palm across his forehead. 'Just over a year,' he said. 'It got particularly busy after the riots. The city went crazy that night. The morning after, Armstrong was here before the sun came up, running the show with a whole bunch of desk jockeys in pinstripe suits. We were trucking kids across town between midnight and three, then sending them BTV between three and four-thirty.'

'How many?'

Esther looked at the boys. 'Two hundred. So far.'

'When the systems were first established and we'd tested them, I was told one thing, but something else entirely happened.' Shade's gaze had gone distant now, as if he were looking through Preston and Mace, beyond Esther and back to some other time. 'It took us a long time to realize how the government wanted it used. Armstrong was insistent. He forced me and I wasn't strong enough to oppose him.'

'Forced you to do what?'

'The scale of it, kid. The scale of it. Especially after the summer of riots; we were putting kids BTV in their dozens. And welfare and support stopped. There was to be nothing in the way of food or drink sent through. But the numbers that kept coming in the vans – it was terrible.' Shade looked at the empty desk again. He was thinking of his brother, Preston guessed. 'I knew it was out of control. But Esther and me – we needed time to think, to work out what to do to stop it. We started sending supplies in secret, using the Blackstone Edge valve up on the moors. I knew if anyone checked the transit records we'd be screwed. But I was buying time. I knew things must be bad BTV because kids kept trying to come back through and we'd find them shaking to death.' Shade looked at his trembling hands. 'I haven't slept in months,' he said. He looked angry at himself. 'I shouldn't be telling you this.'

'It doesn't matter what we tell them now,' Esther said softly. She'd leant close in to Shade, put a hand on his knee. Preston didn't know much about girls, but he knew closeness when he saw it. He reckoned they'd had some sort of thing together. Maybe they still did.

'So when Armstrong runs shutdown,' Mace asked, 'how are you going to get food and water in?'

'We're not,' Shade said. 'Whoever's already BTV just . . .' He found it hard to carry on. His voice was a dry croak. 'They just stay there,' he managed eventually.

'And starve,' Preston put in. 'He can't do that! He's killing them! Nobody deserves that.'

Esther had placed her palms together between her knees and was staring at them. 'The difficulty is,' she said, 'that the project is a prototype. It's secret. There's trial without jury, covert sentencing. Parents and family are given misleading information and denied access to the convicted. And nobody knows about this stuff.'

Preston clenched his fists and stared at the wardens. He suddenly saw the workspaces around him for what they were. Shade and Esther were running a prison from this room. Neither of them looked as if they wanted much to do with it. Neither of them had started out to achieve this. Both had dreamt of doing something good. And yet they came in for each shift, clocked on and kept working.

But even as he considered it, the thought turned cold in his mind. He had no right to criticize them, because he'd done this too. *Go get dead*, he'd typed. He hadn't meant to start something bad. He'd hoped for something better. But it was done now, and when something's done, the only way is forward.

'The only way is forward,' he said quietly.

Esther drew in a breath and Preston could hear it tremble. 'Yes,' she said. 'After tonight, I guess that's right.'

'I need to get Alice out. Just tell me now. Can you get me through?'

Shade nodded slowly. The nightwarden looked shattered.

Esther shook her head. 'It's dangerous, Preston. You shouldn't do it. Really.'

'What's it like?'

Esther blinked, looked at her hands, and picked her words carefully. 'It's like a cave.'

Preston and Mace waited. But that was it. That was BTV: *a cave*. And that was where Alice had gone. And Ryan.

'If I want to go into the valve,' Preston said, 'how long have I got before Armstrong runs shutdown?'

14

'**T**ry this on,' said Shade. He held out a curious folded object. It looked like one of those Velcro arm-straps used to take blood pressure. The ones that doctors inflate with a little rubber balloon – the ones that grip your arm until each pulse of blood feels like the thud of current in an electric fence. 'Careful. It's got a microchip in it.'

'What is it?'

'A databand. Now listen, kid.' Shade gripped his shoulders. He'd gone serious as they climbed the stairs up from the warehouse to a stockroom on the floor above. There were stacks of blister packs, plastic-wrapped goggles and other equipment. It all looked medical: first aid kits, bags of fluid and drips, and the weird armbands – dozens upon dozens of them. Mace had fallen silent as Shade had gathered what he wanted together. 'You cannot get back again without these,' he said, his voice slow and firm. 'If you try coming back without a databand, you'll be just like the boy you saw fitting to death in the car park.'

'How come?' This was Mace, his voice quiet.

Shade was unpacking a collection of these databands, breaking open their plastic seals and loosening them so they were ready to wear. 'Think of it like deep-sea diving,' he said. 'When divers go deep – I mean *really deep* – levels of nitrogen in the blood rise dangerously high. If they come up too quickly, they could die. Now. Where you're going – think of it as seriously damn deep, boys. You try coming back to Manchester in a hurry, you'll arrive in a mess. And you'll go into seizure.' He held up the band, turning it partially inside out. 'See here? The chip reads your blood pressure and hormone levels. And there's a couple of pouches inside the lining. And these little needles . . .' He was indicating a little bristle of metal, like teeth, on the inside of the band. '. . . will pierce your skin and pump you full of the good stuff. You come back feeling nothing more than a bit of jet lag. Maybe a touch of a headache and a fierce hunger. But when you're BTV and you want to come home, you tighten the armband like this –' he was holding it up, demonstrating – 'and you pull this until you feel the needles bite you. That's the key, right, boys? Feel it bite you and you'll be OK. Now. You'll need a few. One for your friend, one for each of you.' He handed over three.

Preston packed them carefully into a shoulder bag borrowed from the stockroom and they made their way back downstairs and across the warehouse floor to the entrance. Outside, the pre-dawn air was chill. There was the beginning of morning in the sky. Across Back Half Moon was the fire door and beyond it, the valve. Preston felt so scared he could almost breathe it in.

Shade cleared his throat, looking at the advancing day. 'If Armstrong runs shutdown,' he said, 'you've got maybe twenty-four hours at most. After that, this valve will deactivate, then bit by bit, all the others too. Drag your feet down there, kids, and you won't be able to come back.'

'We'll be trapped in the pipes,' Preston said, remembering the phrase Shade had used earlier.

The nightwarden nodded. 'Unless there's a valve still open elsewhere. In which case you'll turn up somewhere unexpected. Twenty-four hours, kids. No time for sleeping or hanging around. You get in, you get what you need, you get out again. We have to try to cover our tracks as much as possible before Armstrong's men run shutdown. We'll have to leave you to make your own way to the basement – you'll figure out how to use the valve.'

Preston wiped his eyes and nodded. 'How do we get through the door?'

Shade flashed a set of keys. 'Use this one. And the code for the interior keypad is here. Now – next thing is the goggles.' Shade unwrapped the ones he'd brought down from the stockroom and passed them over. They were big and heavy – ugly rubbery things. 'Try them on.'

Preston looped a pair over his head and straightened them over his eyes and face. They swallowed him up. 'Why do we even need these?' he asked. 'Couldn't we just close our eyes?'

Shade shook his head. 'These are safer.'

Mace raised a hand, pushing his back. 'Listen. I'm not going.'

Preston searched his friend's eyes. 'What?'

Mace bit his lip. 'I'm not going. This Alice thing is crazy, man. Your plan is crazy. You'll be 404 in minutes. You heard what Esther said. It's a cave full of psychos. You've got to be mad. I'm not coming.'

'Jesus!' Preston said. 'What sort of backbone have you got, Mace?' He felt the heat rise in his face, his heart hammering. He clenched his fists. This was typical, this was. Every time it came to the crunch, Mace would be the guy to go missing. All through school – Mace was the one queuing in the canteen while Preston got hammered on the back pitch; Mace was the one doing an after-school detention the night there was a rumble on the bus; the guy who threw a sickie when a show-down was due. 'What about Alice?'

Mace looked at his friend. 'She loves Ryan. She doesn't give a damn about you, Press.'

Preston took a swing at him then. He connected pretty well: a blow just below the eye. Mace gave as good as he got, thumping him on the bridge of the nose so hard all Preston could do was lean against the van shaking stars from his head while Shade shouted and separated them.

'Big-time unnecessary,' Preston said as his vision cleared, wiping the blood from his top lip.

'Major-league unnecessary,' Mace spat, feeling his cheek. 'I'm not coming and that's that.'

'Lads,' Shade said, cold and firm. He had a hand on each of their shoulders, like a father talking to his sons. 'I lost my job. I don't give a damn about your argument. If you want to see the valve, let's do it now. But if you're going to go all soap opera on me, I'll just Sleeptight the shit out of you both and drop you home.'

There was a silence. The sun was coming up and the air was starting to mist.

'I'll go as far as the valve,' Mace said.

The last time Preston had seen the Kepler valve, it had changed him; just the sight of it had tangled his guts. It made you stand up straighter, blink more; it made your back go cold and your skin clammy.

'Jesus,' Mace said as he saw it.

The servers blinked, their fans churning the hot, stale subterranean air. They began the walk towards the raised metal box.

Being near it didn't make things any easier. It was braced by industrial-looking iron girders, raised on a platform of odd rubberized plates, plugged into service pipes in the ceiling and strapped to a workstation to the left of its gaping mouth. The boys halted their inspection there: a functional little desk on wheels, a white tablet, two pens and a shut laptop, three pairs of those saucer-eyed goggles and two books.

Preston stepped forward. His throat clammed up.

Two books. There was a novel. And a little notebook.

The Count of Monte Cristo, battered and rammed with Post its. And Alice's notebook.

For a second, neither of them spoke. Then Mace was talking in a low voice. 'We're in a big underground space beneath the M.I.S.T. building. And we have confirmation that one Alice Wilde has also been here. Item one, a notebook full of mad maps . . .'

Preston swore. 'C'mon, man. Give it a damn rest.'

Mace looked indignant, touched the bruise on his cheek and winced, and raised the phone to his lips. 'My colleague Preston Faulkner is also present. And for the record, earlier he hit me. Twice.'

Preston ignored him. Instead, he flicked through the book. Some of the pages were caught and lifted a little – a breath of cold night air. He looked over his shoulder. A high small window at the far end of the room was open. She'd squeezed through. She'd texted him. She'd dumped the notebook – it was a marker, a trail of breadcrumbs through a dangerous wood – then she'd climbed into the mouth of the big metal monster. Preston swallowed back a hot lump in his throat, thumbing the pages. Then the valve breathed again – a low vibrating stutter that rose in pitch then dropped.

'That is *horrible*,' Mace said. He wiped the sweat from his top lip, his face pale, and stepped back. 'Tell me you're not going in.'

Preston looked up. Two steps led up to a recessed area with a door. He swallowed a mouthful of terror and mounted the stairs. At the top, he turned to Mace. His friend was a wide-eyed statue. Preston felt his fear start to thicken into panic.

Sorry. Going in.

Preston ran his fingers around the edges of the door. The metal was smooth and strong, the gaps in the skin of the machine big enough only for his fingernails. Then it hissed softly, like a sigh. He'd touched something.

The door opened. It was heavy and cold. The interior smelt – weird how associations and memories leapt suddenly to mind – like the inside of a showroom car; new plastic, bleach, a stuffy closeness that somehow calmed him.

Preston could make out a pair of wall-mounted lights behind heavy plastic globes, the sort you might see on rain-swept harbours or on the decks of cross-Channel ferries. Preston took a shaky step forwards, balling his hands and trying to stay calm. Esther's words suddenly came to him –

Kepler valves are bigger on the inside.

Well, this one sure as hell *wasn't*.

There was a modest space, a room the size of a small office. But it struck Preston as being more like a decompression chamber: the walls punched and riveted metal sheets, the floor a metal grille. There was space for – what? – thirty people, Preston figured. Thirty at most, standing shoulder to shoulder as if they were squeezing into a large lift. The place was bitterly cold – strange, considering the heat powering it outside. His breath came out in clouds.

Preston put the goggles on and lowered them over his eyes. The lenses blurred and curved things. He made his way slowly inside, testing the floor uneasily. Those odd creaks and groans – they were coming from somewhere deeper inside its stomach.

The roof was low. The lights flickered just a little. There was a wall-mounted lever, he noticed, with a plastic grip, just beside the door. Preston moved towards it.

'How does it work?' he heard Mace ask from somewhere out in the basement. He sounded a long way away.

'I don't know. Do we switch on the laptop?'

Preston heard Mace lift the laptop screen up and punch a button or two. Preston looked at the door, still standing open – at the basement beyond. He looked at the lever. He held a breath then let it out. He laced his fingers together to stop his hands shaking. And he made his decision.

15

Preston pulled the valve door shut hard until he heard it click. Then he pulled the lever downwards, once, hard. He waited, feeling the pitiful warmth from the wall-mounted safety lights, watching his breath cloud.

For a moment – just seconds – there was the tug of gravity at his bones and he felt as if he were falling. He took a small step backwards, swayed, steadied himself, as if he'd just stepped off a roundabout. Then there was a sharp stuttering flash – supernova bright even in the goggles – that strobed madly for a split second before flickering into blackness. The room became slightly warmer.

It hadn't worked. Of course it hadn't.

'Dammit,' said Preston, turning. 'Mace!' he began. 'It's 404. Open up!' He put his weight on the lever and pushed it back upwards; he heard it release. 'Mace!' he said again, and opened the door.

It was the light that was different at first. When he lifted his goggles up and perched them on his forehead, it wasn't as dark. And it was the sound that he noticed second, the groaning echo as the door creaked open. For a moment or two, Preston stood inside the open valve, looking out. This wasn't a basement.

'Mace?' He felt foolish just standing there, so he took a couple of uncertain steps forwards – small ones in case he was about to plunge out of the valve like a skydiver. Then he was out, and his throat was dry and his stomach had knotted and dropped.

He was in some sort of huge cavern – big enough to bury a pair of long-haul aeroplanes if it wasn't so cluttered with valves. There were thirty, maybe forty of them, all in lines, as if they'd been laid out for a game of draughts.

'Mace?' he said pointlessly. His voice sounded feeble, its echo even more so. This wasn't the M.I.S.T. building. He was underneath it, maybe. *He'd felt dizzy and weird in the valve, right?* That's because he'd been dropping at such a speed. And now he was in a chamber under the city.

Except there wasn't a lift shaft.

And the valve he'd just stepped out of, he realized, looking along the rows, wasn't the same one he'd climbed into. It was smaller than its Manchester cousin, maybe only half the size. And it was considerably older. It had a military-looking blistered exterior. If he'd just ridden an elevator, the valve would look the same at the other end, wouldn't it? *But he'd emerged from a different valve.* The other end was still a box in a Manchester basement. So there were two valves connecting two places, like stations on a train line. And they – what? –

shuttled things between them? Transferred or swapped them?

Preston turned his attention to the others. Even a glance along each row revealed chambers of different types and ages; some crouched lower, some great hulking things with skins of rust. There were little banks of lights arranged above the faces of each valve, displays of lights that flickered and glowed to show these things were alive. The only one blinking, Preston estimated as he took another step down to the smooth concrete floor, was his. No, he corrected himself. There was a second one still going. That was it. The rest were lifeless and silent, as if they were hibernating. Or had already been shut down.

His valve suddenly stopped its guttural breathing, which died to a fuzzy nothing. The silence was almost absolute, except somewhere in the distance – he couldn't tell which direction – was a low, rhythmic rumble. It sounded like a faraway drum, or the thud of a huge heart buried somewhere in the rock around him. The air was dry, almost sandy, strangely warm. As Esther had said: a cave, a vast cavern. Yet he could see. Preston traced the source of the light – *lift your eyes* – fissures and splits in the rock way up high as the walls curved in to the roof dropped sharp slices of light into the hangar.

'Mace?' he said again as he walked. 'You're somewhere miles above me and I'm in a big empty cave.'

Except he wasn't alone down here. He'd seen others go in. Those broken boys in the goggles and the handcuffs – they were down here somewhere as well, right? Fear stirred the contents of his stomach. What if there was no order down here; no governance, just chaos? And he was walking straight into it – the new kid at school watching the gates close behind him and the bus pull away? For a second, Preston thought he was going to lose it altogether. He wanted his dad. He wanted Mace. He wanted a gang of nightwardens.

But it was just him and a shoulder bag and three databands.

Grip it. The goggles made him look as if he'd just arrived. He pulled them off and bagged them. His jacket wasn't needed down here in the odd dry warmth; he packed it away. Then he gave his jeans a couple of turn-ups, dug out his cap, checked his pockets, and shouldered his bag. Across the other side of the cavern was an arched entrance and beyond, a darker corridor. Preston headed for it.

When he drew closer to the archway, he saw it. A tag, sprayed at shoulder height like a sign. Pale grey spray paint, hurried and smudged, but recognizable. A single open-palmed hand with an eye in the centre. The Jupiter Hand.

It was dry. This had been done some time ago. Days, probably. But it meant hope. Preston couldn't help but smile as he ran a forefinger across the design. Ryan had been here. And he'd left this for Alice. He was going to track the two of them. He was going to find them, pass over the databands and then he was going to lead them both home.

In the corridor, the roof was much lower, a kind of soft plaster over rock, as if the spaces had been blasted out and smoothed over. There was an archway to his right, and inside it, a room – smaller this time, but with the same huge space above his head. Preston moved in, treading carefully, and looked up. It was like standing at the bottom of a staircase; the ceiling was three, maybe four, floors above him. And at the top where the walls met the roof, a series of punched holes through which light dropped in broad strokes, illuminating the far wall of the room.

And the far wall was covered in writing.

Preston wiped his eyes. The writing was uneven, jumbled. Notes made in paint – some of it in Ryan's spray paint by the look of it – others scrawled in a pale chalky hand; there were sections of plaster that had been prized away from the wall, Preston noticed, to make palm-sized chunks. Different people had contributed, each with their own handwriting – but one person mostly, by the look of it.

In the centre of the wall, written in big, dark letters, was the word *ARMSTRONG*.

And this word seemed to have a kind of gravity which pulled the other words around it. Lines linked words together. *KEPLER VALVE*, someone had written, and *BTV*. *MIST* appeared twice in two different hands. *Madbox,* someone had put, and underlined it. There were other words, cluttered in clouds or written in lines: *Shutdown?* one said. *Jonathan Shade* said another. *Nightwardens. Conviction without trial. Salt mines?* asked one. In one corner, a series of tally lines had been used to count something off; they stopped at fifty-five. *Old man in the pipes*, said one cryptic note. *Up through the trapdoor* said another. There were names on a different section of the wall – *Gedge, Lewison, Chowdhury, Ellwood, Hoyle*. Then separately, *Rabbit*. And beyond that, hovering on the edge, the words *LONGSIGHT LADS* in a box, and beneath the box – *24-7 watch*. Elsewhere, one note read *NO ACCIDENT*. It had a line to *ARMSTRONG*. *Half-moon*, someone had written. There were a couple of familiar place names too: *Manchester*, someone had put, and *Bham*, *London*. And, strangest of all, something that looked more like a plea: *Robinson Cruso*, someone had written – Preston was pretty sure that was the wrong spelling – then *please get help*. And underneath again, in chalk, *Robinson Cruso please get help*.

Preston let his eyes jump from word to word, phrase to phrase. *What the hell is this?* Prisoners in the movies often chalked off days or weeks using a system of tally lines. Those names could be people who had stayed here in the past . . . except it all looked pretty fresh. No. Whoever had done this – and there were at least seven or eight different samples of handwriting here – wasn't just recording their experiences to kill time. They were trying to piece something together. They knew about M.I.S.T., they knew of Armstrong's connection with the project. They had Halfmoon and Manchester, so they were connecting people and places. Some people they liked – others they seemed frightened of.

Preston was so deep in thought, he didn't hear the foot-steps.

That was his first mistake. Then, something tugged at the edge of his vision – a movement, a shape – and he knew he'd made his second mistake. There was somebody there. Preston's breath hitched and his heart fired.

There was a kid in the doorway. He was all bone and tendon under his T-shirt – shoulders and ribs and sockets. He looked lean and strong, a fair-skinned kid with two little dark eyes under glasses with scratched lenses. A dog tag swung at the base of his throat. His hair was short and red, his nose pinched and pointed. He had a knife. The sight of it made Preston's gut tighten.

The kid stood in a loose slouch, casually, arms swinging, as if carrying a blade was as big a deal as a school bag. He had a broad accent, East Manchester. 'Don't move, screb,' the lad said, his voice nasal. 'Or I'll gut you.'

Preston's knees twitched and shook. He raised his hands, using the gesture to push his bag off his hip and behind his back. It was a mistake.

'So what's in the bag, screb?'

'Nothing.' It came out like a gasp.

'Show me the bag.' The kid raised his other hand, open palm upwards. He had fingernails so badly bitten the tips were cracked and bleeding. 'There's food in there, right?'

Preston fought back nausea. If he lost the databands now, he was never getting back. And neither was Alice. 'Seriously,' he tried, shaking his head. 'There's nothing you want.'

The kid had a hacking laugh, like sandpaper on sheet metal. He stepped forwards and raised the knife. Preston could smell his breath.

'I'll be taking the bag, *bastard*,' said the lad, spitting the last word with fierce finality.

Preston shook violently as he tried to yank the shoulder bag up over his head. He got tangled, feeling the sweat bead on his scalp as he pulled it free. He couldn't hand it over. It wasn't an option. He held it up. His arm was stiller now. 'Listen,' he said, 'maybe we can work something out.'

The red-haired kid grinned into the middle distance, shaking his head, half-whispering something to himself. Then he gave a roar and leapt forward. Preston yelped and threw himself to the floor, falling away from the swing of the blade. He pedalled himself backwards, dragging the bag with him, and made it back to his feet.

'Put it down!' Preston stammered. 'Seriously.' It came out as a babble. 'Please. Wait up a second.' He backed himself into a corner near the writing wall. The kid advanced. 'This is big-time unnecessary,' Preston said, voice wavering with exhaustion. 'Take the bag.'

At this, the kid lowered the knife. As he did, Preston managed to land a kick against the kid's thigh and back off, still clutching the bag. It didn't stop him for long. He came at Preston again, all spittle and fury. There was nowhere to go.

In a second, the knife was at his throat and the kid was in his face, one fist balling up his T-shirt, ramming him against the wall.

The last thought Preston had was for the bag, and for Alice.

16

Suddenly there were others all around him. He heard shouts and a second face appeared alongside that of his attacker – a blond-haired kid with freckles dragged the boy's raised knife-arm backwards. Preston felt himself wrestled to his knees and the lad with the knife was hauled clear, yelling and kicking.

'You try starving us you'll regret it!' he hissed viciously. 'Just you watch.'

A group of them forced the boy down on all fours and kicked him hard. Preston heard his knife skitter off across the floor, and the lad roar with anger and pain. 'Get off!' he spat defiantly, and growled at the group, 'Big mistake, bastards. We're taking the food, or we're taking you out. One by one.' There was more shouting and the lad was dragged cursing out of the chamber.

Preston collapsed against the wall, his heartbeat high and

hammering. He tried to put his head in his hands, but he was shaking too hard, so he pulled his bag close instead and nursed it.

The room was quiet now. The lad with the knife was gone and the others – the ones who'd pulled him clear – were gathering around him. There were eight of them. They looked like the starving kids you see in the bleak films shown between skits and dumb-ass dance routines on charity telethons.

One lad, white, maybe fifteen, had a torn T-shirt hanging loose over an emaciated body. Another looked as if he hadn't slept in weeks, his eyes puffy and bloodshot, his chest heaving as he got his breath back. There was the blond-haired kid who'd saved him – flexing his thin fingers, wincing at his scabbed knuckles. A kid with cracked lips and a line of sores beading his cheeks and nose was wiping his brow and next to him an Asian lad with long dark hair surveyed the scene, shaking his head. Their clothes were thick with chalky dust, their cheeks hollow, their eyes flat and colourless, their little metal dog tags punched with numbers. There was a girl at the front – a black girl with heavy boots, hair bunched in clumps and a checked shirt with the sleeves rolled up. She had her hands in her pockets.

'Who the hell are you?' she said. She had an accent as if she'd been to a good school once.

'Preston Faulkner,' said Preston hoarsely, massaging some life back into his throat. He wiped the spit from his face. 'He tried to kill me.'

The girl smiled bitterly. 'Yeah, well. Fox has been making a habit of that. But, like they say – friends close, enemies closer.' She crossed her arms. 'What did you do to get his attention?'

Preston shrugged. 'I was just reading the wall. He nodded at the writing. 'Is this yours?'

She ignored his question. 'There shouldn't be any more coming through,' she said, her eyes half-shut and suspicious. 'The last gang – McKenna's lot – knew all about shutdown.' She jerked a thumb in the direction of McKenna, the kid with the bleeding lips, before carrying on. 'We've no room for any more. Go back.' There were nods of agreement from the tired faces around her.

'Listen,' Preston started. 'It's just me. There's no more, I swear.'

'Good thing too,' said the girl. 'We're all out of space. So step back into your madbox and go home.'

'I can't do that,' he said. He had to find a reason to stay. The Alice story wasn't going to cut it. He needed something else. 'Is this your wall?' he tried again.

'Go back.'

'I can't,' Preston said. 'Not yet. There's something I need to do before Armstrong—'

'Armstrong?' said the girl. Her eyes widened and she drew her head back. She recognized the name. In the silence, she pursed her lips, blinking. Then, suddenly, Preston saw his advantage. The wall of writing was a group of confused kids trying to join the dots, and he had more answers than they did. If he was going to talk them round, he'd need to trade.

'I can help,' he said. 'I know stuff. I can solve your puzzle here.'

The girl's forehead furrowed. 'Why are you here?'

'Looking for a friend,' said Preston. 'I have to find her.'

The girl ran her tongue along her teeth. 'Arrested? Rioting? Looting?' she asked. 'You got a dog tag?'

Preston shook his head.

'I don't believe him,' said the tired-looking lad. He had a cold face and a filthy silver trackie top zipped up to his Adam's apple. 'He's ditched his tag or something. The kid's all wrong. I don't trust this.' The boy was blinking rapidly, picking at his teeth with his thumbnail, talking into his cupped hand. Yellow fingers. Smoker, maybe. 'For all we know, he could be as bad as Fox and the rest of the Longsight lads.'

Preston scanned the wall. *The Longsight lads*. What had it said up there? He found the message. *24-7 watch*. So Fox was one they were keeping a close eye on. Friends close, enemies closer. Preston touched his bruised throat gingerly.

'I say we give him a chance.' This from a big figure, taller than the others and framed like a boxer with a flat nose and shoulders wider than railway platforms. 'Just my opinion,' he said, his voice unexpectedly gentle, his accent Irish.

The lad in the tracksuit sneered. 'Jesus, Gedge. Go and hug a tree, will you?'

The girl silenced him with a sharp glance, leant against the wall, kicked her feet a couple of times. 'I don't like loners,' she said. 'When they come through in groups, I know what's happening. We can handle it cos they're all scared and we can line them up and sort them all out. But loners? It freaks me. Don't like it.'

'I'm guessing I've not been the only one, then,' Preston said. 'I'm looking for a girl. She's got brown hair. Tall. Alice, she's called. She was following someone else.'

The girl was guarded at first, then she scowled in frustration. 'Dammit,' she spat. 'There's no more room. We're sleeping head-to-toe down here. Unless we find more space, we're gonna end up crushing each other.' Her fists were clenched. Preston could see the line of her jaw working. She walked to the writing wall and looked up at it, hands on hips, and arched her back. The nape of her neck was dark and smooth. She had a wrist full of festival passes and dog-eared friendship bracelets, and a clip-strap watch three links too big for her.

One thing was for sure – he couldn't ask her about Alice now. She needed a reason to keep him, not turn him away. Preston made it to his feet and took a step towards the wall. 'Jonathan Shade let me through,' he said, pointing to the name. 'I know him.'

She turned, interested now. 'What else do you know?'

'I know all about Armstrong.'

The girl's expression went cold and stormy. She looked at her boots, the muscles in her thin arms working. In those silent reactions, she'd made her feelings about Armstrong as clear as if she'd shouted her hatred aloud. 'I don't want to talk about him,' she said eventually. Then she pushed her short hair back. 'Come with us.'

They started walking. A sparse corridor led to a set of stairs. Ahead, the big Irish kid, Gedge, led the way, his broad back blocking the weak light. Above them, metal pipes were riveted to the roof. Water or electricity, Preston guessed. This place didn't strike Preston much like a prison, where were the cells? The big iron gates, alarm systems, high-walled exercise yard fringed with razor wire – all that stuff you saw in movies? Then the corridor opened into a colossal space and Preston suddenly found himself standing amongst a small township of kids.

He held his breath. This was definitely no ordinary prison. As Esther Klein had said – it was a cave.

The place was the size of a sports field, another chamber blasted from the rock. The floor was concrete – clinical, polished, as if it belonged in a hospital rather than a high-security jail. And on the floor, seated in groups, sleeping, sprawling, brawling and talking, were kids. There must have been over a hundred in all; boys mostly, but some girls. And they looked ragged, starving, desperate; the youngest maybe thirteen or so. The room smelt close – stale and hot with bodies and unwashed clothes, and there was a wall of chatter punctuated with bursts of laughter and debate. There were other sounds too: the low rumble Preston had first heard in the valve chamber, and the clanking groans of two huge fans set into either end of the wall high above the crowds, their dark blades rotating slowly.

'It isn't much,' said the slight kid with the blond hair, 'but we call it home.' He gave Preston an ironic wink. 'Lewison,' he said. He jingled the tag around his neck. 'Seventeen double-two six.'

Taken aback by the clamour and stink, Preston stared at the lad for a moment, then recovered his senses. 'Faulkner,' he said. They seemed to stick to surnames here. There was a good deal of coughing, and he saw one kid shivering under another's jacket, another weak with hunger or exhaustion. Elsewhere he sensed pent-up boredom, bad tempers, bottled aggression. A gang were drawing on the walls with chipped-plaster tools next to a hoard of discarded goggles. A lad nearby was nudging his companions, pointing Preston's way. *The new boy.*

Preston's gaze leapt quickly from face to face. No Alice. She wasn't anywhere amongst them. Preston swallowed his frustration and fear.

'We're on the hunt for better premises,' said Lewison, watching Preston's wide-eyed assessment of the place. 'Rabbit's got a group out looking at the trapdoors, due back soon.'

'Trapdoors?' There was another group. Alice could still be here.

'Sounds weird, I know. But there's some doors in the roof out beyond that corridor,' he indicated the far wall of the hall, 'and if we can reach them and get through, there's a chance we might be able to find something to eat.'

Distracted, Preston gazed upwards. Above, the same punched holes in the roof gave out a light weakening as if at the end of a day. That was natural light out there, filtering in through pipes in the rock. He'd assumed to start with that this place was buried somewhere deep underground, but this wasn't subterranean; they were somewhere light could reach. But when he'd stepped into the valve, the sun had just been coming up over the city. Here, it seemed to be fading. 'Where the hell are we?'

Lewison gave a grin. 'Ain't that the question,' he said.

Preston had become aware of the black girl with the checked shirt talking with her group. She dipped her head and bit her thumb as she listened to her advisors and spoke quickly in response, her eyes bright, her gaze steady and confident. He wasn't the only one watching her. Kids in the hall were too.

There was some sort of disagreement emerging between her and the gang. The guy with the tired face and the yellowed fingers was speaking angrily. 'We've no guarantee, though, have we?' he was saying. 'And there's nowhere near enough food as it is. Send the bastard back.'

Gedge was placating him, big hands open and raised. 'Don't we all deserve a chance at least?'

The girl leant forward. 'I think we need him, Hoyle.'

'What, like we needed the other two? When does it stop?' Hoyle blinked rapidly. 'We can't feed the ones we have,' he said. 'And starving out the Longsight lads isn't working, is it?' The kid called Hoyle gave Preston an empty stare, his eyes like black stones. 'Maybe it'd have been easier if Fox had finished him off.'

Lewison pulled Preston away, his hand on his arm. 'Hoyle's a bit uptight,' he said. 'There's been a few loners recently. You're not going to be popular.' He motioned in the girl's direction. 'But Ellwood'll sort it.'

When he'd talked Shade into letting him through, Preston hadn't guessed it would be anything like this. The kids in this room had most likely been pulled out of their houses, swept up off the streets of the city, bundled into vans, taken away from their families. Back home were mothers and fathers, uncles, brothers. *Did this lot have anyone looking for them?*

'On the other side,' Preston said, 'no one knows anything about this.'

Lewison didn't reply. He stared at the room and wiped his eyes. 'I only stole a bike,' he said suddenly, as if it was his first time confessing it. 'Well, a few bikes. I'm quick with my hands that way. Can't resist it, sometimes.' He held up his thin-fingered hands as if they were someone else's responsibility. 'They're all insured, though, aren't they?' he said. 'Bikes. These students come up to study and they've got tons of cool kit. Headphones, sunglasses, tennis rackets. And it's all insured. They get the money back, right?' Preston listened to the turning of the giant fan, trying to conjure some words.

Lewison examined his palms like a fortune teller. 'I only stole a few bikes.'

He'd gone distant, his small face closed up. He said, as if it explained everything, 'I love bikes, me.'

17

The kids in the hall had fallen into tight circles and talk had slowed with the falling of the light. Darkness encouraged a kind of brooding scaling up of character. Maybe each kid was fighting their own slow sadness, thinking of their parents or their mistakes.

Lewison touched Preston's arm. 'You're with us,' he said, nodding towards Ellwood's group in the corner. The room had filled with a kind of liquid summertime darkness through which eyes and hands and faces could still be seen as blue-grey outlines.

After some time, the Asian kid next to Preston gave him a conspiratorial nudge. 'We're all here for a reason,' said the boy, and made a fan of his fingers like a magician. 'All will be revealed. I have seen it.'

Preston was taken aback. 'Seen what?'

'Big mistake,' Lewison said casting aside a pair of

abandoned goggles. 'Never ask Chowdhury "what".'

Chowdhury gave a tolerant little smile. 'There is a law and balance to all things,' he said. 'We've all done bad things. We're here for a reason and we must accept what is coming to us. I for one . . .'

Ellwood raised a hand. 'We've all heard the we're-here-for-a-reason story, Chowdhury.'

Chowdhury blinked his big eyes. People were sleeping now, and voices had dropped to whispers.

Then Hoyle began talking, his face a permanent scowl, his fingers up around his mouth. 'I was just starting cars,' he said bitterly. 'That's all. It was my brother and the others who did the driving. I was just starting them.' Hoyle's fatigue was written under his eyes. He rubbed them with the heel of his hand. 'Course, while I'm there under the wheel hot-wiring, the cops show up and the boys all jet,' he said, 'and leave me behind. I've got three cars started – one of them's this grey Merc. But our kid's long gone by then. I'm under the dash so I only notice the filth when I see they've got their blues on.' Hoyle was looking at his ragged hands, distracted. 'Then I'm in the cells for a bit. But then there's a call comes through and suddenly I'm away in the vans. They put the goggles on. And I finish up here,' he said. 'So, no. I don't accept I've done bad. Wrong place, wrong time – that's me.'

'Yeah,' Gedge said gently. 'Wrong place, wrong time. Isn't that all of us?'

Hoyle scowled at him, and turned to the girl. 'Can't we eat?'

Ellwood shook her head. 'There's still nothing through.' She was addressing them all now. 'The stuff we've saved needs to stay saved. Make sure people know that. If nothing arrives by tomorrow we'll use the reserves.'

'Things are getting bad,' said Lewison. 'You saw Fox earlier. The Longsight lads aren't getting the message.' He shook his head, ominous. 'That knife. He's going to kill someone soon. Maybe we should just share what we've got with them.'

Ellwood was quick and firm. 'No. No way. Not after what happened. They're having nothing. We keep 'em close where we can watch them. But they get nothing unless they give up the weapons.' She spun the watch around her wrist, eyes distant. 'Anyway. Something will arrive tomorrow.'

'It better do,' said Hoyle. 'Or we're dead.'

'How often does it come?' Preston asked. 'I mean, usually.'

'Not often enough,' said Lewison. 'And recently, it's been getting smaller and smaller. For the last week?' He opened his thin-fingered hands out, empty. 'Nothing. There's a bit of water left. Ellwood made us save it. You should've heard the shit she got for sorting that out. Not now, though.'

It was almost pitch-black. Gedge had rolled on to his side, made a pillow of his huge left arm. Preston lay in the dust, fingers interlaced on his chest, listening to the distant boom of whatever. He worried about the Longsight lads – *We're taking the food, or we're taking you out. One by one.* And he worried about Alice.

Somewhere out in the dark, Ellwood had got to her feet and was moving across the hall, whistling soft and low.

'New boy.' It was Chowdhury. 'What's your crime, new boy?'

Preston drummed his fingers and thumbs against each other and didn't reply. *Go get dead*, his fingers said. 'I made a few mistakes,' he said, his mouth dry. 'Nothing I want to share.'

'We're here for a reason, new boy,' Chowdhury whispered.

117

'All will be revealed.'

Out in the shadows somewhere, Ellwood was moving stealthily. Maybe she was looking for something.

Chowdhury said, 'There's ghosts in this place.'

'Ghosts?'

'Robinson Crusoe,' he said.

'What are you talking about?'

'We're not alone here,' said Chowdhury. He touched the bridge of his nose with the tip of a forefinger, checked where Ellwood was, then spoke low and eager. 'There's a free man up through the trapdoors.'

Preston felt an inexplicable lurch of fear. 'What?'

'Through the trapdoors.' Lewison the bike thief had mentioned trapdoors before. 'Rabbit and me got up through them. And beyond them is the place where Crusoe lives.'

Preston laughed at first, partly because Chowdhury was sounding crazy, partly because the dark was making him feel uneasy. His empty stomach grumbled. 'And someone's gone through them tonight?'

Chowdhury nodded. 'Rabbit has. And others.'

Rabbit had been mentioned before. It sounded as if he might be one of Ellwood's lot. Alice could be with them. Preston whispered, 'What's through these trapdoors, then?'

Preston heard Chowdhury's shallow breath. 'There's a white corridor,' the kid said. 'It's bright. And at the end, a kind of doorway. It seems to . . .' The only sound for a while was the lowdown thud that came from beyond the rocky walls, and the groan of the fan blades over the mouth of the vent. 'It seems to pull you in towards it. I went through and I saw a man.'

Crazy talk. 'Robinson Crusoe,' Preston whispered.

Ellwood was still stalking the room out there somewhere. Preston could just make her out, stepping carefully over the sleeping forms of the kids. Whatever she was looking for, she hadn't found it.

'What does she want?' He asked, half to himself.

He heard Chowdhury shift position. 'She's waiting for Rabbit and the others.'

'Are they in danger?'

'Well,' Chowdhury said, 'we've not had the signal on the pipes. Ellwood'll be getting uptight about her boyfriend's whereabouts.' There was the sound of a grin in the boy's voice as he added, "Specially since he's out with the other girl. Anyway, they usually hammer on the pipes to let us know they're all right.' Preston could just about see him as he cocked his head and cupped a hand to his ear ironically. 'Tonight, no echoes in the pipes.' Out there near the pipes on the far wall, Ellwood was listening for contact. Preston watched her shape in the dark, thinking about Chowdhury's words. Waiting for Rabbit. Boyfriend. Other girl.

Then, as Preston shifted position, he remembered something. *Rabbit.*

'Try it,' Alice had said. She'd drawn again, slowly. 'Neat, eh?'

They had been in the Art rooms finishing portfolio stuff over lunch. A warm afternoon with a low sun that made the windows look fogged with crap. The radio had been on. Radiators ticking, the hum of the projector. Still life. It had been – what? – maybe a couple of weeks ago – maybe a year ago; time had stretched and dilated since this whole madness had begun. Preston remembered thinking it was pretty cool, watching Alice draw.

'It's dumb,' he'd said.

'Are you kidding?' She'd grinned. Then she'd done it again. An upside-down 'R'. 'Like when you're up there,' she'd said dreamily as she repeated the shape, 'when you're lifting your eyes, you see the world in a different way. From the top of those buildings, you're seeing the city – you're seeing the world, I guess – from a perspective that no one else ever has. It's all turned upside down.'

They were talking graffiti tags. Ryan's new tag – the inverted 'R'.

'You're joking,' he'd said. And then he'd copied it, angry with her and with himself. Jealously exaggerating it, making it look stupid. 'It's like a rabbit,' he'd said, thinking he was being clever.

Preston thought about that upturned 'R', and the kid they called Rabbit. What if Rabbit was Ryan? It was at least possible, wasn't it? Did that mean Ellwood and Ryan were together? And the other girl? That could be Alice, right?

Except there hadn't been any contact on the pipes.

Preston was immediately up and off through the blackness, heading unsteadily for Ellwood. He moved carefully, checking the dark at his feet, trying not to step on abandoned goggles, tangled dog tags, sleeping kids.

She was against the far wall in a crouch and she knew he was coming, stumbling as he was over ankles and shins. 'Chowdhury send you?' She didn't look up.

Even in the depth of gloom, Preston could see her strong arms and the curve of her back. She had her ear against the pipes, listening for a signal. Her jeans were slung low. His palms prickled as he wondered about how close he should get to her. People were sleeping. If they were going to talk, he

120

wasn't going to do it from a distance. He took a step forwards, thought about going down on his knees next to her, then reconsidered. 'Tell me about the guy called Rabbit.'

She looked up at him. Her face had clouded, her gaze wandered the floor. 'You know him, I guess,' she said, shifting uncomfortably. Preston felt pretty sure this awkward silence had to do with Ryan. He nodded. 'When you described the girl you were looking for, I knew you meant Wilde,' Ellwood continued. 'She came through looking for Ryan. Rabbit, they call him.' She gave a long sigh. 'What a mess,' she said.

Preston felt his stomach tighten. 'So Alice is here?' he said.

'She *was*,' she said carefully. Ellwood rose from her crouch, pushing the creases from her jeans and straightening up. She was taller than Preston, unless he stood on tiptoes. He felt himself blush, though he had no idea why. 'They went up through the trapdoors this afternoon. They still aren't back. And there's been no signal.'

Preston took a step towards Ellwood. 'How bad is this?' he said. He was so close to seeing Alice that the idea that she might have vanished again might have been enough to crush him. He hadn't slept for so long now, he'd started wondering if everything was a dream.

Ellwood looked at her fingernails. 'I'm worried about him,' she said in a whisper. 'I think it's bad.'

They listened at the pipes together for a while, not talking. Eventually, Preston sat with his back against the wall, knees crossed, an arm's length from Ellwood. He thought of Alice and her Get Happy badge and her bike. He tried to imagine where she might be – somewhere up through the trapdoors, somewhere with Ryan. He thought about Chowdhury's tale about Robinson Crusoe, the free man in the pipes; about Lewison the bike thief, with his dipper's fingers. He thought about Armstrong and wondered what kind of man could live with treating people this way, burying a whole bunch of petty lawbreakers and throwing away the key – clearing the streets and winning votes. The politics of fear. And Preston thought about his dad back home – wherever that was – sitting in the flat with that curve in his back and the bags under his eyes, wondering why Mum left.

Ellwood started talking, soft and low; it took Preston a moment to surface. He placed a hand on the floor between them and leant closer. It was too dark to see properly, but he could feel her warmth. 'When you came through,' she said, 'you said you could help. That you know stuff. You know Shade, right?' She drank from a plastic bottle of water and even in the dark Preston could see the watch with the oversized clip-strap slide down the smooth skin of her arm. It was a neat watch – expensive. It wasn't her size.

Then suddenly, a connection clicked. That name – Ellwood.

Mace and he had seen that name recently. *Westminster Politician Assists Police with Enquiries.* Ellwood was the name of a guy involved in some sort of mysterious accident. And then his daughter had gone missing...

'Bloody hell,' said Preston involuntarily. 'You're *that* Ellwood.'

'What?' said Ellwood. Preston could tell she was pretending. She had hard bright eyes usually but they'd softened now. She sat with her feet turned inwards, toes touching.

'I'm so sorry,' said Preston.

She clipped the top of the bottle closed and passed it to

him. An invitation to drink. Maybe down here, sharing the same bottle had ceased to be a big deal long ago. Still, his insides did a weird twist and glow.

'What do you know about me?' she asked.

18

Preston took the bottle, popped the cap. The neck was warm from the touch of her hands. He put it to his mouth and drank thirstily. In the silence, Ellwood made a check of the pipes again.

'Only what I read on the internet,' Preston said. 'You've no tag. I'm guessing you're not here because you looted a high street after a bunch of stupid riots.'

She rubbed her arms. 'I'll tell you,' she said after a moment's thought, 'but this is a trade. I need your help.'

Preston nodded. There was a long silence. The slumbering shapes around them shifted. When Ellwood leant forward and in the half-dark, Preston could see her face properly. The arch of her eyebrows, dark eyes, the little dots on her lobes where her ears had been pierced. He liked her. The realization came to him sharp and quick and he winced at it, thinking of Alice.

'My dad,' Ellwood whispered, 'is a member of Parliament. *Was* a member of Parliament. I guess you already know this stuff.'

Jacob Ellwood, the name in the article. 'Some of it, yeah.'

'He worked closely with another guy – high up in the government now. You said you know him. Christopher Armstrong.'

'I met him. Just recently.'

'Figures,' Ellwood said. 'Anywhere law and order is, you'll find Armstrong. He's been working with a company called M.I.S.T. based in Manchester – you'll know those guys as well, I'm guessing.'

'Technological prototyping and development for criminal justice,' Preston recited.

'Right.' She waved a hand into the blackness around her and said, 'This is Armstrong's project. An alternative prison system. It's obvious really, when you think about it. Our prisons are full. It's costing us a ton to maintain all those ancient buildings. There needed to be a cheap alternative. Well – one easy way to save money is to remove prison staff, right? Forget rehabilitating convicts. Just dig a big hole and abandon them.' Ellwood's face was set stern and troubled again. She knotted her fingers together over her knees.

'And your dad?'

Her head dipped before she spoke again. 'He worked on the project with Armstrong for a while. But he didn't like it. Especially after the riots that summer. Armstrong started putting gang members away, then kids with bad families who lived in the wrong neighbourhoods – like that's *their fault* – then looters, then just kids like Lewison, Hoyle. Yeah, they'd done some pretty bad stuff but . . . here?' she said, raising a hand to the roof. 'No one deserves this, right?' She looked at him, direct and urgent, her eyes brimful of belief. She was biting her lip. Preston would have agreed to pretty much anything then. He nodded. 'Anyway. Dad couldn't live with it. He wanted to blow the whistle.' Ellwood gave a sad shrug. 'But Armstrong wouldn't let him. Things got worse. There were huge arguments around that time. Angry phone calls. Dad threatened to go to the press.' Ellwood wiped her eyes and beckoned for the bottle. Preston passed it and she drank. 'Crazy talk. Mum was dead against it but he wouldn't listen. And then, one night . . .' She faltered, and Preston thought she might be crying. He was paralysed by indecision. He almost touched her – got as far as extending his fingers – but as if to save him from some disastrous misjudgement, Ellwood held out the bottle and said, 'Dad was killed. But I don't think it was an accident.'

'So you started doing some digging.'

'Yeah. I did. The cops said he was over the limit. But Dad had quit drinking – he hadn't touched it for over a year. And when I tried to find the other vehicle involved, I got nowhere. In the end I asked Christopher for help.'

'You mean Armstrong?'

'Yeah. Mum was in pieces. She was no use. Sasha – my sister – she was at university. Christopher was a family friend. Dad and him were always together. We used to talk now and again . . .' Ellwood tailed off.

'So you think that by asking him – by telling him what you suspected . . .'

'Yeah. He knew I was getting close. He didn't show it, of course – God, no. He was a brilliant liar. But underneath, he knew I was dangerous.'

'So – what happened?'

'One night I . . . I woke up down here,' Ellwood said with a bitter half-visible smile. 'Can you imagine what that felt like?'

Preston felt a cold dread as he thought about it. 'How long ago was that?'

'Weeks. Maybe months. It's hard to tell in a sunless hole.'

'And . . .' Preston shrugged. 'What's your plan?'

In the dark she seemed to debate whether he deserved to know. Preston held his breath and waited. When she spoke, she was alive and glowing with conviction. 'We're all going to break out,' she said. 'And we're going back up to the surface. Then we're finding Armstrong.' She licked her lips slowly, deliberately. 'And we're gonna kill him.'

She held his gaze for a second or two. Preston felt that high, hot wire of fear in his chest. The girl was all fuelled up – twisted and hyper. He couldn't look anywhere else, even as he felt the shoulder bag against the small of his back. Three data-bands and a hundred kids. Preston finished the water and wiped his chin. If he was to save anyone, he'd need to tell Ellwood about the databands. There'd be a serious fight over who got to go home and who didn't. It was another conversation he didn't have the courage for.

'So that's why I need your help, Faulkner,' Ellwood said. To his surprise, Preston found the palms of his hands were damp and he rubbed them against his jeans. 'You know stuff, and I need to know it too,' she said. 'We haven't got much time. The food's almost gone.'

Further off, a gang of lads were sitting shoulder to shoulder, backs to the wall. One had glasses on. Was that Fox, grinning out there in the dark? *One by one.*

Ellwood wiped her mouth. 'Like I said, we haven't got much time.'

Preston considered the empty bottle in his hands. Even water was a carefully guarded resource down here. Shutdown meant the nightwardens wouldn't be able to deliver food and drink. He remembered Mrs Scott – his History teacher in Year Nine – saying that civilization was only one meal deep. Preston hadn't had a clue what that meant at the time. Even brainbox Alice had needed two goes to explain it to him afterwards. Now, Preston knew what old Scott was on about. As soon as the food and water ran out down here, there'd be no such thing as civilization or order. It'd be every kid for themselves; it'd be half-starved Longsight lads refusing to give up their weapons, gathering in the dark. Preston felt the databands and goggles press against his back in the bag. There was the start of a plan in his head, just a fragile little thing. If he could get three people out, they might have time to come back with more databands and rescue the rest. He'd just need to choose the two that came with him.

Preston must have slept, sitting next to Ellwood, back to the wall, legs up, arms around his knees. He knew he'd been asleep because he woke suddenly. The chamber was still and silent. Preston waited a moment, watching the shapes of sleeping prisoners, working out what might have woken him. Then he heard it. Low breathing, nearby.

When he turned, there was a shape up close, a kid at a crouch moving stealthy and steady. Preston froze, his skin suddenly cold. He could have reached out and touched the shape – the lad was moving across him towards the sleeping Ellwood. She was just beyond, curled up and senseless. Vulnerable.

The figure was Fox.

It took Preston a second to marshal his thoughts. Fox was light on the balls of his feet – delicate like an acrobat. One hand was on the floor, balancing him. In the other, Preston saw the shape of something curved. It was a knife. As Preston's eyes got used to the fuzz of the dark, he could make out the shape of the kid's face and the lenses of his glasses, the sheen of sweat on the back of his neck.

Preston swallowed his fear and checked Ellwood without moving his head. As slowly as he could, he adjusted his position, feeling the dull ache of cramp in his calves as he readied himself. His stomach gnawed and grumbled as he made fists of his hands and held his breath.

Fox was closer now, a liquid shape like a predatory animal.

Somehow Preston knew. This was an assassination. If he didn't move now, Ellwood would die silently, a cold hand over her mouth, a blade in her belly.

Preston shifted position, biting his lip. No one else seemed to be awake out there in the dark. He moved quickly. Two quick strides were all he had to get some momentum going. He threw himself forwards, hard and low, shoulder first. He struck Fox around the waist, bundling him over on top of Ellwood. She woke gasping and kicking, instinctively pushing them off. Preston went down, his arms around the attacker. He didn't know where the knife was – he couldn't make out the shape of the kid underneath him in the blackness. He pushed down on Fox's back with all his weight, praying a hand wouldn't wriggle free and a blade open him up.

'Jesus!' Fox said through his teeth. 'What you doing? What the hell you doing?'

Ellwood was alert now. 'Faulkner,' she said. 'What the hell?'

Preston loosened his grip and Fox kicked himself clear, rolling on to his arse and sitting, the knife gone. He was a practised liar. 'You get your hands off me, screb, or I'll chop you up,' he hissed.

Ellwood said, 'Fox. What's happening?'

The kid gave a yellow grin. 'New boy jumped me. All uptight and paranoid, man.'

'What are you even doing here?'

'Taking a walk.'

Ellwood pulled her knees up towards her. 'Walk somewhere else, yeah?'

Fox shrugged. 'Whatever.' He brushed the dust from his jeans and stood, then winked. 'Nighty-night, ladies.' He gave Preston a leer so sour it made him shiver. Then he turned and picked his way into the darkness between the limbs of sleepers.

Preston let out a trembling breath, watching the kid go. 'He had a knife,' he said when Fox had vanished into the gloom. 'He seriously looked like he was coming for you. What have you done to piss him off?'

Ellwood bit her fingernails. Her hands were shaking. 'It's been getting bad for a while,' she said. 'I don't want weapons. We can't have blades. Fox and his boys wouldn't give them up. Things got nasty.' Ellwood was spinning her father's watch again, intense. 'Gedge thought I handled it wrong. Maybe I did. But I figured we could force them to surrender.'

'You've been keeping food from them?'

Ellwood nodded slowly. 'It was the only control we had. We need control.' She ran a hand through her hair and it stood up, tangled and brilliant. 'Guess we're losing it,' she said.

They sat in silence for a long time after that.

There was a hand on his shoulder. It tightened, shaking him. Preston blinked groggily and wiped his mouth. It could have been hours later, could have been minutes. Lewison was standing over him. Ellwood had gone.

'Heads up,' Lewison turned. He turned, indicating the far corner of the hall. There were figures in the mouth of the corridor, holding each other up. 'Rabbit's back,' said Lewison with a grin.

19

Across the room, kids were up on their feet, crowding the returning figures. Preston craned his neck, his heart strong and hard under his ribs.

Then he saw them.

It was Ryan he recognized first, the older boy stooped with fatigue. And Alice was walking a few steps behind. Alice had her hat on, her hair in bunches under it, her jeans with holes at the knees. The sight of her was like drinking adrenalin, a rush that made him want to run across the room and bear hug the breath out of her. He couldn't stop smiling, but then his energy seeped. He had to tell her about the text message. He ran a palm across his dry lips and held his breath.

He'd rehearsed it a hundred times over. *I have something to say that you need to hear.* Then, *I made a terrible mistake.* Then, *We all make mistakes, right?* Then maybe, *Don't punish me for this. Let me explain.* But whenever he rehearsed it, the ending was bad. It didn't matter how much he adjusted his words, it was always: *How could you do this to me? I thought you were my friend. I hate you. I'll never forgive you.*

Ellwood went forward to Ryan. There looked to be a moment of bungling reluctance, one that held the two figures apart. Then Ellwood put an arm round the taller boy's shoulder and he stood stiffly, placing a hand on hers, pulling her towards him just a little. Alice folded her arms and hung back a bit. Then the awkward moment was over, and all around them, kids began to rise to their feet, leaning in, craving news. Preston felt a complicated knot in his chest. He tried to swallow it down but it persisted, partly a burn of bitter satisfaction at seeing Ryan and Alice so distant. It was clear there was something between Ellwood and Ryan – something young and awkward – and that Alice was bruised and seething, but that too tugged under his ribs, made him uneasy. He bit his thumbnail until it stung and bled. After a time, the conversation seemed to stop and there was movement. Ellwood was leaving the big open cave and heading back towards the corridor where they'd first arrived. Ryan was following, and so were the others now: Hoyle, Chowdhury, the big lad Gedge and the rest of her close team of advisors. The kids in the cave, though, they dropped away, returned to their places. At the head of the delegation, Ellwood walked shoulder to shoulder with Ryan, Alice a few steps behind. Alice turned and saw him.

Preston raised an open palm in greeting, straining every sinew to exude cool. He felt an involuntary grin split his face. Alice broke away, started towards him.

*

When he held her she felt thin and frail, her cheekbones

133

sharp against the side of his face, and her breath came in a rattle, as if she was ill. Preston had played and replayed this moment in his mind since Alice had gone missing. The real thing wasn't what he'd expected. In his imagined versions, she'd even kissed him on the cheek. But the real thing was colder and sadder. Alice looked exhausted and cried quietly. 'Press,' she said, holding him at arm's length to look at him. 'This whole thing is a nightmare. Some of them are only children. What are you doing here?'

He wasn't expecting the question. The answer seemed obvious. 'I came looking for you,' he said.

Alice laughed. It was a laugh that should've sounded joyous, but it carried a kind of pity in it.

'What?' said Preston.

'You shouldn't have bothered.'

Preston felt himself colour up fiercely. She sounded ungrateful but he didn't know why. 'What's happened?'

She blinked tears from her eyes. 'God,' she said quietly. 'What *hasn't* happened?'

Preston suddenly felt as if they were two strangers. 'Ryan OK?' he tried, immediately cursing his stupidity.

Alice scowled. 'Oh yeah,' she said darkly. 'He's been amusing himself.'

'What's wrong?'

'Why not ask Miss High and Mighty,' Alice said. Then she closed up, biting her fingernails. 'Sorry,' she said. Then, 'I have to help some of the younger ones. They're frightened.' She turned and walked back towards the group.

Preston took an uncertain step to follow, but faltered and then stood, foolish and alone, feeling the whole room watching him. Lewison rescued him a moment later.

'C'mon. It's the meeting in the writing room. She wants you there.'

They were gathered around the writing wall in a loose half-circle, Ellwood was at the centre, one hand in the pocket of her jeans, one hand open-palmed against the words on the wall, fingers touching *ARMSTRONG*. When she saw him she gave him a nod – a slight, almost imperceptible, signal of her approval.

Ryan paused and gave Preston a look, a cold-eyed upward tip of the chin that was the only indication they'd ever even met. To Preston's left, Lewison was jumpy and curious, eyes everywhere. Hoyle was standing opposite, his scowl a mask. Dwarfing him was Gedge. He gave a nod. 'New boy,' he said by way of greeting. Alice had kept her distance from the group, Preston noticed, arms folded and gaze downward.

Ryan was talking freely. 'So we found another squad of madboxes,' he said, a tremor of excitement in his voice. 'Seriously.' There was a collective *yes*, a silent fist-clenching moment of relief. Ryan grinned. 'There's maybe a dozen and they look alive.'

'Seriously?' hissed Hoyle.

Ryan nodded. 'There are problems,' he said. 'We need to get through another set of doors. But when we do – those madboxes . . . they're lit up like Christmas lights.'

An impromptu cheer went up, and the room echoed to swapped expressions of relief. Ellwood held a hand aloft and the discussions broke up again. She gave a smile, one that seemed to take in everybody. Preston liked that smile.

'This is good news. And right now, we need good news,' she said. She paused, then added, 'There's been no more supplies through.' She'd addressed it mostly at Ryan and his group, but the effect was the same on everyone – a collective groan of despair.

'There's gonna be war for what's left,' said Hoyle. Someone else swore loudly. Someone said, 'We're going to starve down here!'

'This is the man responsible,' said Ellwood over the hum of voices, her hand on Armstrong's name. 'He's shutting down the madboxes and we're being left for dead. He's the enemy, right? So when we get through, he's the one we need to target.'

'We're closer than we've ever been,' said Ryan. Someone had handed him a bottle of water and he'd thrown back half and seemed revived; he stood taller and straighter. 'We'll need to go in groups. The journey's a difficult one. There's some strange stuff up there,' he said. 'There's no pipes so we couldn't signal. It's all very . . .' He paused. 'The building gets very different. But if we get through the doors, we could all be out in hours.'

'The children need to go first.' It was Alice, biting her lip. 'We need to get the younger ones out.'

All out in hours? Children first? This wasn't what Preston had expected. It was as if no one here knew that entering a valve without a databand was suicide. Preston felt the sweat prickle on his scalp. He was the only one who had the full story. He had to tell the group.

Chowdhury was speaking now and Ryan was shaking his head, his lip curled in frustrated anger. 'We're here because we have committed crimes,' Chowdhury was saying, his voice soft and humble. 'We have to accept that. We've sent six frontmen through and they promised they would be returning to help us. So why leave?' Voices clamoured at this and

Ellwood had to wave them down. 'We must give them time,' Chowdhury continued. 'They need our faith in them. They'll be back.' There were murmurs of agreement; a skinny kid to Chowdhury's right nodded his assent. Someone clapped him on the shoulder.

In the end, Preston couldn't stop himself. 'They won't,' he said, clear and calm. At first the group were taken aback – *the new kid speaks* – but then Ellwood, eyebrows curved high, gave a cautious nod. Preston broke the tension of the silence. 'Your last two frontmen went through a few nights back. I know that cos I saw one come through the other side of the valve.' Ellwood's face changed at this – the line of her jaw tightened as she checked the responses of the crowd. The writing room was silent. In the icy grey light, Preston could feel everyone's eyes on him. 'He didn't make it. None of them made it.' He hadn't thought ahead sufficiently to realize fully what the response would be. These were fellow prisoners – volunteer frontmen who'd taken a risk for the others. They'd never see them alive again. Heads dropped and feet shifted. Someone swore bitterly.

Then Hoyle spoke through his ragged fingernails. 'How can you be sure?' he said. 'You could be lying. To keep us here.'

The idea seemed crazy, but the faces of the kids in the writing room told another story. Lewison frowned, looking across at Hoyle. 'I'm not lying,' Preston said with feeling. 'Why would I be lying? I'm trying to help. I saw one kid come through. The nightwardens had the other one too.'

'Nightwardens,' said Ellwood. She turned to the wall, tracing the connections. Preston watched her, feeling the suspicion in the room. 'Shade, right?' she said.

Preston nodded.

'I heard that name too,' said one of the kids.

'There's three of them,' Preston said. 'One's Shade, one's an American woman called Esther. There was a third I didn't meet. Shade's brother, I think. But he wasn't around.' Ellwood rolled a finger at him, encouraging more. 'They guard the outside of the valves – the madboxes – but they don't expect anyone to make it out. Not alive, anyway. You can't.' Preston found himself having to raise his voice as he spoke; others were calling, jeering. He felt his face flush and a line of sweat travel the length of his spine.

Ellwood said, 'Hear him out!' She still had control, Preston reckoned, but it was tentative. Her voice was firm and objections petered out. 'He knows things we don't. It's possible the valves were designed this way. It sounds like the kind of thing Armstrong would plan for.'

Hoyle was playing with the zipper of his trackie top. 'Here's an alternative story,' he said. 'Let's say new boy's one of them. One of these nightwarden people. They're not happy that our frontmen have got out. They've sent this guy down to stop us.' Hoyle got a murmur of approval for this and pushed on, stabbing a yellowed finger at Preston as he did. 'So just as we're about to make an escape, you show up to tell us it can't be done.' Ellwood tried to calm him, but Hoyle, wiry and exhausted, skeletal, was breathing deeper and thrusting his chest out. 'You're part of the problem, new boy. We've got a solution right here!' He thrust an arm out in Ryan's direction. A cheer went up at this. An actual full-throated cheer.

'Hang on,' Ellwood said, her voice sharp. But the feeling in the room was changing and Preston could sense it sharp and clear. It felt supercharged, flammable.

There were upraised arms directing insults. Chowdhury almost had to shout to be heard. 'This fighting gets us nowhere! We must wait here. There are enough supplies to keep us alive for days yet . . .' But he was clamoured out by jeers, opinions and warnings.

'Let's go for the trapdoors!' someone yelled. It might have been Hoyle.

'Let's go through now!' came a shout. 'Get the goggles!'

Ellwood tried to get control again but the exchanges had got ugly and she was drowned out. When Chowdhury held up both arms and called for peace, someone hit him and he went down. There was a surge in the shape of the group. Preston tried to pull himself clear. Someone kicked him. He could hear Alice screaming something. There was a sort of scrum.

Then Ryan was shouting something – yelling at Ellwood, his face close to hers, and she was shouting back, and the energy went out of the fight and the room stilled around the two of them. 'We're going!' Ryan was saying. 'We're going now! That's what we need to do. For Christ's sake, Chloe, don't bloody *overthink* this like you do everything else!'

Ellwood straightened up. 'Overthink?' she said, her voice high and taut. 'Someone's got to do the bloody thinking down here!' She stabbed a finger at him. 'If I'd done a bit more thinking,' she said with furious sarcasm, 'maybe I wouldn't have ended up—'

Ryan gave an indignant laugh. 'Right. So it was all a mistake, was it?' He struck the flat of his hand against his chest. 'Now I've done all the hard work, I get cast aside, do I? Who's the new crush now, Chloe?' Ryan pointed at Preston. 'Faulkner's got the inside track and suddenly he's God's bloody gift, is he?' He spun round and paced.

Preston looked at Alice. She was standing at the edges of the group, and she'd closed up, made herself small – her shoulders hunched, her head down. Her expression was one of studied devastation. She was working her jaw, biting back rage and tears.

Ryan continued. 'There's a dozen madboxes up there and they're alive! They're working!' There were cheers from the assembly at this. Hoyle raised a fist in the air and roared his agreement.

Ellwood had to blink tears from her eyes. She'd lost this one, it was clear. 'Ryan, please. Wait. It's not safe.'

Ryan turned to the group. 'I'm going,' he said, pushing back his hair with a pair of perched goggles. 'I'll check it's safe. If it is, I'll get word to you all. Who's coming?' he said. 'I need volunteers.'

It was Alice who raised her hand first.

20

When Ryan saw her, his expression changed. He seemed suddenly aware of what he'd said and done, and his eyes softened. He nodded his agreement. Hoyle volunteered too. Chowdhury nursed a cut on his forehead and glowered. Others wanted to be in the second wave – cowards who needed someone else to die for them. Some weaker kids just got turned away.

The stand-off lasted while Ryan's little group rested and made preparations. The writing room had calmed, the crackle of violent energy dispersed. Ellwood sent Chowdhury over with three bottles of water and a couple of tins of food, which the three of them shared as they talked in low voices, Ryan laying out his plan, Alice listening silently, Hoyle asking questions. Preston watched from a distance, feeling stupid and helpless. Twice he began the walk over to their corner, ready for an argument. But twice he hesitated.

'Faulkner,' said Ellwood, placing a hand on his elbow. 'His mind's made up. You won't change it.'

'But it'll never work,' Preston said.

'So you said. Tell me again.'

Lewison said, 'You were saying they can't get through, yeah?'

Preston nodded. 'Armstrong's set it up so you can't go back through a valve without being killed. It's like diving, or something. Coming back up too quickly. I have to stop them if they're planning on trying it.'

'I tried,' said Ellwood.

'Yeah,' said Preston. She deserved to know the truth. If he was going to help her, he needed to tell her about the databands. This was a secret he couldn't keep by himself, no matter how hard the conversation would be. 'I've got something to show you,' he said, checking Ryan's group were absorbed in their planning, then swinging the bag from his shoulders. 'There's still a way we can do this, but it's difficult.' He dug in his bag, past the balled-up jacket and goggles. Three databands. He pulled them out.

Ellwood's eyes widened and they crouched low around the bag, protecting it from the gaze of others. Lewison craned his neck to look. Preston lowered his voice. 'You get through alive if you wear one of these,' he said. He picked one up, demonstrated. 'There's a tiny computer checking your vital signs with a pouch of medication attached, and a row of sharps that stick into you here – an injection system. It takes a few minutes to work and then you throw the valve switch and you're through.'

'Bloody hell,' breathed Ellwood. 'How many have you got?'

Preston packed them away, nervous hands trembling. 'Welcome to my dilemma,' he said. 'There's three.'

A couple of hours later, Ryan's group left. Preston watched them go. Alice didn't look back. Lewison went to check on Chowdhury. Ellwood, back from checking the hall, returned her attention to the bag on the floor between them. 'Where did you get them?' she asked.

'Nightwardens. They use them to come through when they drop off food.'

Ellwood gave a desperate laugh. 'They won't be using many, then.'

'You know what? Shade seems an OK guy. Esther's all right too. I think they've been leaving more supplies than they should. They kept talking about shutdown like it was something they didn't want.'

'Yeah, because they lose their jobs.' Ellwood scowled and traced a finger through the dust on the floor.

'It was more than that. They wanted to help.'

'Then they should have given you more bands. What's the use of three?'

Preston's stomach gave a growl and he stood up. 'Maybe I can come back with more,' he said.

When Ellwood stood up she was close to him. He wanted to touch her but he hesitated and she spoke. 'You should go,' she said. 'Join Ryan's expedition. Do what you can to stop them. I'll follow on.'

'Come with me,' said Preston. He did his best to keep his voice casual. It still came out like a plea. 'You'd be better at talking them out of it. And you know where the trapdoors are.'

Ellwood gave a sad smile. 'I don't think so,' she said.

'Whatever me and Ryan had – we haven't got it any more. Besides,' she added, 'I need to stay for a while. Word's got round. The natives are restless. It's down to me to give the last of the food out.'

Back in the hall, there were kids muttering in their sleep, boys with parched lips dreaming of rain, half-awakes in desperate debate. There were the Longsight lads, watching and waiting – the red-headed Fox with the battered face and the glasses. There was a kid on his own with a face like a car crash, crying for his mum.

It was Lewison who showed Preston as far as the long, low corridor at the far end of the hall and waved him off. Behind him, some kid had fainted and a few others were shouting for help now, calling for water.

In the darkness of the corridor, pipes were riveted to the roof alongside old industrial strip lights in heavy iron and glass cases. After a dark kilometre or so, it opened into a high-ceilinged silo. And up there, ten metres above the floor, were two recessed squares. One still had a door. The other was an open hatch. These were the trapdoors.

Discarded metal objects were cast about directly below the openings. Alongside the ragged-edged food cans that had been fashioned into decent tools, Preston could see other abandoned implements – belts with metal fasteners, dog tags broken from their chains, bunches of keys: stuff that had been used to hack an ugly, pock-marked upward route of irregular handholes into the wall. All the way up to the trapdoors.

And there were three figures using the holes to climb.

Ryan was ahead and was picking his way upwards, one

handhold at a time, reaching, testing, then hauling himself closer to the hatches in the roof. There was about three metres to go, Preston calculated. It was a perilous-looking journey. The holds, hacked from the chalky plaster, crumbled at their edges. Showers of grit and dust fell in mazy drifts as the three climbers toiled upwards. Hoyle was second, watching Ryan's progress carefully, pausing to rest with one foot pressed into a depression and his spare leg hanging free, neck craned. Alice followed, her hat crammed into her jeans pocket, her hair loose and dusted with chalk, bare arms straining.

Their concentration was entirely on the climb; three silent, gasping figures heaving themselves towards the trapdoors, hand over hand. Once near the top, there was an awkward readjustment necessary so the climber – Ryan in this case – could reach for the lip of the hatch in the ceiling with one hand whilst clinging on to the highest handhold with the other. With a scramble and a swing, he was up and through, legs pedalling wildly, then he was lowering a hand, white with plaster dust, for Hoyle.

Below them was Alice. She was shorter, her build more delicate – the move towards the hatch was harder for her. She reached out, her right arm taking her body's weight, the floor ten metres below her.

Then something went wrong. It must have been her grip; a clod of plaster broke free, sending a shower of debris down into the room. Her balance went. She windmilled wildly, reaching for Ryan's hand, and in a horrible parody of a slow-motion swan dive, seemed to be falling.

Preston ran hard, making for the wall.

Above, he heard her scream, and Ryan shouting

instructions. As Preston reached the first handholds and hauled himself upwards, he half-expected to hear the dull crunch of her body hitting the floor. But she was still up there, suspended. Ryan was yelling at her to calm down. Alice let out a high shriek. Preston climbed, scrambling recklessly from hold to hold, arms and legs burning. He was weak with hunger and fatigue, and his eyes stung with sweat and dust. He could hear Alice breathing hard now, dry terrified sobs. Preston craned his neck as he pulled himself up. Ryan was bent at the waist, his upper body over the lip of the hatch, both arms taking Alice's weight as she swung above the drop. Her grip looked as if it were loosening and Ryan's gritted teeth and desperate eyes confirmed it.

Preston pushed himself on, exhausted.

When he reached her, he had no time to think or feel. High above the hard floor, he pushed himself under her legs, stepping upwards as he did so. Alice's kicking feet slithered against the bag on his back. Preston strained, his fingers tightening against the hacked handholes.

Then her weight vanished, suddenly – she was through. Preston clung to the face of the wall, feet tucked into one hole, fingers crammed into the fissure of another, taking great dusty gulps of air, hoping some strength would return to his arms and allow him to move. He was dimly aware of a fuss above him – Ryan shouting, Alice holding an arm out – but when he finally had the courage and energy to look up, it was Hoyle he saw first, his face a malignant frown. 'Jesus,' he hissed. 'New boy's come to join us.'

Preston closed his eyes against the sweat dripping from his brow. 'Screw you, Hoyle.'

Ryan and Alice were above him at the trapdoor, side by

side, offering their arms. With all the strength he had left, Preston held himself steady and began to reach towards them.

'Thanks, Press,' said Alice, hand outstretched, face all relief and wonder. 'Come on. You've really got to see this.'

21

Through the trapdoor, everything felt different.

There was a white hall with a polished floor and lights lining the roof. Preston took a moment on his back, taking it all in.

The corridor was clean and white. Everything was all right angles – all plush interior, like a hotel. It smelt like disinfectant. Alice touched his arm. Her hair was plastered to her forehead, her cracked lips bleeding. She'd brought a half-bottle of warm water. They shared it in silence.

Ryan crouched over him, sarcasm curling his lip. 'Guess the boss sent you,' he said. 'Come if you have to, Faulkner. But don't think you'll change the plan. You won't.'

Preston made it to his feet and somehow found the will to walk, trailing plaster dust as he went. Dizziness swung the space around him and he had to lean against the wall, leaving a filthy shadow of grime. At the end of the long white space,

Ryan pushed open a pair of swing doors.

What came next changed everything.

Preston arrived last to find Ryan, Hoyle and Alice robbed of speech. There was an open space. There were glass-fronted cabinets with interior lights. A wall-mounted fire extinguisher, a muster point. And, weirdest of all, there was a set of escalators.

They were hissing and creaking in the big space, revolving endlessly like a hamster wheel in a cage. No one spoke for a long time – even Ryan and Alice, who'd already seen the place, were reduced again to disbelieving silence. Somewhere near them, that deep and regular boom he'd first heard when he emerged from his valve had increased in volume. It wasn't mechanical, Preston realized – it was something organic.

The place smelt of floor polish and air conditioning and it looked like a shopping centre, or an underground train station. There was something dreadful and cruel about it, something inhumanely unfair about two such different places being next to each other. Ryan said, 'It's up here.'

Preston followed towards the escalators, unsteady, swaying like an astronaut. The ride upwards was ridiculous. Four kids, faces blurred with grime and lined with fatigue and hunger, clothes torn and twisted, staring shell-shocked as an escalator carried them as calmly as if they were shopping for kitchenware.

At the top was a reception area.

'I don't believe this,' said Hoyle.

There was a big, white, curved sweep of desk with a telephone and a computer. A deep-blue wall-mounted sign, glowing a little, like neon, announced, *Welcome to Axle Six*. Underneath, it said, *Technological prototyping and development for criminal justice*.

There was a waiting area. A low table and comfortable chairs. The place was a polished and glowing front for some sort of company that traded in prisoners. This was the kind of sanitized, guilt-free space that hid a horror beneath it, like the foyer of a mental asylum. Except there was no one here. Whoever had built this wasn't hanging around to take responsibility. Shutdown meant closing both ends of the Kepler valve.

Ryan pointed. 'This is the way out,' he said.

To begin with, it looked as if he was walking towards an opaque black wall. Preston couldn't get his eyes to register. Then, as he stepped forwards, the jumpy reflection of the reception lights shifted, and his whole perception of the black wall changed.

It wasn't a wall at all. It was big glass doors.

Looking out was like changing the way you thought about everything. Like when you're convinced you're moving because the train opposite you is pulling out of the station – and it's only when it's gone and the platforms around you are still that you realize you're the stationary object. Preston stared.

That sound he'd heard – that deep, rolling boom – it was the sea. It was the thunder of breakers against a sheer cliff wall. Outside there was a storm. It was lashing down in sheets against a curved concrete loading bay. There was space for trucks or cars and what looked like a landing pad for helicopters. It was hard to make it out because it was night. The four of them cupped their hands against their temples and pressed their faces to the glass. Out there, beyond the entrance space, ornamental shrubs and grasses were being whipped about as wind tore at the greenery.

Past them, a steel fence rose up around the space – thick vertical struts, conductors and wires, which meant it was electrified – then, further beyond, Preston could make out a cliff edge in the velvet blackness, and a black body of water beating the rocks below.

Across the compound from them, a short dash away, was a second building, glass-fronted, inside which were Ryan's valves. He'd been right. There were a dozen, all lit up. Shutdown hadn't reached them yet. They could be the way out. No wonder he was fired up.

All they needed to do was find a way through the doors.

'This isn't Manchester,' Preston said, his breath clouding the glass.

Alice dropped her forehead against the cold, black surface. 'The Count of Monte Cristo,' she whispered. It was the first thing she'd said for ages.

Ryan said, 'What?'

Preston remembered. 'It's the prison on the island, right?' The book she'd been reading – the story of the prison off the coast of France. He looked out into the darkness.

He was pretty sure that wasn't France out there either.

Ryan spoke. 'That's our way forward,' he said, finger on the glass.

What happened next was quick and crazy. Ryan turned and strode across the reception area, vaulted the desk and manhandled the receptionist's chair back. All Preston could do was watch as he swung it like an axe – an ordinary office chair with castors – and slammed it hard against the glass with an animal yell.

He may as well have tried to dent metal with a feather.

He staggered backwards, dropped the chair – the plastic

casing of the seat had shattered – and swung it again. It split into bits on contact with the glass and spun away. Ryan pitched the distorted remains across the reception floor and put his hands on his knees, breathing heavily. 'There's got to be a way through these doors.'

'They're electric, right?' Alice said. Her gaze was on a wall-mounted panel. There was a shoulder-height keypad and a little grille to speak into. 'Is there a code or something?'

They crossed to the wall next to the doors and stood in a half-circle, staring at the problem. 'Anyone handy with this stuff?' Ryan said.

Hoyle grinned. 'Well,' he said. 'I'm pretty good at hot-wiring cars.'

Hours later, it was clear the system was rather more sophisticated than a Mercedes-Benz. The first hour had been spent in gouging the front panel free, working in shifts trying to prise open the casing of the keypad using the same tools that had hacked a chain of handholds into the wall below the hatches. It was Ryan who did it eventually, giving a great shout of victory as the housing split open and he pulled it free, fingers bleeding. Beneath was a rubber membrane, a motherboard, and a tangle of wires as delicate as a nervous system.

Hoyle peered at it. 'Holy shit,' he said.

The following hour was the slowest of Preston's life. His knees ached, his stomach grumbled, and the silent storm beyond the glass raged ceaselessly. He spent the time exploring the reception area. He checked the phones – they were dead – dug through desk drawers and tried to start the sleek desktop computer.

No luck. Until the little plastic card with a magnetic strip.

Preston found it tucked against the back of the top drawer of the receptionist's desk and pulled it free.

'Hey, Hoyle,' he said, holding it up. 'There's not a slot for a keycard, is there?'

'Course not,' spat Hoyle, sweating over his work, his yellow fingers probing and pulling, detangling wires, following them to their source in the wall. Preston pocketed the card, spirits sinking.

After forty minutes, Hoyle had the motherboard out, though it was still connected to the machine by a maze of wiring. Then he was decoupling and recoupling connectors, using his dog tag as a makeshift blade, cutting the fine copper free from its plastic and twisting wires together.

He'd been on it almost two hours when the explosion came.

There was a flash, a bright cloud of light that burst from the wall. Hoyle was cast backwards like a doll, arms flung outwards, silhouetted against the spray of vivid whiteness, then he was on the floor and there was a loud bang.

The lights went out. There was a horrible smell of fused plastic and burning circuitry. Only the outside lights remained on; enough to see Hoyle on his back and Ryan over him. As Preston moved forwards, there was an unfamiliar clang and shudder, and the interior lights came back on. They were a third as bright, pale red. Emergency power. A generator somewhere.

'Hoyle?'

The lad on his back was stirring, and then up on his feet, Alice steadying him. 'I'm OK,' he was saying. He sounded drunk. 'Get off me. I'm sorted.' In the red light, he shrugged aside any help and moved forwards, peering at the circuits, wincing at the burns on his hands. Eventually, he said, 'Interesting.'

Then he started again, slower this time.

'You sure you know what you're doing?' said Ryan.

Hoyle turned. 'I do now,' he said. He flexed his fingers, staring at a tangle of connectors. 'This will either kill me, or get us through,' he said emotionlessly. 'You guys ready?'

'Any final words?' Ryan said.

Hoyle gave him the finger and returned to work. A moment later he'd located what he wanted. 'Right, then,' he said with finality. 'Let's go.'

They stared in mute silence as the thin kid in the tracksuit bent over his work one last time. There seemed no sign of fear in him. As if it didn't matter that much one way or another. He touched something against something else. There was a crackle and click.

Then the great glass doors opened.

The wind entered and charged in circles, sweeping the floor with rain. The sea roared like an animal above the crash of the undergrowth. Ryan, who was closest, was knocked backwards by the force of the storm.

'Oh my God!' said Alice slowly.

Hoyle was almost pulled forward, a paper boat caught in a dark current. Preston guessed it must be the first fresh air he'd tasted for months. He stepped out into the storm, his clothes flapping against his thin body. Ryan followed.

The air was warm and laced with salt. Preston had to steady himself as the storm tore at his hair and drew tears from his eyes. They crossed the loading bay. A sheen of water rippled on the concrete and drains broiled beneath their feet.

Preston's shoes were quickly soaked through, and his clothes stuck to his skin. The sea seemed all around them, roaring from all directions, as if they really were on the island in Alice's book. Above the compound the electric fence undulated in the wet wind.

Ryan was at the second building now, head dipped slightly as he considered the glass doors. The sea boomed again and the ground seemed to shift with the force of it. Beyond the glass, the gaping mouths of the boxes. Their lights were shivering and blinking with energy. They made Preston think of router lights, the kind that meant a strong connection. Hoyle was running the sharp sides of his dog tag around the edge of the glass doors, looking for a gap. The doors were lighter and thinner, less protected – but there didn't seem a way in. Ryan swore loudly, beating the glass with his fist.

Then Preston remembered the card he'd found. He dug into his pocket, checking the building around its glass doors as he did so.

And there it was: a wall-mounted card reader protected from the rain by a hinged bulb of plastic. Preston stepped forward. Even Hoyle gave a bitter grin as Preston held his breath, lifted the rain-soaked flap and ran the card through the slot.

The doors hissed apart. The group entered, one by one, part breathless, part relieved, and part terrified.

22

Inside, the air was dry and musty. Dust drifted in corners. The scuff of old boot-tracks meandered between the machines – the final checks of the staff before shutdown, Preston guessed.

Hoyle was jumpy with energy. 'This is it,' he said, checking his goggles and pulling them over his head. 'This is the way home. Any one of these could take us out of here for good. We can do it right now, yeah?' He began pacing up along the line of valves. Their low gurgling hum was like a vibration beneath the pounding of the water along the cliff face. 'First thing I'm gonna do when I get back is swipe some food,' he was saying, flashing a skull-like grin. 'Can't wait. C'mon. We're out of here. Which one do we pick?'

Ryan was considering the machines carefully, biting his thumb. 'We need to work out where they take us, first,' he said. 'And when we're happy it's safe, we'll need to get people up in groups,' he said. 'Even if only one of them takes us home, if we brought people up in twenties, we could get the first lot through pretty quickly, assuming everything's working, then go from there.'

'Kids first, remember,' said Alice.

Hoyle spat on the floor and shook his head. His eyes were dark and suspicious again. 'Kids first? I don't owe those people anything,' he said, jabbing a yellowed finger in the direction of Axle Six. 'I don't even bloody know them.'

'Hoyle, calm down,' said Alice.

'I'm out of here. What was Faulkner's story? That all our frontmen are dead? Well, now we've got a whole new squad of madboxes and we need to prove he's lying, right? So I'm your man. I'm going through.' Hoyle widened his palms and gave a sarcastic shrug. 'We're not running a kindergarten, Wilde. So, no offence, but screw the kids, yeah?'

Alice looked at Ryan, her eyes wide, an appeal for sense. Ryan raised a shoulder and looked for a second as if he couldn't muster the strength. Then he spoke. 'Chowdhury'd have us wait, but that's senseless. With no food coming, we're all going to die.' He pushed his hair back. 'Ellwood's too obsessed to think straight. Like Hoyle says, someone's got to go first. Why not him?'

'Jesus, Ryan!'

This was it, Preston thought. If he was going to stop this madness, he'd have to do it now. What had Shade said? *Where you're going is seriously damn deep. Come back in a hurry and you'll go into seizure.* Hoyle and Ryan were going to turn up in an alleyway in Manchester shivering and dying. He'd have to explain about the databands. He had no choice.

He swung his bag off his shoulder. 'Listen,' he said. Ryan

didn't. Hoyle was halfway up the steps of the first valve. 'Listen!' Preston shouted.

Hoyle turned. With his goggles on, he looked monstrous. 'What now?'

Ryan rubbed a hand across his beard and blinked tiredly. 'More bad news, Faulkner?'

'You won't get through alive,' Preston said.

Hoyle started laughing, a curdled sound with only malice in it. 'So you keep saying, new boy, but I ain't staying here to starve.'

'There is a way, though,' Preston said. He was holding his bag up now, raising it like a prize. Hoyle stopped. Ryan was silent. 'You wear them.' Preston's heart was knocking like a rocking chair. 'Up around your arm like a band. The night-wardens told me about them. There's a little pouch of drugs in them and it stops you dying.'

'What are you on about, Faulkner?' Ryan had thrust his hands in his pockets and was regarding the bag suspiciously.

'The databands,' Preston said. 'I've got some with me.'
Some. Jesus, that was a horrible butchering of the truth.

'Databands,' said Hoyle, deadpan. 'Were you planning on mentioning these at any point?'

Ryan held out a hand. 'Let's see, then.'

Preston swallowed hard. There was a part of him desperate not to do this. He couldn't give them all away. He wanted one for Alice, one for Ellwood, and, dammit, *one for him*. Ryan wasn't in his plans. There was no way he was handing them over. But he could show them at least, and try and stop this.

He unstrung the top of the shoulder bag and widened it, dropped a hand inside and felt past his jacket, the goggles he wore in the valve, and . . .

Shit.

He checked again. He pulled out the coat. Hoyle was saying something cutting but he couldn't even hear. The goggles hit the floor and he dug again, getting frantic. *Oh, God.*

There was icy meltwater in his stomach and his legs liquefied. It was near-impossible to stand upright. The databands were gone. Everyone could see it on his face. Preston tried not to weep with the panic of it all.

'Well,' said Hoyle. 'That's convenient, isn't it?'

For a moment, Preston couldn't figure it out. He'd had them with him all the time. When he showed them to Ellwood, he'd made damn sure he didn't hand them over.

'Someone's lifted them,' Preston said. The group was fracturing and splitting, attacking itself. Starvation did that kind of thing. *Who'd done it? Ellwood, maybe? It didn't seem likely. Who else had been there? Chowdhury? Lewison?*

'I can't see any reason to stay, then,' said Hoyle with breezy arrogance. 'I'm out of here.'

And he climbed the last steps up to the gaping mouth of the first valve.

The next few seconds were complicated:

Hoyle's weren't the only footsteps. It took Preston a moment to realize; someone else was crossing the loading bay, the rhythm of running boots just audible above the hum of the valves and drumming rain.

He was the first to turn.

Out in the storm was a figure – a tall, strong girl. It was Ellwood, head down against the driving rain, a silhouette against the blood-red of the generator lights. She'd followed, like she said she would. Preston felt his hopes kindle.

She squeezed through the gap they'd made between the doors. Her dark skin was beaded with water, her hair pushed back from her face in a tangle. She was breathing hard after the climb to the hatches. She saw Preston looking back at her. 'Axle Six?' she began, but faltered when she saw what was happening.

Alice saw it too. 'Hoyle, no!' she screamed and broke into a run, taking the steps of the valve in one leap. Preston only had a moment to register that it meant that Alice believed him. He left his bag and ran too. Ryan was following Hoyle up the steps.

'Hoyle!' shouted Ellwood. 'Wait!'

Back in the basement at M.I.S.T., Preston had shut the valve door before he threw the switch that activated it. There'd been the click of the shifting mechanism before the thing had shuddered into life. But this was a very different deal. The valve door wasn't even half shut. As he ran, Preston could hear a voice from inside echoing tinnily. 'It's cold in here.'

Alice was at the mouth of the valve now, hauling the closing door back open. Ellwood was next to get there and a shoving scrum developed, Ryan pushing Ellwood back, yelling, 'Let him go!'

Ellwood slipped under his arm and in through the closing door, trying to pull Hoyle out.

As Preston got there, Ryan blocked his path. 'Let him go!' he shouted again, and followed his words with a great furious barge. Preston grabbed at Ryan, tugging him clear, and the two of them went down, Ryan with his arms low around Preston's waist. They rolled over a couple of times, elbows and knees jarring and bruising, and they bumped down the metal steps. Then, they were clear of each other, on their knees, and Ryan, wild and fuming, lunged at him and missed. Preston swung a fist and felt the crunch as it connected and in return, took a blow hard in the gut. Preston was 404, winded and gasping.

Up at the mouth of the valve, the door was still open, Ellwood wedging herself in there to stop Hoyle shutting it. Then it all got way worse; the valve changed its voice and the deep gurgling hum became something more like a guttural roar. Hoyle must have thrown the bloody lever.

The valve blurred and juddered, as if it was speeding up somehow – Preston had to blink, that hallucinatory feeling coming again: hunger, lack of sleep. It was still open, and Ellwood was half inside, pulling Hoyle back, when the sound of the valve pitched upwards to a weird scream and Ellwood was thrown clear, falling hard to the floor.

Alice gathered herself first, checked the half-open door, and looked inside. There was a horrible silence for a second or two as her breath came in great desperate gulps. 'It's empty!' she shouted, her voice breaking. 'He's gone. Jesus. He's out. He's free.'

He wasn't. He was dead. But Preston didn't care about Hoyle any more. It was Ellwood he was thinking of. She'd been almost inside the thing when the lever was thrown.

He dropped to his knees next to her, and suddenly, she reminded him of the kid on the table – the one Esther had brought through. He fought back a nauseous panic and flexed his fingers, thinking. Where was the nearest doctor, the nearest hospital? Preston leant in close to her, wondering whether to give her the kiss of life. But – *thank God* – she was breathing. He could hear it. Close up, it was furious and shallow. And when he touched her chest, he could feel her heart stuttering under his open palm. Maybe she was starting the fits and judders he'd already seen the other kid experience. The rattling teeth, the shuddering muscles. But this seemed different. She was loose and still. And she was alive.

Ryan was at his elbow now, then Alice too, the three of them crouching over her, Ryan checking her pulse, two fingers against her neck. 'No no no,' he was saying, low and guttural. Alice was silent and white-faced, biting her lip.

'Recovery position,' Preston said, holding her head, his upturned hands a makeshift pillow. Ryan had a half-bottle of water with him and they tried to get her to drink but it spilt down her chin and pooled in the little dip of dark skin at the base of the throat. Then Ryan tried speaking low and soothingly to get her to wake up. She wouldn't. Her breathing got shallow and shifting, her dark face unnaturally pale, her pulse weak.

Inside, Preston felt suddenly and utterly ruined. Ellwood was the reason he'd been able to see a way out of this. She was going to be the one who could return with fire and fury, and bring Armstrong down. Without her, any advantage had evaporated. All that was left now was surviving this.

He had to get her to a hospital. Which meant he had to go back through the valves. Which meant he somehow had to get the databands back. And he needed Ryan and Alice to help him, and for that to work, he had to tell them everything. Every bloody thing.

23

He needed to do two things: clear up the whole text message thing and then explain the databands. And then at last it would all be out and Alice and Ryan could hate him with every fibre, but at least it would be over.

He took a shaky breath, his face on fire. 'There's something I need to say.'

Alice tucked her hair under her hat wearily. 'We need a plan.'

'I need to tell you both some stuff first.'

Ryan was checking Ellwood's pulse. 'What?'

'I was the one who sent the text message.'

'What text message?' said Alice.

'You'd left your phone at my place,' Preston said. 'And Ryan had sent this text and I sent the reply.' It was horrendous to watch. Alice went from kind of puzzled to horror-struck to furious. 'It was a mistake,' he carried on. 'I knew it as soon as I did it. That's why I came here – to apologize.' Preston knew he couldn't rescue this one. Alice looked tight, sharp, cold.

Ryan had made the connection now too – his face had darkened and he'd pulled his head back in that way people do when they want to distance themselves from you. 'Jesus Christ, Faulkner,' he said, his lip curling. 'You're a nasty piece of work, you are.'

'It wasn't like that.'

'Yes it bloody was. I sent a message asking for help. You saw it, Faulkner. And you sent a reply.' His voice was uneven now. 'You split us up,' he said.

Alice looked at him with such an intense disgust he could hardly bear it. He'd lost her friendship for ever and he felt a shame so sharp and deep that it seemed a hard and permanent part of him like a skeleton. *To hell with everything.* 'There's something else as well.' Then he just started talking. He went through the whole thing Shade had – the bands, the way they worked, the microchip, the needles, the drugs, shutdown. How, if they could help him find the bands, he could get three people out, right now. Ellwood and two others. They both watched him with a terrible kind of contempt, but they listened at least.

Alice spoke first. Not out of malice, just a flat statement of fact. 'Three,' she said. 'Some of those kids down there are like thirteen years old. Three's not enough.'

'I know,' Preston said. 'It's a big decision.'

'A big decision?' Ryan snorted. He looked tormented. Perhaps the whole blade of guilt in the guts thing had started for him too. It was Ryan's fault Ellwood was hurt, after all. 'Damn right it's a big decision!' he fumed. 'And when the rest of them find out, Faulkner, it'll be more than a big decision, it'll be a war.'

Preston wiped his eyes. It made no sense limiting damage now, he needed to do things the way they needed doing. 'We've got to get those three bands back,' he said. 'That way, I can get Ellwood to a hospital. She's the only one who can help bring Armstrong down, and she's sick.' Preston swallowed hard. 'That means we've got room for one other person. So who's it to be?'

Ryan and Alice looked at each other. Alice inflated her cheeks and let out a long sigh. She looked like she was going to say something but didn't.

'Why you?' said Ryan.

'What do you mean?'

'I'll get Ellwood to a hospital,' said Ryan. 'Me and Alice'll deal with it. You stay here and make sure there isn't a war. How does that sound, Faulkner?' He gave a malevolent glare, watching for a response.

Preston pulled a face. 'C'mon,' he said.

'You'll have to do better than that.'

'Leave it,' Alice said.

'No, let's hear him out. Faulkner's got all the ideas, apparently.'

It was partly hunger, Preston guessed – his stomach felt as if it was trying to eat itself – partly sleeplessness, but suddenly all he could remember was this activity they'd done in Ethics once. It went like this: an imaginary hot-air balloon is running out of fuel and is falling towards the earth. All ten passengers are going to be killed by the high-impact crash as it strikes the ground. But here was the catch – if six people jumped out, taking their own lives, the remaining four would be collectively light enough to drift harmlessly to safety.

There was a lawyer, a doctor, a drug addict, a footballer, a bunch of others. Which ones would you encourage to sacrifice themselves, the teacher asked, and why?

Preston had never paid that much attention. Now, crouched next to a dying girl and fighting the howl of panic in his head, he wished he had. He thought about Shade, about the warehouse workroom and the stockroom full of goggles and kit. 'Stop dicking about, Ryan,' he said. 'Ellwood needs a hospital. So it has to be her. And it has to be me because I'm the guy who knows Shade. I know where he keeps the rest of the databands. I know where I can get a load more. So it's me, her, and one other.'

Preston didn't wait for an answer. Instead, he lifted Ellwood carefully. He could feel the girl's heart beat against him as he hauled her up. It was an ungainly moment. She was tall and strong but her legs were useless, and for a second or two he held her like a doll. Then he managed to stoop beneath her arm and stand upright.

'Where you taking her? The valves are here.' Ryan said.

Preston shook his head. 'Who knows where they lead?' he said. 'I need to go back through the one I came in.' He hitched Ellwood up again, struggling under her weight.

After a moment of brooding silence, Ryan joined him.

They left the valves and worked their way slowly back out into the wind and rain, Ellwood strung between them, heading for the red lights of Axle Six.

The walk, with Ellwood between them, was long and hard, and the descent back through the trapdoor was backbreaking. They left the clean white spaces of Axle Six slowly and carefully, manoeuvring Ellwood's weight between them as they lowered her through the hatch into the fetid darkness below. The air was warm and close and stank of rank bodies. It was like a descent into hell, Ryan sweating and swearing as he secured his footing, then called up to Preston, one hand gripping the lip of the chalky hole hacked from the wall, the other raised up to catch her. Preston, his hands under her armpits, lowered Ellwood towards him from the trapdoor above. Ryan pinned her to the wall as Preston swung his legs through, found his footing and they descended slowly, Alice calling out the positions of the hacked-out handholds. In the close, damp darkness at the bottom the three of them collapsed, Preston pouring with sweat and coughing out dust, so weak with hunger that he had to lower Ellwood to the ground and then sit, wiping his wet face with trembling hands. Alice had fallen into a solitary silence, staring at her fingernails and thinking.

'I'll stay,' Ryan said eventually. His face was a smear of plaster dust and sweat, his hair white with it. 'I can keep control of the food we've got left and . . .'

Preston shook his head. 'The last of the food will already be out,' he said.

Ryan licked his cracked lips and winced at the pain of it. 'So how long would you be?'

It was difficult to say. He'd come out at M.I.S.T., he'd find Shade and ask for help. Shade would know what to do. Then he could be collecting the databands and he could be straight back through for the big-time prison break. *Except there was shutdown.*

What if the valves weren't working any more once he got home? What if he couldn't get back at all, and everyone left behind was left behind for ever? The thought was almost too much. Preston felt his heart do a weird flutter and he felt faint. If he didn't eat soon . . .

'How long would you be?' This time it was Alice asking.

'I don't know for sure. Maybe another day.' *Assuming Armstrong hadn't pulled the plug already.*

Alice knotted her fingers together, then said, 'I'll stay.'

'No way,' said Preston.

But Alice continued, 'I can make sure the younger kids are kept safe. I'll stay.'

'It should be me, Al,' said Ryan. He looked at her with tenderness. 'I screwed everything up for us down here. I'll stay.' Alice held his gaze for a long time, her face unreadable.

'This is stupid,' Preston said. 'We haven't even got the bloody databands yet.' He fought his way to his feet, groaning at the effort of it, legs and back aching, stomach gnawing. It was either Ellwood, Chowdhury or Lewison. It had to be – they were the only ones who even knew the bands existed. When he showed them to Ellwood, he'd made damn sure he didn't hand them over . . .

Then it made sudden sense.

Lewison – that's who it was. What did he say about stealing bikes? *I'm quick with my hands that way. Can't resist it, sometimes.* 'It was Lewison, the bastard,' Preston spat. 'He lifted them. C'mon. If we find Lewison, we've still got a chance.'

The final stretch of stinking corridor seemed to last an age. The hall was alive when they arrived back, a fever of bad panic in the air. The food and water had been set up in the centre of the hall. Chowdhury was there now, unpacking the last of the tins and bottles, a couple of kids helping. Groups were making ragged lines, but they broke up when eyes turned to the corridor and the prisoners saw them returning.

They could hardly carry Ellwood a step further, and as they made it into the hall Preston felt his legs sway. He couldn't lock them, they wouldn't straighten, and he had to lower the girl's limp shape. There was no strength left. Ryan set her down as crowds gathered, and questions came fast then. What had happened? Was she dead? Were there monsters? Did the madbox eat her? Was there a way out? Hoyle – where was Hoyle?

They handled it between them in the end, sharing the story, their voices cracked and mostly crowded out. Someone passed a half-finished bottle of water and they shared it, talking slowly, picking their words carefully.

'She's still alive,' Preston said, sheltering Ellwood from the push of the crowds. 'But we need to try and get her some help.'

Ryan was giving an exhausted account of Hoyle's disappearance. 'He went through,' he finished. 'I don't think he'll be coming back.'

Preston asked, 'Where's Lewison? Anyone seen him?' He couldn't get an answer. Shrugs and silence. Most kids stayed near the food in gaunt and defeated groups. 'Where's Lewison?' he said again.

Then one set of kids suddenly broke away from the gathered groups and headed for the corridor. One of them had an armful of tins, another some water.

'Hold up,' Ryan said when he saw them. 'That's not a good idea. We need to stay here.'

The kid at the back turned. It was Fox, with his scratched glasses and his angular, bruised face. The Longsight lads. 'You gonna stop us?' he said. Some of the others were watching now. This wouldn't have happened yesterday, with Ellwood still around. There were rules and routines: places you could go, places off limits.

'You can't go,' Ryan said.

'You can't get through the valves,' Preston shouted in support. They needed to control this. The group stopped again. All four turned, looking almost ready to listen.

'He's right,' said Ryan. 'The valves nearly killed Ellwood. You can't go through.'

'I don't remember anyone putting you in charge,' sneered Fox.

'Wait . . .' Preston started. He was going to say more, when he remembered – the door to the room of valves had locked behind them as they left. The card was in his pocket.

But before he could tell them, there was something else.

This time it was a commotion over by the food and water because Chowdhury – who had been talking, Preston realized, his voice steady and constant – started shouting. 'Hey!' he was saying. 'There's a distribution model. Hey!' Preston knew what he was going to see before he turned around. Now the boss was gone, there was a fight starting.

The Longsight lads took off, heading for the valves. Ryan started chasing, but then faltered and came back to protect Ellwood as the crowd began a feral surge.

'Calm down!' Preston tried. 'Just hang on a minute!' But he was swallowed by a sideways movement towards the supplies – all shoulders and sharp elbows, some pushing, others jostled helplessly along. He could hear Alice shouting something, Chowdhury saying, 'Stand back!'

Preston tried to find Lewison in the breaking and grouping. There was no sign of him. Someone nearby had gone down and someone else had fallen over them, legs knotted.

There was a scream from somewhere near the ground; a kid was getting a boot in the face, clawing at the legs descending on him, trying to pull himself clear.

By the time Preston had pushed his way to the edges of the scrum, it was chaos. The hall was nothing but a shifting mass of roaring groups. Across the centre of the space, the place where Chowdhury and Alice had been, was a swollen smudge of spilt water, split and leaking plastic bottles cast about. There were fights at the edges of this dark grey stain, scuffles and brawls for the bottles. The same had happened with the food: cans and packets of stuff had been torn open, tipped out. One group were tearing the plastic husk of wrapping from a tray of tins, shouting and shoving to get access to it.

Civilization was only one meal deep.

Alice emerged from the ruck, hair streaming, wiping the back of her hand across her bloody nose. 'What do we do?' she said. 'It's crazy!'

There were shifts and surges in the crowds. One group had started throwing empty cans to deter attackers. Another gang had backed off, dragging a haul of sealed bottles. A third lot were wearing goggles; they'd turned themselves inhuman. Ryan appeared, pulling Ellwood, hands looped under her armpits. They settled her in a quieter corner. Someone gave her water but she couldn't drink. Her pulse was weaker again.

'I need to find Lewison,' Preston said.

'I'll help,' said Ryan. Alice stayed with Ellwood.

Preston picked his way through the chaos, checking faces. One group were sitting it out, watching with weary horror. Some small thin kids – lithe little rodent boys – were tracking the progress of fights and then scurrying in to swipe a bottle or a can. One lot were working as a team, with two or three of these runners bringing trophies back for a group who'd occupied a corner. The kid who'd been trampled earlier had got himself clear, his T-shirt soaked with spilt water, big black boot-marks on his tiny ribcage.

Lewison was nowhere to be seen.

Preston scanned the hall and caught sight of Ryan, who gave him a hopeless shrug. Over by the corner where he'd sat with Ellwood and her gang just the previous night, Preston saw Chowdhury. He made his way across, picking a route that avoided a violent scrum that had broken out over a couple of tins. His stomach tightened and ached at the sight and smell of the food – what looked like cold soup and tinned potatoes. One kid was hunched eagerly over a can of it, shovelling in the contents with a trembling hand.

Preston didn't want to contemplate what some prisoners might do to survive once supplies were gone. But if he couldn't find Lewison and talk him into giving the bands back, he'd be finding out. The thought made him twist with terror. He made a silent promise to himself there and then, circling the edge of the hall and staying away from the fighting, that if he ever had the chance to get Armstrong back for this, he would.

Ryan had already reached Chowdhury when Preston arrived. The kid had taken a further beating since Preston had last seen him. He tried to smile but his lip split. He indicated his eye, which had puffed and closed up. 'Some people won't listen to reason,' he said by way of explanation. 'There's a simple mathematical way to divide it all. But I've yet to convince this lot,' he said, his face clouded. 'Ryan was telling me about Ellwood. How is she?'

'She needs a hospital.'

Chowdhury put his head in his hands. 'You know, she was right to be worried about the Longsight lads. They jumped me.' He wiped his good eye and paused. 'What will we do without her?'

'Chowdhury. Listen – this is important. Where's Lewison?'

He frowned. 'He left just after you did.'

Preston's heart began a long, slow downward fall. 'Left where?'

'Ellwood gave me the supplies to sort out. I was busy dealing with it. Lewison went back to the food valve to see if anything else had come through, I think.'

Ryan said, 'And have you seen him since?'

Chowdhury shook his head. 'Soon after you came back it all kicked off,' he said. 'I didn't . . .'

Ryan closed his eyes and exhaled – a steady, exhausted outward breath. Then he asked the question Preston had felt creeping up behind him for some time, the question that had been nagging and gnawing at him as he carried Ellwood back. 'Faulkner,' said Ryan. 'Did Lewison know how the bands worked? The needles, the top of the arm – that stuff you told me?'

Preston had been trying, but he couldn't remember what he'd said. And he also couldn't remember where Lewison had been when he said it. Preston's chest felt suddenly empty. If Lewison knew how the bands worked, he might not be here at all any more. He nodded reluctantly. 'I think so,' he said.

Chowdhury said, 'What's happened?'

No one said anything in reply.

The fighting subsided in the end and Preston made his way across the hall to the valve room. That was where the food valve was, Chowdhury had said. Lewison might be somewhere in there.

Preston was the solitary standing figure. Like the riots – the ones on TV out in Birmingham and London and Paris and in Manchester too – there was a limit to the energy a crowd could expend; it didn't matter how hungry or abused or desperate they were, eventually they couldn't carry on. The centre of the hall, around the spillage, was empty now. Debris littered the open space and around its edges, groups of frightened, starving kids huddled together for safety. Whatever was going on, Preston thought, this was its final stages.

And now the databands were gone he was a prisoner too, just like all the others.

He dragged himself across the hall towards the writing room. Beyond was the valve room where he'd first emerged almost twenty-four hours ago. It already felt as if he'd taken a lifetime of punishment.

He made his way up the short corridor towards the writing room, and was making to turn right and head into the half-darkness of the valve room and begin his pointless search for Lewison when the hallucinations started. It was the hunger and sleeplessness playing their tricks again. This time it was voices. Actually, a single voice pursued by a bunch of echoes. A familiar voice too, coming from the writing room.

'I'm in a massive open-plan room with a big high ceiling,' it was saying. 'Curious markings decorate the far wall, the desperate scrawl of abandoned prisoners. Literacy levels down here are low.'

Despite everything, Preston felt his heart inflate and hope rise. He laughed; he couldn't help it. He had to wipe his eyes. He walked to the archway of the writing room.

And there, Elliot Mason was speaking into his phone and gazing starry-eyed at his surroundings.

'Mace,' Preston said. Mace turned, and suddenly his face was all grin. He still had his goggles, pushed high up into his hair, and his databand already on. He was real. Preston's knees nearly went, but his heart was full. 'What are you doing here?'

Mace, his phone at his chin, said, 'My colleague Preston Faulkner also present.' Then, suddenly serious, added, 'Shade sent me. Shutdown's been started and accelerated. He told me to say that all the valves will definitely close down today. Even the food ones.' He dipped his head in the direction of the valve room. 'Most of the ones in there are already dead. I came through the M.I.S.T. valve like you, but we're seriously short on time, brotherman. He's going to keep it open as long as he can, but it's going offline any moment now.'

So this was it. All valves closed. There wasn't even any more food coming. Just as he'd thought. Armstrong had condemned a hundred kids to death. 'Mace,' said Preston. 'Tell me, please God, you brought some databands.'

Mace shrugged a bag from his shoulder. 'Sure,' he said.

Preston nearly wept. 'How many?' he said. It came out as a croak.

'I've got mine here,' said Mace patting his right arm. 'And there's three more. You, Alice and Ryan. Sorted. Where are they? We need to move.'

Ah, dammit dammit. Preston ground his teeth. *Ellwood needed one. Someone was going to have to stay.*

'What's up, Press?'

Preston tried to swallow but his throat was sandpaper. 'There's someone else coming back with us,' he said. 'It's complicated.'

Before anything else, he had to get Ellwood and Ryan and Alice across the hall without attracting attention. It was near-impossible, hauling Ellwood between them as they were, the toecaps of her boots etching lines in the blood and water behind them. Suspicious eyes followed them. Soon, Preston knew, the Longsight lads would be back. They'd have found they couldn't get through the final door to the valves. They'd be nursing a fury.

In the writing room, Alice hugged Mace and cried. Mace stared wide-eyed at Ellwood as Preston lowered her against the wall where, only hours earlier, she'd spoken as the leader. Ryan shook Mace's hand and there was an awkward telling of stories – brief, emotionless stories that fell far short of the horror. Mace spoke into his phone a lot while everyone else passed round his water and shared his chocolate with trembling reverence. Preston tried not to burn up with the fear of everything, rehearsing what he needed to do, how quickly he needed to do it. Databands and goggles. Back through the valves. Everyone out. It didn't feel as if it were possible. But it had to be; he had to get them all clear and free. And then there was Armstrong.

'I'm staying,' said Alice as they finished. 'I've talked it over with Ryan and I'm staying.'

Preston felt his heart seize up. She wouldn't make it alone. 'No,' he said. 'Please.'

Ryan cleared his throat. He was standing close to her. Close like he used to back at school. 'I'm coming back for her.'

'I'll stick with Chowdhury until you do,' Alice said with a pale smile. 'It's decided.'

Preston wanted to speak. But Alice didn't look at him any more. He'd forgone that friendship now, and he'd have to pay the price.

Inside the valve room, it was dark. But one valve was breathing and its light was a low glow.

Preston rode the relief, and Mace led them over, then turned his back to it and opened his bag. 'Put them tight around the top of your arm,' he explained, handing out the databands. 'There's needles. It'll hurt. Itches like hell, too.'

Ryan cursed, struggling with the Velcro straps, pulling it up over his wrist and scowling. 'It bit me.'

'Yeah,' Mace said. 'That's good. You need to feel the bite.'

Preston looped one up over Ellwood's arm, lifting it clear of her body, pushing the band into place and tightening it. There was a catch in her breath as the needles punctured the dark skin of her upper arm and that, Preston guessed, could be a good thing. He checked the band, his face close to hers, worked a pair of goggles carefully on to her forehead, then moved her towards the valve, her shape in his arms feeling both curious and familiar. Mace followed. Alice hung back, eyes wet with tears while Ryan held her close. Preston gave him a few moments. Then Ryan broke the embrace, held Alice's hands in his and spoke soft and low to her. He turned to face the line of boxes.

The food valve was different from the M.I.S.T. one – it was older and smaller. The pattern of lights wasn't like the others. Up there across the compound, those valves had big bright displays, all pyrotechnical flickers and blinks. This old beast, though, had a single dull yellow eye to the left of the door – an elliptical glow the solitary indication it was still alive. Alice was crying now. Preston checked his goggles and took a step forward, ready to enter the dark interior.

That's how close they got to leaving.

Then someone appeared out of the dark, a shape made of shadow. A step forward, and the kid was all bones and edges. Strong shoulders and arms, short red hair, glasses over small black eyes. Behind him, a clot of darkness broke into three other figures. They were back.

'OK,' said Fox. When he spoke, his voice was like a hacksaw – his words somehow a statement, not a question. 'Which one of you bastards has the keycard?'

25

Preston knew everyone would look in his direction.

Ryan had inadvertently raised his eyebrows at him, staring across Ellwood's slumped figure, an accidental betrayal. Alice was staring at him wide-eyed and terrified, the Longsight lads grouped either side of her.

Mace, on the other hand, didn't know what on earth was going on and recorded the fact, his phone at his chin. 'We've been joined by a small group of fellow prisoners,' he said.

Fox stared at the newcomer. 'Who the hell are you?'

Mace blustered onwards. 'Under the mistaken impression we have some sort of keycard.'

'Mace,' said Preston. 'Just stop.'

'New boy,' said Fox, flashing his teeth. 'All eyes are on you.' He held out a palm and flexed his fingers. 'Hand it over.'

Preston didn't have long. His stomach flipped like a skimmed stone. 'I don't know what you're talking about,' he said.

Fox laughed. 'Yeah,' he said bitterly. With that, he turned to one of his boys – a squat kid with a rat's face who read his leader's glance like semaphore. The kid grabbed Alice, pushing her arms backwards and down, crushing her wrists together behind her back. Alice winced and gasped, her face a picture of terror. Fox picked at his teeth with filthy fingernails. 'Hand it over, screb.'

Preston held up a hand. 'I get it. OK. Stop.' He gave Ryan what he hoped was a meaningful look. Behind them, the open valve was a matter of feet away. They'd been so close.

Ellwood's breathing was faint and shallow. Preston checked the databand with a hooked finger, careful not to draw attention to it. Ryan whispered something so quietly, Preston couldn't hear it. Was it something like, *'What are you doing?'* It sure as dammit wasn't a vote of confidence.

But Preston couldn't see that he had any choice. 'Maybe I've got it somewhere here,' he said, rising and fake-checking his pockets.

'Correction,' said Mace into his phone. 'It seems my colleague Preston Faulkner does indeed have the aforementioned keycard.' He looked up at Fox. 'I can only apologize.'

Mace withered slightly under Preston's glare. Preston patted his jeans stupidly, preserving whatever time he had left. He lifted out the card. 'Your lucky day,' he said. His voice sounded hollow. He readied himself. Most of what followed was going to hurt. 'Catch.' He flicked his wrist, sending the card across their heads in an arc.

Fox couldn't help track it as it spun, eyes upwards.

That's when Preston ran at him, and barrelled him down in a great charge. He knew the knife was in his back pocket. He wrestled it free as they fell and threw it clear. The

181

Longsight lads leapt into action then. Alice was discarded and they flew into the fray, teeth bared, directing vicious kicks. Ryan was amongst them too now. Mace had given up commentating and was running for the ruck.

Some school fights are for show – one kid getting held back by a mate, doing the let-me-at-'im dance while the other kid snarls and whips up the crowd. Other fights are quick and humiliating: two or three well-placed punches and a head-butt – one kid getting frogged big time and retreating. Others are all pile in, dirty as hell, PE changing room fights – teeth and hair and barely enough room to swing a fist.

This was one of those.

The key was, Preston knew, to stay close, wrestle hard, protect your eyes and make sure the bastards didn't knacker your goggles. That's what he did. He was on the floor with Fox, rolling over and over, kicks raining in. Then Ryan was somewhere close, giving some kid a hiding. Alice was trying to pull Fox off him. Mace shouted, 'Big-time unnecessary!' and then hit someone on the nose. Preston threw punches hard and quick, trying to escape Fox smothering him. Nothing made contact with any force. Someone was tugging at his hair with a fist. He threw an elbow back, felt it make contact. Someone's nose gave a horrible splitting sound and a voice screamed in pain – Preston couldn't see who.

Then he had Fox's hands at his throat. Fox was digging his thumbs into his windpipe, a big grinful of spit close to Preston's face. Then Fox was gone, and Ryan was pulling him back by his tags, pummelling him with a mad roar. Alice was kicking like crazy, one of the Longsight lads on the floor cursing and swearing.

Everyone had lost their minds. The cave had turned them

into animals.

'We're going!' shouted Mace. He was at the door of the valve, goggles on, roaring. Preston was exchanging blows with the rat-faced kid and caught him a good one on the chin. Then someone was on his shoulders, both arms around his head and he was spinning, his vision obscured. He heard Mace shout, 'We're going! C'mon!'

Alice was helping him now. He knew it must be Alice because someone spat, 'Bitch,' as she hit him.

Ryan's voice had joined Mace now. 'Press! C'mon!' and, 'Alice, run. Leave!'

Preston backed into a valve hard, crushing the kid hanging on to him, sending an elbow back into his face. Alice was backing away, free now, her nose bloody. The Longsight lads were down. Two of them, anyway.

'Go, Alice!' Ryan shouted. 'Go! Find Chowdhury!'

Alice wiped her face, gave a wild wave, then turned and ran.

Ryan was pulling Ellwood across the threshold of the valve. Mace was at the door, shouting, beckoning. Preston started to run. It seemed to take an age, a dream where sprinting at speed is like wading through gluey fluid. Then his legs went and he skinned his knees as he fell. He made it up again.

He was at the door now. Inside, the light was burnt orange and the air was so cold he could see his friends' breath cloud. He could see Ellwood on the floor, Ryan pulling a pair of goggles down over her eyes, Mace at the lever. He turned to close the door behind him.

Fox was at his face with a knife.

'Don't move a frickin' muscle, screb,' he spat.

Preston froze, his heart somewhere up in his throat. Mace

could throw the lever now, even with the door half-open, and the three of them would get away home. He'd be thrown clear, half-dead, and Fox would cut him up.

Except Fox did something strange instead. The lad paused a second, pulled the blade clear, and pushed his glasses back up his nose. 'Let me in,' he said. 'Let me come with you.' Preston choked on nothing, trying to make words come. There was a steady stream of blood from a cut on his forehead and he had to wipe it from his eyes. He wondered again if he was dreaming. 'Please,' said Fox, lowering his knife-arm further.

Preston licked his lips. There was a time – maybe just a couple of days ago – when he would have done the right thing. He reached for his own databand, ready to peel it off and hand it over. He ran a finger along its edge, heard the Velcro begin to tear. He knew what the right thing was – he had to hand the band over to Fox, send him in his place and stay with Alice.

But he wasn't going to do that, he realized. Things had changed. He thought of the balloon debate.

Then he punched Fox hard in the glasses and shut the door on the cave as the kid stumbled backwards down the valve steps, his dropped knife clattering away.

'Let's go,' said Preston.

The light flickered, and the valve began its breathing. Preston fumbled his goggles on. There was that strange feeling again; the curious sensation of movement, as if somewhere beneath them was a travelator.

The valve was working.

It was shuttling them, swapping them – spinning its chambers like a gun. There was the unholy stutter of flashing light, bright enough to burn his eyeballs. Preston felt weirdly seasick. In the half-light, he saw Mace lose his balance a bit and grab Ryan's arm. The two of them spread their feet and balanced like passengers standing in a railway carriage.

'I feel horrible,' Ryan said. 'Has it happened yet?' He placed a hand on his stomach. 'I'm going to be sick.'

'Wait,' said Preston. 'You'll feel the band in a sec.'

He prayed they would.

In a second or two, it happened. There was a strange tightening, as if it was hardening against their skin. Then he felt the sharps drive in. His upper arm went suddenly very cold. He blinked away a strange dreamy dizziness.

Mace had winced and brought his hand up to his arm. After a moment he said, 'We're done, right?' Scratching the band, he announced, 'We're home.'

It was Ryan who pulled his goggles down over his chin first, opened the door and peered out. 'It's quiet,' he hissed. 'It's dark out here.' There was a slow pause. 'Smells different. And it's like totally silent.' He slipped his head and shoulders outside. 'There's no one out here,' he said. Then he was through.

Preston pushed his goggles up, stooped over Ellwood and raised hers carefully too. Her head lolled. As they moved her outside, Preston could see the dark silhouettes of his friends. Ryan, the tallest, with his hands on his hips, looking upwards as if inspecting something; Mace with his phone out, lining up a voice memo. 'This is difficult to explain,' he said, stilted and slow. 'We aren't . . .' He cleared his throat, lowered the phone for a second and then raised it again. 'We aren't in the right place.'

26

They lowered Ellwood on to the cold concrete floor, making a pillow of Preston's jacket. Her breathing was shallow and shifting. She was in bad shape. They stood, and took in their surroundings.

They'd entered the valve in a basement under M.I.S.T., a long, dark open-plan space with blinking banks of tech, high windows and a heavy fire door out into the sunken garden. *But this? This wasn't supposed to happen.* They were standing in an icy-cold cramped room. The ceiling was low and rattling with rain, the walls exposed brick. The valve they'd emerged from looked like a rust-encrusted old prototype, angular and ungainly. To its left there was a desk with scattered, curled Post-it notes bleached of their colour, a chair on castors, a telephone with no dialling tone – Ryan was checking it – an empty filing cabinet and, across the far side of the space, huge wooden pallets with polythene-wrapped packages on them – canned food and water. There were hundreds of them: tinned meat, cheap soup, potatoes, all plastic-wrapped for transport.

This must have been one of the valves where the food supplies had gone in. Esther had mentioned one out at Blackstone Edge. Preston found his voice. 'The others must be shutdown already. The valve redirected us. Maybe this is the last one still open.' *And maybe they'd come within minutes of being trapped in the pipes.*

The far wall was a floor-to-ceiling panelled shutter, like a garage door. Preston tried the button mounted on the wall next to it. Nothing. Maybe the motor had stopped working. Mace crouched by Ellwood, a hand on her shoulder, checking her breathing, while Preston and Ryan worked their fingers underneath the door. They heaved upwards and it shuddered and screeched. It moved a little. Mace joined them.

'On my count: one, two, three,' said Ryan, and they hauled again. There was a gap now, just thirty centimetres or so. Enough to squeeze through. Ryan lay on his back and began to work his way under. 'Gimme some more room!' he panted. Preston and Mace hauled the door up another few centimetres, and a few more again. It was old and rusty and squealed on its tracks. 'Hey!' Ryan said. 'Lift your eyes, man. Taste this air! It's beautiful!'

He was through and out into the blackness beyond. They heard him crouch and lean in, his shoulder against the outside of the door.

'Where are we?' Preston said. 'What can you see?'

There was a moment of silence. Then they heard his voice. 'You're not going to believe this.' They checked Ellwood, then Preston and Mace pushed their way under, wriggling on their stomachs.

They were back in the real world again and it was stunning.

There was a car park edged with a high chain-link fence. The wind, sweeping across the tarmac in icy-wet sheets, buffeted the side of the building. The air was clean and bone-chilling. Some way off, invisible, a motorway hissed with traffic. There was a gate bound loosely with a padlock and chain. And there was a van, a white Transit with regular UK plates and missing wheel trims.

Beyond the fence were moors. Blackstone Edge. Preston took a couple of steps forward, watching the dark contours of the landscape. It was British moorland all right – empty, bleak, familiar. The few trees that huddled around the building soon thinned to low, gnarled bushes and then to spongy peat and wet grass.

Mace was at his shoulder suddenly, shivering, his back to the rain, phone tucked in under his chin. 'A moody moor at midnight,' he said. 'The glittering lights of a city in the distance. We could be literally anywhere in the world. Perhaps we're even strangers treading the surface of a distant planet . . .'

'That's Manchester,' Preston said, pointing.

Mace stopped speaking for a moment and sighed. 'My colleague Preston Faulkner also present,' he said, before returning to his dictation. 'We have emerged at a different place. I don't know how to explain this, but I swear I didn't come in at this point. It seems there could be some sort of underground train working beneath the city and we've stumbled across a top-security transportation system. . .'

Preston scoffed. 'C'mon, Mace. Get real.'

Mace paused the voice memo with a wet finger. 'Manchester's aborted plans to develop an underground are the stuff of legend,' he said. 'There's a huge pit under Piccadilly Gardens. There are ten kilometres of nuclear bomb-proof tunnels under Chinatown, brotherman. I am one hundred and sixty per cent serious.' He fixed Preston with an earnest glare, then spoke into his phone again. 'An eerie light plays across the underbelly of the clouds over the scene before me. This phone says it's just gone four a.m., but I don't know if it's accurate . . .'

'We need to get to Shade,' Preston said, turning. He was thinking of the little pouches of drugs in the databands: could more be administered after an accident and still help someone pull through? 'He can help Ellwood.' He made his way back across the slick tarmac. Ryan, who had been out at the edges of the compound, pressing his face against the fence to examine the world beyond, was returning too, a hunched figure with his hands in his pockets.

Preston nodded in the direction of the van and said, 'Can you drive?'

Inside, Preston cradled Ellwood's head, bending in low to check her. She seemed alarmingly still. There was the slow in-out of breathing, but it seemed tired and fading.

'I can see the Beetham Tower out there,' Ryan said, rifling the desk drawers. 'Manchester's a few kliks off, down that way.'

'We need to get her to Shade,' Preston said. 'He'll know what to do.' Preston wasn't sure he believed himself, but added, 'He's been looking out for us, after all.'

Ryan grunted. 'You've a weird definition of *looking out*,' he said. 'This is the guy who built the madboxes, yeah? I'll be more in the mood for battering the dude if I ever get near him

. . . Ah!' He turned, lifting a set of keys from the desk drawer. 'Check these out!' he said, spinning them around an extended finger. 'If these fit that rust bucket outside, maybe we're in business. Come on.'

The van smelt of spilt petrol, coolant, chemicals. Frost patterned the inside of the windscreen and Ryan had to scrub at it with the sleeve of his jacket, his breath coming in clouds. Preston helped lift Ellwood into the back, holding her gently under the arms, Mace at her boots, and pulled the door shut with a slam.

Up front, Ryan struggled with the wheel and seatbelt. The seats were soft and pockmarked with cigarette stubs, the dashboard dusty. Mace got in next to Ryan, soaked from opening the gates in the rain, and used his phone to pull up a map and give some rudimentary directions.

The vehicle grumbled and shuddered and came to life. Only one headlight worked. 'Christ,' Ryan complained. 'This thing's scrap. C'mon!' he urged, the gears scraping. The van began to move, reluctantly.

They didn't bother closing the gates. Preston watched the road unspool behind them as they dropped slowly down an uneven track, the suspension groaning as it bounced them, the moors banking high on either side as if the road had been cut into it to disguise the route. Sometimes, when his dad had driven 'over the tops', as he'd called them, Preston had noticed an occasional solitary landmark and wondered what it was. There might be a substation for the TV mast further south, or a small outbuilding used by the water board near one of the steel-grey moorland reservoirs, but other than that, the tops were a wilderness. The existence of a small, fence-bound compound up here wouldn't attract any attention. It was a good hiding place for a reserve valve.

The track emerged at the edge of a road so thin it looked as if it might crumble into the peaty banks of sedge grass flanking it. Ryan stalled the van a couple of times. The engine was damp. He gunned it again, cursing. Soon, they reached a broader road – at least this one had catseyes and markings – and began heading down the valley towards the city suburbs below.

'What if the cops stop us?' Mace said as they hit a steady, rattling speed.

Preston thought of his dad and his heart shuddered. 'There won't be any patrol cars up here,' he said.

Ryan held up a hand. 'Quiet a second,' he said. He was checking his wing mirrors and everyone held their breath while a pair of headlights drew up behind them. There was trembling silence in the van while they waited for the car to overtake and relief when it sped off ahead of them.

'She's getting worse, I think,' Preston said, checking Ellwood. 'We'd better hurry.'

They dropped through a couple of deserted moorland villages and then the housing began to thicken. Old factories and textile mills started cropping up, along with pubs and post offices. They sat and listened to the engine turning at a pair of traffic lights at red, or heard the squeal of the ancient wiper blades and the cough of the heating system as Ryan drove them into the city through housing estates towards high-rise tower blocks. The radio didn't work at first, just hissed and crackled, but as the moors fell away behind them and the street lights and billboards of the centre came closer, Mace fiddled with the dial until a local station emerged from the fuzz.

They caught a five a.m. news bulletin. It was Wednesday, Preston realized as they listened – three days since his first night-walk on Sunday – he'd been BTV for just twenty-four hours. Shade's deadline had passed, he realized. Alice and the others were trapped in the squalor and stink with no way out. They had to get the valves open again.

Suddenly, his attention sharpened. 'The search is intensifying for a group of missing Manchester schoolchildren,' said the announcer in the grave voice reserved for stories that might end badly. 'Police have declined to make any further comment about a number of leads they are following in their attempts to ascertain the whereabouts of four teenagers, all of whom attend the same school in the Millennium Quarter.'

'We're famous,' Ryan said, deadpan. They were passing under a flyover now, and there were signs of life on the streets: a group of students making their unsteady way back to their dorms on Oxford Road, a couple of guys at a taxi rank laughing and punching each other's arms, a cop car that made the blood freeze up until it drifted off at the next set of lights.

'Justice Secretary Christopher Armstrong has caused controversy among politicians and supporters of the New Conservative Party,' the announcer continued, 'following his failure to rule himself out of a leadership challenge when directly questioned at a press conference in Manchester yesterday.' Preston raised a hand and hissed everyone quiet. 'Speculation is mounting that Mr Armstrong will use the party conference, which begins in Manchester later today, to announce his candidacy, a move that commentators say will divide the party. Mr Armstrong, whose strident views on law and order have gained him support from far right pressure groups, is set to announce bold proposals to strengthen the

UK's criminal justice system in his keynote speech this evening.'

'This evening,' Preston repeated as the announcer covered another story. He'd forgotten all the party conference preparations his dad had been involved in. Politicians and aides, reporters, TV camera crews; it was all building up to the keynote speeches. And that was tonight.

'Armstrong,' Ryan said. 'Is that the guy who Chloe thinks is . . .?'

'Yeah,' said Preston, cradling her head on his knees. 'The man who killed her dad.'

The wipers squeaked and the engine grumbled as they idled at a set of lights. Mace said, 'But what can we do? I mean, just us?'

Preston bit his thumb, thinking.

One way or another, it all had to end tonight. He just needed to figure out how.

27

'We saw it in the news,' Mace explained to Ryan as they drove. 'There was this story about Jacob Ellwood – Ellwood's dad – being killed in a car crash, and Armstrong helping the cops with their enquiries . . .'

Preston took over. 'But she knows it wasn't an accident. And Armstrong sent her BTV when she found out.'

'So now we've got her back . . .' Ryan started.

'We have a weapon,' Preston finished. 'And she's still alive, just. So if we can somehow get her fit and well . . .'

Ryan carried on, nodding, '. . . we can use her as proof that this guy Armstrong is a nasty bastard.'

'Exactly.'

'So let's get her to a hospital. We get her to Salford Royal. Or Manchester Royal Infirmary.' Ryan was checking the wing mirrors, planning a route. 'Then I get some of these bands you were talking about, and I go back for Alice.'

'Wait, though,' Preston said. There was no easy answer. Everything was a gamble. 'They'll recognize her, won't they?'

Mace placed a hand across his forehead, realizing. 'Ellwood's a missing person. It's been in all the papers.' Mace knew more than anyone else how the story had been covered. He'd obsessed about it enough in the days and weeks after she went missing – bored the hell out of everyone in the canteen with it. 'She's been on TV bulletins and stuff. What if the hospital staff recognize her?'

'Yeah. And the cops come steaming in. We'll lose her for good.' Preston watched Ellwood. Her eyelids had started a sequence of weird flickers. She was still with them, at least for now. But how long had they got? 'And then we can't get back at Armstrong,' he finished. He thought about Ellwood the night she'd told him everything. That unquenchable fire in her – the passion for revenge. Could he just deny her that? Leave her at the hospital and hope she was OK? Or by delaying, was he killing her?

'C'mon boys,' Ryan said. 'I haven't got long. I need to go back for Alice. Give me a decision here. Which way do I go?' They were approaching the city centre now. The sky was pale and clearing. A bus laboured past them, its interior lights illuminating a sealed bubble of commuters, heads bowed, checking phones. The van drifted to a halt at the lights halfway down Cross Street. A bakery was opening for the day. In the damp shadows of a bookshop doorway, a man shifted in his sleeping bag. Preston checked Ellwood's pulse. There it was: weak, but steady. Anxiety squeezed his chest shut. What would Ellwood want?

'C'mon,' Ryan urged. The lights were changing. 'I haven't got long.'

'M.I.S.T. is left here,' Preston said, leaning forward, indicating a turn-off.

'What about the hospital?' Mace said.

'We can't risk Ellwood being recognized. She's hanging on for now,' said Preston. 'First, we need to find Shade.'

Ryan eased the van, its engine coughing, into Back Half Moon. The walls either side were close and high, washed in yellow headlamp light as they made their way forward. The echo of the vehicle made Preston nervous. Getting caught now would be a disaster. Ryan rounded the corner in the alleyway, pulled right into a tight space, and when the van stalled again, decided against restarting the engine and yanked the handbrake up.

And there was M.I.S.T., white-faced in the pre-dawn glow of the garden's uplighters. It was weird to see the place again. He had only walked down Back Half Moon Street for the first time three days ago. And in that short time, his whole world – not just his world, actually, *the entire world* – had become a different place. And there was no undoing that short walk.

'That's where we went in,' Mace said, pointing at the basement doors and the valve beyond. It seemed a pointless observation but at the same time, something utterly confounding and strange.

Ryan said, 'Me too. I saw these kids in lines.' He pushed his hair out of his eyes and leant forward across the steering wheel.

'We need to find Shade,' Preston said, cradling Ellwood's shoulders.

*

Preston knew something was wrong before they got out of the van. The fact they'd come out up on the moors at the dormant valve – that, he knew, was a bad sign. It meant that Armstrong had finished running shutdown and that the valves at M.I.S.T. were already dead. But Preston didn't expect what he found when he padded carefully through the gate and up to the doors where, just a few nights before, Shade had first ushered him into the world of the nightwardens.

For a start, the door was open and banging idly. Inside, the lift was dormant. They struggled up the stairs with Ellwood. She felt heavier, sagging between them, hard to carry. Mace checked her pulse again, but couldn't find it and after a flurry of panic, Preston had to lean close and put his ear against her lips before he caught a breath. At the top of the stairs they shouldered open the swing doors and Preston moved in to the space backwards, his muscles weak with fatigue.

The warehouse was an empty shell.

Mace, who had Ellwood's feet, almost dropped her as he made his way through. In the end, it took everything they had to lower Ellwood gently.

Preston stayed on his knees for a long time.

'There was a whole office here . . .' Mace was saying as he walked in slow small circles, waving his goggles at the emptiness. 'There were chairs over here, a table here. Where's the vending machine? Where's the TVs?'

No one talked for a long time. The grimy panes of the warehouse windows glowed with the cold dawn. There were rectangles of discoloured concrete where the furniture had been. He'd skipped the hospital and instead brought a grievously sick girl to a stripped-out goods warehouse with nothing in it. The computers were gone; the TVs, workstations and cabinets. The databands were gone. Ellwood was going to die here in this pointless space, and Alice was trapped BTV.

It took everything he had not to roar with anger or dissolve into tears.

Ryan was on his knees, head down, hands splayed in the dust on the floor. He raised his head, blew the fringe from his eyes. 'So where are these bands, then? How do I get Alice out now? She'll die in there, Faulkner. Alice will die.' He wiped the tiredness from his eyes, smearing his face with grime.

Preston knew if he didn't grab this thing now, no one would. They'd fight each other, they'd blame each other; they'd rage and fume and then the anger would wane and they'd just drift. They'd call their parents, the police – there'd be tearful family reunions and press conferences.

It couldn't end like that. On a godforsaken island somewhere there was Alice, Chowdhury, Gedge, the others. There was a whole crew of kids running out of food and breathing each other's disease whilst somewhere else Armstrong would be shredding documents, burning folders, scrapping hard drives and emptying offices to make sure no one ever found out about his little experiment. Would Ryan talk to the press? Would Mace tell his story? Preston grimaced. It wouldn't much matter if they did. They had no proof. The nightwardens were gone. The prisoners were never making their journey back home. Who would believe them?

And if they were to talk, Preston thought, maybe Armstrong could make something horrible happen.

The thought was like an icicle. Armstrong would come and find them and finish them. Preston watched the gentle flicker of Ellwood's eyelids and wondered if she were dreaming; his fingers pressed the dark skin of her neck, finding the soft pulse of life there. *What would Ellwood say if she could?* She, more than anyone, would know what the man was capable of making happen. Some faceless team of hired guys in black suits and gloves was surely coming to wipe them out.

Very soon – in a couple of days maybe – Ryan would be found dead, his broken body splayed in the shadow of some tower block he'd planned to climb. *Urban exploration craze gets out of hand. Unfortunate teenager killed in tragic fall.* Mace might be a traffic accident. And him?

Preston's mind was made up. If they didn't act now, they were just waiting to die.

'Listen,' he said. 'We can still fix this. It isn't over.'

Mace said, 'It is, Press. Look around you. Let's just go home.'

'No.' Preston forced himself to his feet. 'We can't do that. Once Armstrong knows we're out, he'll come and find us.'

Mace looked up at the ceiling and let out a long breath. 'We're 404,' he said. He looked as if he'd been tipped up and emptied out. There was nothing behind his eyes except fear and despair.

'C'mon, Mace,' Preston urged. 'What did the radio say? About Armstrong.'

Ryan gave them a bleak look. 'There's the party conference,' he said. 'Armstrong's giving a speech there.' He closed his eyes. 'Doesn't help Alice, does it?'

'What are you thinking?' said Mace. 'That we get Ellwood there?'

Preston shrugged. *Was it possible?* He touched Ellwood's wrist, then lowered his face towards hers, so close he could have kissed her. He felt her shallow breath on his lips. If they sat around, there was no way she'd recover in time. 'First, we need a doctor,' he said. 'Anyone know any doctors?' He looked at the people around him. The answer was obvious.

Mace spat, wiped his eyes. 'We've got no one,' he said.

Then everything changed.

'Not quite true,' said a voice like sandpaper from somewhere behind them. They all turned. Preston knew that voice. He felt his heart fill. There were footsteps.

A figure was crossing the dusty space towards them. A stooped figure. A tired one.

It was Jonathan Shade.

28

Preston thought he was going to cry.

His throat tightened and his eyes itched. Shade leant over Ellwood, checking her pulse and listening to her breathing. Once he was satisfied he looked at the others, his hollow face dark with sadness and regret.

'I knew about the Ellwood girl,' he said. Preston wondered if the nightwarden slept at all – how he must feel as he closed his eyes. The burden of everything must be too heavy to bear. Innocent kids had killed themselves trying to escape his prison. Now the ones left would starve slowly to death.

No one knew what to say, so no one said anything.

Shade couldn't look up. He seemed to be addressing the floor, flexing his fingers, occasionally checking the empty place around him as if he were still amazed to find it stripped. 'I never meant this to happen,' he said. 'I didn't wake up one day and think – I'll be a prison warden. That's not how life is,' he said. 'Most people you see every day – those people you see coming into town on buses – they didn't want to be doing what they're doing. They're trapped too.' He stopped, took a breath. 'Some people might have a bigger cell than others, but we're all still in prison.' Shade was talking about choices not spaces, Preston realized. There had been this series of choices in front of him over the last week – and he'd made all the wrong ones, bad choice after bad choice. The text message started it and they all came tumbling after that one: the lies to the police, the arguments with Mace, the valve, the databands. Ellwood half-dead, Alice trapped. Choices, not spaces.

Shade started up again. 'And in this game,' he continued, 'you can't travel backwards. Whatever it is you've done –' he gave a shrug, his eyes cold – 'is done. All I can do now is try and fix my mistakes.'

That was it, thought Preston. Life was turning out to be a whole bunch of mistakes you tried to fix. He cleared his throat. 'Shade. We need your help,' he said, 'fixing some other mistakes.'

Shade's eyes shone as he blinked away his sadness. Then he laughed a dry, tired laugh. 'I'm in,' he said. 'There's a lot we have to try and repair.' He extended a hand then, fixing Preston with that magnetic gaze of his. 'Let's shake on it.'

For a second, remembering that first time, Preston had to check the nightwarden wasn't wearing gloves. He wasn't.

They shook, and Preston gripped the older man's hand confidently. They were all on the same side now, no matter what had come between them before this moment.

'I need databands,' Ryan said. 'And I need to go back through.'

'It'll take some time,' said Shade, 'but I can help there.

More than you think.'

'And we need to help Ellwood,' said Preston. Shade listened intently as they recounted the accident, his face clouding then clearing. 'I was thinking of all the medical stuff you've got in the stockrooms upstairs,' Preston explained as the tale drew to a close. 'I figured you'd have some idea of what . . .' He tailed off, his heart thumping fearfully.

Shade rubbed his chin thinking. 'Most of the stuff – the drugs and meds – they're gone. There's a couple of hundred databands still in storage up there, ten boxes of goggles and a bit of Sleeptight. But that's it. I've managed to keep the Black-stone Edge valve open. We haven't much time, but if I can bust it all out of storage, there's enough kit to get you back BTV. Though that's not going to help your young friend here.' He walked to the window and stood with his back to the room, his hands clasped behind him. Then he turned, face set, his decision made. 'The Royal Infirmary used to supply the whole project,' he said. 'All our stuff was made up by drugs companies and dropped at the hospital. Armstrong didn't want any awkward questions being asked of M.I.S.T., so it was all delivered there. No one could make the connection.'

'Is there someone there you could contact?' Preston felt a gleam of hope.

Shade scowled. 'Armstrong will have closed all that off now the project is on shutdown,' he said. 'He'll be destroying the evidence trail.' He thought for a second. 'I know which part of the hospital we need to get the meds, though.'

'Where?'

Shade was remembering, staring into the middle distance. 'I went with Esther once when our supplies ran out,' he said. 'There's painkillers, antibiotics, statins. If we could get someone in . . .' He patted his pockets, pulling out a pen and paper, and began writing. 'The Ellwood girl needs this,' he growled, holding up a scribbled list.

'Aren't you going to get it?' Preston felt the fear tighten like a fist in his chest.

Shade shook his head. 'No,' he said. 'That bit I'll leave to you.'

'Shade,' said Preston, cradling Ellwood, 'C'mon. You've got to help us. We might get the wrong stuff. You know where to look.'

'There's more than one problem to deal with. There's your man here,' Shade said, indicating Ryan, 'and his databands. That's something I need to put right too. I've enough in stock to clear out the whole of Axle Six but it'll take a few hours to unpack it all and get it ready. If I can get up to the moors this afternoon, I can get BTV before Armstrong realizes we've kept it open. I can get everyone out. I have to try.' He checked his watch. 'Morning shifts have started. Take the hospital first. Follow the instructions on the paper. Find a way in. Steal the meds. Get it all back here and treat her. I'll be here to help for a while at least. But for now,' he finished, 'there are things I have to fix.'

'I'll come with you,' said Ryan.

Shade paced a second, shaking his head. 'No,' he said. 'Think about it.' He began laying his plan out with all the knackered patience he had left. 'Once you've sorted the meds, get to the convention centre. That's where the party conference is tonight, yeah? That's where Armstrong will be. Watch the place. Figure out a way in. Don't get seen, don't get caught. Surely we're all thinking the same thing here, aren't we?' He looked up at them. 'Well, aren't we?'

There was a silence.

'Yeah,' said Mace. Then he added for clarity, 'We're thinking about how Armstrong might be funding secret donations to military groups using the Federal Reserve, right?'

Shade blinked, cleared his throat. 'No,' he said, raising a single finger for emphasis. 'We're not thinking that.'

Mace scowled. 'Well, we should be.'

Ryan said, 'You're thinking we might show up at the party conference?'

Shade wiped his forehead and nodded. 'Soon enough, Armstrong will know you're out. None of us is safe. We need to get to him before he gets to us. So, yeah, I'm thinking we all show up tonight, and we announce our presence. We make it uncomfortable for him. We expose the whole project in front of the cameras. We bring Armstrong down just by being there.'

'But we'll never get in,' said Ryan. 'The security will be massive. Cops, TV crews...'

Shade raised an eyebrow. 'You're the Jupiter Hand kid aren't you?'

'Yeah,' said Ryan.

'C'mon,' Shade said with a laugh. 'We need you here. I can handle Axle Six alone. But you and your lot have found ways into a whole bunch of places under tough circumstances, haven't you?' He fanned his hands out. 'Be creative. Take someone with you, scope out the convention centre, find a way in, hunker down.' He made it sound easy. 'And for God's sake don't get caught.' Shade flashed them a grin. 'This is up to you now. I have to stay here, get the databands ready. If things go well, I'll be with you tonight. But before that, I need to go BTV.'

29

It was late morning by the time they got there, so the car parks at Manchester Royal Infirmary were full and the front entrance was busy. They wolfed a plastic pack of supermarket sandwiches, relishing every bite, as they watched the building. Three sliding doors hissed constantly back and forth as patients and visitors came and went.

Ryan checked the list again, squinting at Shade's hurried scrawl. 'Faulkner,' he said. 'Which is the best way in if we're to get to the second-floor stockrooms?'

Preston had been making a silent assessment of the hospital as he ate. He took the list of instructions and studied it. 'We could try getting in further along. It's the eye place – you know, laser vision correction and stuff. We could use the main corridors to work our way back,' he said. 'It looks too busy to go straight in here.'

Mace checked his watch. 'It's past eleven. We need to be

quick,' he said. 'Let's go.'

The Royal Eye Hospital adjoined the main building, but seemed quieter. A group of student doctors were sharing coffee by the entrance. Reception was empty. A nurse in a white coat, hairnet and blue plastic shoe covers was pushing a trolley of files.

'Which floor again?' Mace said as they made their way across the entrance hall, their footsteps echoing. Ahead were two lifts and a grey-haired man at an information desk.

'Can I help you?' he asked.

Mace stuttered. 'We're here to see our gran,' he said. 'My mum's texted us the ward number.' The guy nodded and, when the phone at his desk started ringing, turned his attention to the call.

The lift doors slid open on the second floor and they stepped inside. They emerged to a series of sanitized and polished corridors. Coloured signs – blue, purple, lime green, orange – directed them to the Acute Referral Centre, towards Opthalmic Imaging, or in the direction of Electrodiagnosis and Ocular Prosthetics. Big displays heralded '200 years at the forefront of global eye care'. 'Help us celebrate our bicentenary', declared an arrangement of banners and information boards.

Preston knew that to falter would invite curiosity. Nurses, cleaners and doctors were moving swiftly from one unit to another. If a group of unidentified kids loitered about, Preston knew, someone would soon spot them. Whatever they did, they'd need to do it confidently.

'This way,' Preston said. They began the walk back towards the infirmary departments, swapping whispered suggestions to each other as they went, trying not to refer to Shade's instructions too openly.

'That looks like it,' Ryan said as they passed. 'Keep walking.' There was a canteen only a handful of paces further down. Customers were coming and going. There was a cleaner in overalls driving a machine with a rotating disc for polishing the floors. They reached a junction and U-turned their way back again.

Preston tried not to appear obvious. It was just a pair of doors with two glass panels and a magnetic lock – one of those doors that opened from within once a buzzer had been pressed. Through the windows he could see a corridor beyond and a member of staff working at a desk, a hunched shoulder pressing a phone up against her ear. She talked and typed at the same time.

They walked on again, then back once more and took a table near the door in the canteen, where they sat with a hot chocolate in a Styrofoam cup watching the midday news cover the build-up to the party conference on a wall-mounted TV. 'And worse,' Mace finished as they passed the cup between them, 'how do we get past the woman at the desk?'

'We could wait for someone to come out,' Ryan suggested, eyeing the TV, watching for the time.

'Don't fancy our chances,' Preston said. His hands were jumpy. He bit his nails. 'How about some sort of distraction?'

Mace finished the chocolate slowly, thinking it over. 'I'm with you.' He licked the chocolate from his lips. 'I look lost and confused, ask a load of weird and wonderful questions . . .'

'. . . and one of us gets past while you're at it,' finished Preston. The friends looked at each other for a moment, not quite believing what they were about to do. Then Ryan flattened the cup slowly and deliberately, folding the polystyrene over until it became the shape of a wedge. 'This,' he said with a grin, 'will come in useful.'

Preston and Ryan watched as the woman at the reception looked up, responding to Mace's open hand against the glass of the door.

Mace gave a grin and a stupid wave, then mouthed a lot of nonsense at her. The door buzzed. In his right hand, Mace held close to two quid in change, and this he scattered about his feet as the door opened. 'Damn!' he said. 'Sorry! One second . . .' The woman watched patiently as he scooped up the cash. And as he did, Mace jammed the folded cup into the gap between the door and the floor. It wouldn't hold long. Ryan crouched low, and began a crawl forwards, staying out of sight. Preston followed suit. 'Sorry!' Mace called, making it to his feet and moving towards the desk at a jog. 'I'm all over the place! I'm looking for my gran, you see.'

The woman at the desk looked bored, blinking. Preston made his way through, following Ryan, crawling carefully along the corridor, keeping Mace between him and the receptionist.

Mace was pushing on. He dropped his coins on the desk in front of her, being careful to obscure her view. 'Sorry,' he said again. 'I've got an obsessive-compulsive disorder, see. I have to have my coins in . . .' Mace paused, improvising, '. . . date order. If you'll just give me a second, I'll . . .' he began checking each one, announcing the date of issue aloud and then pocketing it carefully. 'Even years of the nineteen-nineties go in the front right pocket of my jacket,' he explained. Preston crawled on, his stomach gnawing and his hands trembling. 'Odd years from the two thousands go in front left . . .'

'Can I help you, young man?' the woman said. Preston could see she had steel-grey hair and lined cheeks. Her lips were crabbed and severe. It didn't look as if she was buying Mace's story. 'My gran,' he said feebly. Behind him, Preston heard the door close. The temporary doorstop had come loose.

Ryan had made it as far as the curved reception now, and pushed himself tight against it under Mace's feet. Preston joined him, brushing Mace's leg and disrupting his flow. Dammit, he actually looked down. For a stupefied second, the two friends gaped at each other. Preston stared up at Mace from his position on all fours, making a fearsome face at him, eyes wide and pleading. Mace remembered himself and looked again at the woman. He smiled, trying not to blush. 'I can't find my gran,' he said weakly.

Further up the corridor was the ward, and some open stockrooms. Ryan nodded towards them, and the two of them made their way forward as swiftly and carefully as they could, listening as Mace tried the emotional approach. 'She's ill,' he was saying about his imaginary gran. 'I saved up these coins to buy her some flowers or something. But I can't find where they're keeping her.'

'Have you a ward number?'

Mace was working his magic. 'I've forgotten it. If I could just buy her something nice . . .'

'There's a shop on the floor below.'

Preston kept up his crawl, wincing as his trainers squeaked against the polished floor.

'One from last year!' said Mace. He was on to his coin story again. 'If they're less than four years old, I keep them in my shoes,' he explained, and began demonstrating, unlacing his trainers. 'You'll have to excuse my socks . . .' he said, bent double.

That did it. 'Yes, well,' said the woman rising from her chair. 'Perhaps you could organize your coins later. If you'll follow me, I'll point you in the right direction for the gift shop.' She began to make her way back up the corridor towards the door, massaging her back with chubby hands as she did so. Mace scooped up his change in a fist, shoved it into his pocket, and gave Preston a wink. Then he followed.

Preston tucked himself against the wall at the back of the walk-in stockroom, shoulder to shoulder with Ryan. He was already checking the medication, the dog-eared list in his hand. He was finding it hard to hold it steady, Preston noticed.

The walls were lined with open shelves and glass-fronted cabinets, and an array of blister packs, plastic bottles, prescription boxes and packages were stacked and stock-checked, signed off and sequenced in lines. The labelling didn't make it easy to work out what they were looking at. He leant across Ryan to examine Shade's scribbled instructions. *Vico-parastatin*.

A minute or two passed. Outside, Preston could hear the squeak of rubber-soled shoes on polished hospital floors. The phone at the reception desk rang. They had to abandon their search and press their backs against the far wall of the room as a doctor in a white smock passed by. *Dammit, that was close.* Preston let a breath go and wiped the sweat from his palms on his jeans. If they got caught here, no amount of smart-arse storytelling was going to get them out of it.

Ryan hissed, 'Yes!' and pointed. Vico-parastatin. Preston nearly cheered – relief consuming him as he bundled a handful of boxes into his bag. He pulled the rest of the stock forward, trying desperately not to dislodge the neat stacks of labelled boxes and pots. But his hands were shaking stupidly and his fingers felt thick with guilt and fear. A couple of pots tipped and one hit the floor.

And – *dammit, dammit* – the cap popped off and a bunch of blue pills slid in a thousand directions. Ryan cursed as he squatted to try and gather them up. It was hopeless; they'd skimmed and spun everywhere. And now there was someone coming, the regular beat of footsteps. Big strides. A dark-skinned guy, a male nurse in a green uniform, pulled up, surprised, nearly dropped his clipboard. Preston felt his legs buckle.

For a second, the guy didn't know what to say. There was a couple of teenage kids in his stockroom, stealing drugs. He swore. 'What the hell do you think you're doing?' he said, his shock turning to hard outrage, his forehead creasing and his black eyebrows converging.

Preston pushed the bag behind his back, speechless. In the end it was Ryan who cleared his throat and somehow found the composure to say, 'Who, us?'

30

Preston and Mace watched the darkening sky through the grubby windows of the empty warehouse. It was nearly four now; pretty soon the traffic up Deansgate and Cross Street would thicken and the cars would queue their way out into the suburbs, little metal boxes in the rain.

The steal could've gone better, that was for sure. It had taken everything he'd got to sprint clear after Ryan had shouldered the nurse to the floor. And the guy had been so damned furious he'd followed for ages, yelling after them. At one point a couple of orderlies had joined the chase, which had been useful, in a way, because it made it easier for Mace to spot them and join the escape. But when Mace had taken the stairs near outpatients on his arse after a comic slip, it looked as if they'd be caught. Then a couple of ambulances tore in to accident and emergency at once, sirens whooping, and somehow, they got free during the melee that followed. The trek back across town had been slow and nervy, the lads leaping for cover at the sound of every siren.

Preston left Mace at the window, bit his fingernails and paced in a pointless circle around Ellwood. She was still unconscious, a coat rolled into a pillow for her head, a blanket from the third-floor stockrooms across her body, her eyes flickering a little under their lids as if she were dreaming. Ryan had checked on her, spoken to Shade, and then made his way across town to the convention centre, where Preston had agreed to join him. Preston checked Ellwood's pulse again, touching her wrist and feeling the blood push back against his fingertips.

Shade came down from the upper floor, his tired tread heavy on the stairs. After Ryan had gone, he'd spent another half-hour clearing out the rest of the storage spaces up there. He seemed distracted as he packed a heavy bag with sealed plastic packets of databands, counting them in batches of twenty, packing them tightly, checking and double-checking, adjusting his goggles. 'Right,' he said, finished at last, putting his kit to one side. 'Before I go, let's see the meds.'

Preston and Mace unloaded the blister packs of vico-parastatin. Little glass vials – Shade called them ampoules – of clear liquid that you could safely snap open; a couple of syringes in sealed plastic bags.

He nodded his satisfaction as he checked them.

Shade's hands were surprisingly steady as he flicked the tip of the syringe lightly a couple of times, chasing the air to the top, and nudged the liquid out. He looked at Preston. 'Ready?' When Preston nodded, Shade pressed the metal to Ellwood's forearm.

The boys watched as the plunger dropped and the medicine entered her system. When it was done, Shade placed the empty chamber on the floor and rubbed his palms together slowly, watching. He placed a gentle hand on Preston's arm. It took him a moment to see what the nightwarden wanted, until he realized how hard he was holding Ellwood's shoulder. He loosened his grip. He was a frenzy of suspended breath and taut tendons. Mace paced, prickly and energetic.

'What will happen?' Preston said. He cleared his throat, adjusted his position, making sure the girl was comfortable.

Shade rubbed his chin with a cupped hand. 'It could be as long as a couple of hours before we know. But oxygen levels in the blood should stabilize. Pulse will strengthen and breathing will deepen and get more regular. Like I said,' Shade spoke levelly, 'it'll be a couple of hours. Put her down, kid.'

Preston felt himself blush. 'Yeah,' he said.

It was a tormented wait. There was something on Preston's mind and he couldn't let it go. He smoothed Ellwood's blanket. 'Shade,' he said. 'When I went through the valve, I arrived at this cave. There were all these big dark rooms that looked like they'd been dynamited out of the rock.' Shade sat crossed-legged next to Ellwood, checked her, then tucked his knees up and nodded. 'And the kids over there were all sleeping together, head-to-toe in this room, all getting ill and half-starving to death.' Preston realized as he was speaking it would be hard for the warden to hear, and stammered his way to the end of his sentence. 'One of the last things I saw down there was this massive riot for food . . .'

Shade's eyes had lowered. He was biting his lip. It took him a couple of goes to get his voice started. Then he said, 'We started hearing rumours about shutdown months ago. So we stockpiled cans and bottled water and kept them out at the Blackstone Edge valve. Then we'd try and get through every week or so.' His voice had dropped to an exhausted rasp by the end. 'Armstrong was bound to find out sooner or later. He was spending a lot of time at M.I.S.T. We had to stop the deliveries. I'm sorry I've not been able to get any more through. Is everyone still . . . alive?'

Preston nodded, hoping so. Then, he told Shade about the trapdoors, how they'd carved recesses in the walls and hauled themselves up there. He described the long white corridor and the escalators.

When he described the foyer of Axle Six and the black night and beating sea beyond, Shade's expression darkened. Preston reached the end of his description. 'So where *is* that place?' he asked.

Shade took a long time to answer. 'I don't know,' he said.

Preston frowned. 'C'mon. Seriously – where is it? Who built it?'

'We didn't build it,' Shade said, weighing his words very carefully. 'My brother and me just . . . found it.'

It took a long silence for that to register – for Preston's thinking to sift through it all, trying to make it fit together. 'Found it,' he said. He remembered the third desk – the empty one back when the warehouse was the headquarters of a prison system. He'd asked Shade who it belonged to. *My older brother*, he'd said. 'So you and your brother opened the valve and that place – Axle Six – was just *there*, on the other side?'

Shade brooded silently. 'You're asking me,' he said, 'like I'm the guy with all the answers. I'm not.'

'I'm asking,' said Preston, pushing his luck, 'because there was a kid BTV who said we weren't the only ones down there.'

The corner of Shade's mouth twitched. His eyes went big and still. 'What do you mean?'

'The story goes there's an old man out there,' Preston said. 'The kids call him Robinson Crusoe.'

Shade turned away.

Ryan studied the exterior of the Manchester Central Convention Complex. He was scanning and planning. Preston, exhausted by the wait at Ellwood's side, had walked up Deansgate in the rain to join him. As he stood watch, he found his attention returning to the big curve of the roof – an upturned boat with a hull of patterned glass. It used to be a railway station way back, he remembered his dad telling him once, designed with this grand high roof for the rising steam from the engines. Now that big glass curve would look down on a stage and a hall, a media centre, meeting rooms, galleries and press areas. Above the two boys was a white clock face at the apex of the building's curve, hanging like a full moon: 4.55 p.m. The conference would be starting in two and a half hours, tops. Beneath the clock a flat-roofed foyer projected out across the stone-flagged pedestrian area. A string quartet were tuning up just inside the doors. TV crews hauled equipment back and forth. Vans pulled up, disgorged their kit and moved on.

Preston knew Ryan loved climbing, but he couldn't imagine any way the guy could get up on to the curve of the roof, no matter how clever and fearless he was. Surely the way in would have to be somewhere else. The raised paved areas and steps in front of the building were thronged with cops and partitioned by temporary barriers for queuing. No chance of walking in the front doors looking like a member of the public.

So that left the sides of the building, and maybe the service entrances to the back.

That's where Ryan had turned his attention as well. They sheltered in the steel and glass doorway of the Bridgewater Hall, looking out through the gathering late afternoon gloom across the crowds of people and traffic.

'There's the underground car park,' Ryan said, nodding towards a curved drive which dropped down from street level into dark vaulted spaces. There was a barrier, a pay-point and an attendant. Prices had doubled for party conference week. 'I guess there might be a way in from there.' Ryan paced and bounced on the tips of his toes. He was sharp and fired up – running on fear and excitement. 'Looks like they use the back of the place for deliveries. There must be food and drink – champagne and oysters and all that stuff, right? Where does that go in?'

They took the steps up to the station and watched as articulated trucks unloaded at the back of the centre. There were two temporary Portakabins for extra security teams. Six guys with shaved heads and heavy raincoats were checking off deliveries with a handheld scanner.

Ryan cursed. 'I need a bit more thinking time,' he said. Preston looked at his watch. Ryan grimaced at him. 'I know, I know,' he said. 'No time left. We need a plan.'

Back under the eaves of the Midland hotel, Preston, cold and hungry and wound tight with fear, found himself thinking again of Ellwood – and then of Shade. Armstrong had taken everything from the nightwarden: his job, his liveli-hood, his reason for working and living. He'd had the buildings stripped, the assets removed, the accounts frozen, and the valves shut down. But Shade seemed to have some-thing left – some dark and brooding determination to set things right. Preston remembered the news article on the radio – the one that they'd heard on the early bulletin about Armstrong's speech, the radio saying he was *set to announce bold proposals to strengthen the UK's criminal justice system*. Tonight was Armstrong's keynote speech, Shade had explained. Everyone would be there. TV cameras, reporters, newscasters, press and photographers. If there was a better place to lift the lid on Armstrong's brutality, Preston couldn't think of it.

Then his thoughts turned to Alice, Chowdhury, Gedge and all the other kids on the other side of the valves. There was a whole world hidden underneath the streets and the big curve of the convention centre roof and the sounds of the kitchens of the Midland hotel and the taxi rank and the girl holding her dad's hand as she jumped over the cracks in the pavement.

They had to do this or those kids would never come out again. They had to find a way in, and quick. But they needed Ellwood with them.

'I'm going back to check on her,' he said.

Ryan was so deep in thought, he didn't even respond.

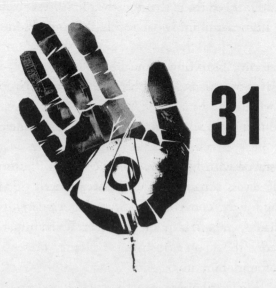

31

It was nearly six o'clock when Ellwood's hands moved.

One arm was shifting in the dust. Preston dropped to his knees and lifted the wandering arm. Mace listened to her breathing.

'Easy,' said Shade. 'It's a good sign, yeah. But we're not done yet.'

Preston looked at her dark skin and strong face – the high forehead and cropped hair. Her eyelids were jittering like someone half-awake. Then she went still again and Preston stared at her for a long time, his head crowded with competing pictures: Alice, Ellwood. Old friendships, newer ones.

Shade's face clouded after a while. He checked his watch and scowled. Then, when he couldn't pack and repack his bag of databands any longer, he knelt next to Ellwood, ushering Preston aside.

'What's up?'

Shade checked the girl's pulse, then lifted her eyelids gently one at a time, examining her pupils. 'It might be nothing,' he said.

Mace said, 'Do we need another injection?'

Shade shook his head. 'Don't want to risk an overdose.'

'So what is it?'

'Should be happening quicker than this,' Shade said.

Mace stayed with Ellwood, and once again Preston flogged himself across town, fighting the weary ache of his bones, heading for the convention centre. Night was closing in. If Ryan hadn't cracked it by the time he reached him, they were doomed.

He found him in brighter spirits. 'Borrowed a phone charger from a kid in McDonalds,' he said as Preston reached him. 'And look at this.' Ryan prodded his phone with wet fingers, tucking himself in under the eaves of the hotel. Ryan held the screen out.

'What is it?' Preston said as he leant over.

Ryan demonstrated. 'Helpful website, eh?' he said, bringing up a complete floor plan of the building before them. It showed the interior spaces; sections were labelled – Central Hall, Charter Suite, Exchange Foyer, Auditorium – and when you clicked, the map spun and grew as you swept low across the rooms and into a computer simulation of the interior.

'This,' he said, 'was made for us. Watch.' He held the phone up, planted himself in the centre of the pavement, orientated himself and the screen, and then began examining the scene ahead of him and cross-checking it with the floor plan. 'There's interior photos as well,' he murmured. 'And nice helpful little descriptions.' He quoted as he studied the plan: '"Purpose-built state-of-the-art eight-hundred-seat auditorium fitted with high-specification audiovisual systems." That'll be where the speeches happen, then. And the front section here has . . .' He peered at the screen, wiped the rain from it, '"break-out rooms for networking." Whatever that means.'

'So what's the way in?'

Ryan held up a finger and made another silent examination of the floor plan. Then he straightened up. 'We need to be over there,' he said, pointing, his voice fizzing with excitement. 'If I can get on to the foyer roof – that bit's flat at least – I reckon I can find a way in through service pipes or vents. Then to the Charter Foyer and the Gallery,' Ryan turned, holding the phone out for Preston. He tapped the screen. 'See this bit here? There's cloakrooms, service rooms, toilets and storage.'

Preston nodded. He got it. Those areas would have fewer delegates, and so less security; rooms which might give them somewhere to stay hidden while they worked out what the hell they were going to do next.

Crucially, though, they needed Ellwood with them. All of this would be for nothing if they didn't have their secret weapon. She had to be with them all the way. 'So how are we going to get Chloe in?' he said. The name sounded odd as he spoke it. 'Ellwood, I mean.'

Ryan gave an exasperated sigh. 'If I can find a way in through the roof, I might be able to get access to a fire door or a service entrance . . .'

They spent another fifteen minutes pacing the exterior. It got harder as the place got busier. The entrance steps were a congregation of politicians, diplomats, assistants and aides, all meeting and making their way through the glass entrance into the open spaces beyond. TV cameras, each with lighting rigs and the convention centre's exterior spots, threw harsh shadows against the rain-washed paving.

Eventually, Ryan found what he was looking for: a quieter half-shadowed corner. There were three roll-top catering bins that provided precious cover and a door – locked, of course. The place was overlooked – everything was overlooked unless you were an urban explorer – but Ryan seemed satisfied that if he was lucky, he might be able to find his way inside, and to wherever that door was.

'Right,' he said. His voice, Preston noticed, was trembling. He was as frightened as everybody else. This whole thing didn't seem any less stupid than it had a few hours ago back in the warehouse. 'I'm going to wait here, watch the crowds, see what security do. You're going back to check on Ellwood, right?'

Preston nodded. 'And Mace and me get her here by eight.'

Ryan bit his nails and checked his watch. 'Eight. Right. So be at this door. Stay out of sight.'

Preston nodded. 'Got it.'

Ryan shifted from foot to foot awkwardly. 'Good luck,' he said. He held out his hand.

Preston shook it. 'Thanks,' he said. 'You too.'

The last thing Preston saw as he made his way through the rain towards Back Half Moon Street was Ryan, hands in his pockets, goggles round his neck, looking up at the white face of the convention centre clock, examining the curve of the building's roof, working things out.

Planning his most important climb.

When he got back, it was almost seven. Ellwood hadn't stirred.

Shade had roped Mace into checking the van with him and the two of them were now sitting in a tense silence, the preparations long since complete.

'Listen,' said Shade after they'd checked her again. 'I can't hang about any longer. I'm heading up to Blackstone Edge. It's an old valve. It shuttles slowly. It could take me a good while to get through. We can't risk Armstrong's tech team realizing it's still open.'

'Stay for a while,' said Mace. '*Please.* I mean – what do we do when she wakes?' He stumbled a little. 'If she wakes.'

'If she wakes,' he said, 'You'll be fine. If she doesn't . . .' Shade checked his watch, abandoned his sentence. 'I'll get to the convention centre as soon as I can. Assuming everything goes smoothly I could make it there by nine. Let's hope I'm not too late.' Shade bit his lip, then crossed to Ellwood one last time, crouching and checking her. Preston watched the warden's face, looking for signs of hope. There weren't any. 'Dammit,' hissed Shade, pressing a finger against the girl's neck. 'This isn't working.'

He went then, silent and brooding.

Preston and Mace were left alone amongst the scuttling spiders and the dust and echoes, listening to the last of the rush hour traffic. Seven-thirty. It was dark outside now, and the empty warehouse was amber with thrown street light. If they didn't do something, they were going to be very late to the convention centre.

'Mace,' Preston said. 'You'd better go and meet Ryan. I'll follow.'

Once his friend had gone, recording a memo as he went, Preston paced the floor, hands in pockets to stop himself chewing his nails. It was nearly eight now. Armstrong would be taking the stage soon, Preston guessed. Making his speech. He felt dread tighten in his gut. If Ellwood didn't wake soon, she'd probably never recover. It'd be like a coma, or brain damage.

Then it happened. Ellwood's heel scraped against the floor. Preston spun round and stared.

Jesus. She moved.

Preston hurried to her. It took him a few moments to find the pulse; he was too nervous. Then he felt it thump against his thumb and it felt strong and steady just as Shade had said it would.

Then Ellwood suddenly drew in a big breath. Her chest filled, her arms flexed, her head came up. She'd broken the surface like a swimmer. Her eyes were closed, but her pallor was gone now. She was coming round. Preston wiped his eyes, let out a shaky breath.

'Hoyle,' she said. It took a second to figure out what she was saying, what she was re-living. She opened her eyes, blinked rapidly and said the name again. Her lips were cracked and bleeding. Preston tipped water against them and she drank.

'We're in Manchester,' Preston kept saying. 'You're safe.'

'Hoyle.'

'No,' said Preston. He had her nursed in his arms. 'Hoyle's not here.' Preston didn't want to think about where the hell Hoyle was.

Ellwood spluttered and spat, then tried to sit up.

'Faulkner,' she said eventually. Preston felt a crazy kind of pride. She remembered him. 'What happened?' He gave her his best soothing smile. She pushed the water away. She was upright now, and her eyes were clear, as if she'd brushed away a bad dream. 'Armstrong,' she said. 'I need to find him.'

Ellwood was back.

32

The walk through Manchester was slow. Partly because Ellwood was exhausted and shivering, partly because they queued for out-of-date pasties at a bakery at closing time – bought half a dozen with a crumpled fiver – and partly because the girl kept looking up and around, watching the lights of the buildings, feeling the rain on her face, staring at parties of drinkers and office workers, smiling at her freedom.

It was just after eight by the time they got to the convention centre. The bins were arranged in lines along the side of the building near the kitchens. Preston sent a quick text: *Here*, cursed his dying phone battery, and crouched down. Ellwood ate greedily and finished a bottle of water, stronger now. As they waited, they watched the little bright boxes of the rooms across at the Midland hotel, arranged like a honeycomb of cells. Now and again, a figure would cross the yellow space between the curtains and be silhouetted there. On the top floor, a man was leaning from his window, smoking and talking on his mobile.

From where they hid they could see the taxicabs filing up, the passengers stepping carefully across the rainwater in the gutters, the camera crews and reporters delivering their bulletins; they could hear the string quartet playing when the doors hissed open and shut.

The service door behind them opened a crack.

Ryan's face appeared. *Thank God.* The gap widened, the metal grumbling and rusty. No one had used this particular back way for a while. 'It's not much,' Mace said from inside. 'But we call it home.'

Ellwood and Preston slipped inside. There was an awkward four-way embrace that Preston extended beyond necessary, feeling a wild kind of relief at being with his allies. 'Long story,' he said into the tight space between them.

'You OK, Chloe?' Ryan asked.

Ellwood tousled his hair. 'I've been better.'

'Hi,' Mace introduced himself. 'I'm Elliot.'

Ellwood smiled at him, warmer now, stronger all the time.

'We've brought food,' Preston said, the paper bag of stale pasties in his fist.

They were in a breeze-block service passageway, musty and dry. A battered store cupboard, an old fire extinguisher and a raincoat were the only signs of recent use.

'Through here –' Ryan explained through his food, pointing down the passageway – 'there's a couple of stockrooms and the toilets. Most of the doors are locked and the rest of the building's just huge open spaces full of people. The ventilation shafts were dead easy really. But from here on in, it's going to be hard. There's loads of security. Big guys in black jackets.'

Ellwood, who'd been examining their bolthole carefully as Ryan spoke, flicked her eyes meaningfully upwards. When Preston turned and followed the girl's gaze, he saw the problem. There was a wall-mounted CCTV camera tucked into a high corner up there. 'It might look old,' said Ellwood, 'but we can't gamble on it not working. Let's stand here.'

They pressed their backs against the wall beneath the camera, well clear of its line of sight, relishing the pasties, groaning with delight at the luxury of it all. 'Been thinking,' Preston said, swallowing. 'There'll be speeches and stuff, won't there? Debates, talks, presentations, that sort of thing. They've got to start soon, right?'

'So?' said Ryan.

Ellwood picked up the thread. There was a light behind her eyes now. It was partly the meds, partly the sustenance, partly the zeal that came with being close to her goal. Armstrong was nearby, and the knowledge of that was in her every gesture and decision – in the clear force of every word she spoke: 'So things will quieten down then and we can start to move about a bit. We need to find out what's going on, and where he is.'

Ryan wiped his greasy fingers and swiped his phone alive. He checked the floor plan again, cursing the internet speed. 'Yeah,' he said, putting it together. 'We'd need a conference programme. A running order or something.' He pocketed his phone, pushed the hair out of his eyes. 'We're gonna have a hell of a time hijacking Armstrong's speech if we don't know when or where it's happening.'

'Exactly.'

Ryan rubbed his eyes. 'Maybe . . .' he started. He'd noticed the stock cupboard. The padlock was only small. 'Gimme a hand with this, will you?'

Together they kicked at it, wincing at the noise, nervously eyeing the camera. The door gave pretty easily and a nest of spiders scattered. Preston tore the filmy webs aside and rummaged, working quickly. There were gloves, a high-vis bib and safety helmet, a couple of cans of paint, gaffer tape in gunmetal rolls, some matches.

Mace spoke into his phone. 'We're in a service corridor, breaking into a cupboard. Sadly, there's nothing to help us here.'

'Hang on.' Ellwood had seen something. 'That sign.'

Preston pulled it free of the junk and wiped it down on the sleeve of his jacket. It was a grubby, plastic-coated metal thing that read, 'Out of Order' in bold and beneath, 'Manchester Central apologize for any inconvenience caused during maintenance work.'

'This, plus the tape . . .' began Ryan, his eyes lighting up a little.

Preston grinned, reaching for the gaffer tape. 'Yeah,' he said. 'It might give us a place to hide, at least for a while.'

Ryan bit his fingernails, thinking. 'We need somewhere spacious,' he said. 'Somewhere luxurious with a decent PC and better web access. A nice little hidey-hole. We stick the sign up on the door and no one will disturb us.'

'Great,' whispered Ryan through a dark, sarcastic grimace. 'Just great.'

There was just enough room for four of them in the toilet cubicle. It was all they could find in the time they had. At the end of the service corridor where they'd entered, Ryan had shown the group what lay beyond a set of fire doors: the wide-open convention centre spaces, rooms the size of aircraft hangars under the high arched roof, blue carpets with corporate designs, and white walls hung with black-and-white photographs.

And then there were the people. There seemed to be thousands of them milling out there – women in dinner dresses with their hair up, men in suits, straight-backed waiters with trays of little pastries, girls in black catering uniforms deftly weaving through the crowds with champagne, camera crews and media types, assistants with phones making frantic calls and checking the news websites.

There was nowhere to hide out there, no way they could scout out a nice little office and tape an 'out of order' sign to the door. 'Besides,' Preston had hissed as they watched the ebb and flow of the crowd. 'Why hang an "out of order" sign on an office door? There needs to be working parts for something to be out of order.'

So they'd all reluctantly agreed.

It was the Charter Foyer gents toilets – the closest and quietest space they could find. The four of them stood for a moment, arms around each other's shoulders in a kind of crazy kinship, staring at the tiled floor at their feet.

Preston felt Ellwood's closeness and wondered whether he maybe loved her.

Then they started talking in low whispers, partly to force down the fear, partly to make sense of it all, partly planning the final few hours of their togetherness before it would all end.

Ellwood was sharper with every minute, thriving on the fear. 'If we can get hold of a conference programme we can work out what's happening when,' she hissed.

'And people leave stuff around, right?' Ryan said. 'If we're lucky, someone will leave a programme and we'll be able to . . .' Before he could carry on, the outside door opened and someone crossed the tiles in polished brogues.

Terror stifled them into silence. Ryan, Preston, then Mace all lifted themselves slowly and carefully up on to the toilet seat, backs pressed against the cubicle wall, so their feet wouldn't be seen. Ellwood followed suit, crouching between them. It was ridiculous. The four of them held their breath, curled up and silent.

A second man entered. There was some brief talk and a mobile phone rang. A voice began a series of confirmations and instructions. Someone cleared his throat and told an incomprehensible joke. Scratchy laughter. Then the doors swung shut again and silence descended.

They lowered themselves carefully. 'We could have put this sign up on any bloody door we liked,' Mace said. 'And we chose this.'

The next half-hour was excruciating. Every minute or so, the four of them were forced to mount the toilet seat as silently as they could, hold each other up, heads silently down, waiting as conversations meandered on and phone calls were made. Then they'd descend again to their more comfortable standing position – slowly and silently, hoping they'd counted the men in and out correctly – then check the 'Explore our Venue' section of the website again, swap an idea or two about where they might go next, fret about where the hell Shade was, whether Alice was safely home yet, then the doors would go again and they'd be hauling themselves upward and the cycle would begin anew.

They were rewarded, eventually. After a period of promising silence, Ryan peeped over the door of the cubicle and saw a booklet abandoned near the sinks.

'Thank God,' he said as he shut the door behind him again and held it aloft between the four of them. But then, in their eagerness to look, and because of the closeness of their arms and hands, they conspired to knock it out of his grasp as he tried to open it, and the conference programme fell between them and then Ellwood, trying to shift her position, accidentally kicked it along the floor and it spun away into the next cubicle.

The outside door opened for the millionth time and the four of them immediately raised themselves up off the floor to stand, almost heartbroken, on the toilet seat, all furious at each other. Ellwood ground her teeth, her eyes ablaze. Preston stared at the anonymous tiles on the wall, blaming himself. It was his upraised hand that had knocked it out of Ryan's grasp, wasn't it? He couldn't be sure.

They were all so preoccupied and angry, they weren't counting in and out. They'd lost track of who was there and who wasn't. Had the bloke with the stupid ringtone gone yet? What about the one with the sore throat who'd been gargling paracetamol? That stock trader in a shitty mood? After a period of silence, Ellwood gave him the nod and Ryan lowered himself down to the tiled floor, delicately, holding his breath.

Silence.

He let it out. 'Jesus,' he said, his voice bitter. 'I'll have to go and get it now. That was your fault, Faulkner.'

It was whilst Ryan was speaking that Preston realized they'd dropped to the floor too soon. There was someone still out there. His heart fired hard and fast. Ellwood had realized too. Her eyes went wide and furious. Ryan put a hand across his face, wincing.

'Who's that?' said a stern voice. A guy, middle-aged, maybe. 'Who's in there?' he barked.

The group looked silently at each other, each willing someone else to say something clever. Ellwood raised a critical eyebrow. It had to be one of the boys who answered, given where they wcrc. Mace cleared his throat and tried a husky voice. 'It's just me,' he said. He improvised, blushing. 'I'm helping a friend.'

'Good God!' barked the other voice. There was a pause, long and cold and dreadful. Then he said, 'I'm calling security. I'm calling security now.'

The outer doors swished open and shut.

'Bloody hell,' said Ellwood.

That pretty much summed it up.

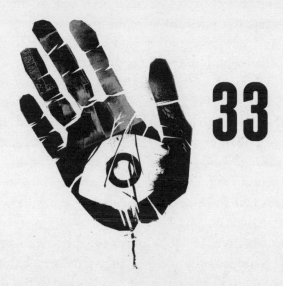

33

There was no alternative. When the guy went, they had to move quickly. Ellwood slid the lock free, swearing at their stupidity, and they piled out. The toilets were empty. Ellwood pointed in the direction of the dropped programme and Mace checked the cubicles for it.

Then they had to go.

This was it, Preston thought as they loitered at the door. Out into the open. It would all end very quickly and painfully if security were close. Ellwood sensed this too and took a deep breath. Then she pulled the door open and sneaked out.

Outside, the conference had begun. Speeches and meetings were underway, and the crowds had dispersed. Across the open blue of the carpet near the bar area were a group of men drinking and talking. A gaggle of journalists were hunched over a video camera checking their shots from earlier, and the sound guy was sorting out his microphones.

Most of the security must have been out in the entrance foyer; there was one chunky bloke in padded black and that was it – all quiet except for the low babble of the drinkers and the muffled sounds of meetings and presentations.

To their right was a place Preston recognized from the online map as the Gallery – a broad corridor lined with black-and-white photographs. The doors off to the left and right were meeting rooms, but the map showed smaller units down there too. Ellwood knew it as well; she cocked her head in that direction and they began a light-footed jog away from the main hall and entrance foyer, along the gallery towards the smaller spaces.

One was free, its door propped open with a wooden wedge. Mace raised a hand as they passed it, halting their nervy progress. They retreated inside, closing the door. No lock, Preston noticed.

Inside, they talked in low, relieved whispers. The meeting room had a small central table with a vase of flowers on it. There was a smartboard and a projector.

Between them Mace opened and flattened out the official event programme. 'This thing'd better be worth it,' he said, flicking through the pages with trembling fingers. Soon, he found it – a full-page summary of the evening's events.

The five of them leant closer.

Ellwood got there first. 'Here.' She placed a fingertip firmly on the page. 'He starts at nine.'

'What's the time?' said Press. His phone was dead.

'Eight forty,' Mace confirmed. 'So where do we have to be?'

'Somewhere called the Exchange Auditorium,' Ryan muttered, studying the programme. He had his phone out. He clicked a couple of times. 'Purpose-built eight-hundred-seat lecture hall,' he read aloud. 'It's . . .' he looked up, getting his bearings, '. . . a couple of minutes along that way.'

Mace rubbed his eyes. 'So do we try and get in there now and hide?' He looked at each of them expectantly. 'Or do we like – burst in later?'

For a second no one spoke. There was no plan. This was as far as their thinking had got. Preston looked at Ellwood expectantly.

She scowled. 'This is my battle,' she said. She'd gone cold and indignant. 'If you don't want any part of it, Faulkner, fine. I get that.'

'No,' Preston said. 'That's not what I—'

'Well pack it in with the stares, then. It's not like I'm *made of answers* here.'

Preston swallowed, not sure what she wanted. 'Whatever,' he said.

Ryan curled a lip. 'Jesus, you two,' he said.

'What's that supposed to mean?' said Ellwood. The tiny room fell still then. Mace took a step backwards, as if the extra distance might help. Preston thought about that moment back in Axle Six; the whole rebellion thing when Ryan stalked off with Hoyle in tow. *Don't overthink this like you do everything else*, he'd yelled at her. For a second, it looked as if this was going to be payback. But she just stayed silent, staring at him.

'It means,' said Ryan slowly, 'that you're doing that whole Chloe Ellwood thing again, but with Faulkner this time.'

'The *Chloe Ellwood thing*?' she said with fierce emphasis.

Ryan simmered. 'Yeah. The thing you did with me.' Ryan looked coldly at Preston. 'Don't get involved, Faulkner. It'll mean trouble.'

237

Ellwood gave a hollow laugh. 'You know what trouble is, Ryan?' She crossed her arms. 'You're all cut up about cheating on your girlfriend and now you're trying to blame me. But I don't remember you putting up much of a fight at the time.'

'Bitch.'

Ellwood stabbed a finger at him. 'Where is she now, Ryan? Ditched her again, have you?'

Ryan exploded at that. He threw himself across the table at her. The vasc of flowers went down in a spray of cold water. Mace grabbed his arms, trying to restrain him, but Ryan pulled himself free. Ellwood stepped backwards, evading his grasp.

Preston leapt between them, arms out, separating them. The noise was going to attract attention. 'Stop!' he hissed. 'Both of you!'

The heat went out of it all as suddenly as it had come. Ryan stepped clear of the table, pushing the hair out of his face, shrugging Mace off his back. Ellwood wiped her eyes. Her hands were shaking.

Preston said, 'We don't have to like each other, right?' Silent stares and brooding. 'But we need to keep it together for another hour and then it'll all be done.' Mace was trying to tidy the flowers. 'We need to keep moving,' Preston said. 'If security know we're here, they'll find us eventually.'

Ryan seemed convinced eventually. He swore a couple of times under his breath. Then he checked the floor plan on his phone again. 'OK. Let's see what this auditorium looks like,' he said, straightening his clothes.

Ellwood nodded.

*

They made their way out of the office, bunched together. Their line of sight was broken by the curved white wall of the meeting rooms to their left, so they couldn't immediately check what was going on in the Gallery and Charter Foyer beyond – they had to sneak forwards, Ellwood at the front, Preston and Ryan following, and dip their heads round the corner for a moment.

Preston watched a guard move further down the Gallery, walking ponderously with his hands behind his back, looking at the photography. Ryan turned back to the group and gave a nod, and they moved out into the open, walking swiftly, heads down. Preston felt his pulse scamper, but soon they were across the exposed space and against the doors of the Exchange Hall undetected, tucked up against the lush greenery of a couple of broad-leaved indoor plants. There was a low table with a slew of abandoned drinks and three empty chairs. Ellwood looked through the glass panels of the hall doors – ducking down and scowling.

Ryan referred to his phone again, squinting at the floor plan, then looked up at the doors. 'Through here,' he said, 'is the hall. Then, out of the far doors, we come to the Exchange Foyer. From there we can get into the Auditorium.'

'It's busier in there,' Ellwood said. 'Is there another way?'

'Not according to this,' Ryan held up his phone. 'Through the hall, out the other side.'

Mace was at the window now. Preston joined him, glancing swiftly at the space beyond and pulling back. 'Dammit,' he said.

Mace nodded, agreeing with the assessment. Beyond was another large exhibition space: a high curved roof, a bar area, groups of circular tables ringed with leather chairs, an area of relaxed seating across the far side. And the double doors at the far end that Ryan was talking about.

But there must have been thirty people in there, grouped informally around the tables towards the front of the space. They had tablets, newspapers, briefcases and drinks. Some sort of discussion or debate was going on.

'They've got their backs to the doors,' Preston said hopefully.

'All they've got to do is turn, though . . .' Mace murmured.

Ryan said, 'Could we crawl?'

'Across a hundred metres of carpet with no cover?' Ellwood said, ducking back from the window with a scowl. Ryan bristled, clenching his fists. Ellwood calmly checked her father's watch: 8.45 p.m. 'Fifteen minutes,' she said, ignoring his slow-burning resentment, 'then it'll be all change, and these spaces will be full of delegates.'

'So what's the plan?' said Mace.

'OK. Let's walk through,' Ellwood said. There was a pause. Ryan snorted at her. It sounded ridiculously simple. 'We just walk. Really calm. Look like we belong here.'

Ryan indicated his clothes. 'Are you kidding?'

Preston scowled. They were all grime encrusted and stinking. He indicated Mace's goggles, perched in his hair, and his friend pulled them off and pocketed them. Still, this was never going to work. Mace raised his phone to his chin. 'We're about to infiltrate a high-security conference of the country's most powerful politicians,' he said into it, 'by walking in the front door with a cheery wave.'

'Put it away, Mace, for God's sake,' said Preston.

'My colleague Preston Faulkner also present,' hissed Mace, disappointed. 'And others, too.' He held the phone out in the centre of their huddle. 'Introduce yourselves, guys.' Nobody spoke. Ryan looked ready for murder. 'What?' said Mace.

Against the clock and in the absence of any other plan, they lined up, hearts hammering. Ellwood first, Ryan second. Then came Mace, then Preston bringing up the rear. They were all terrified. They readied themselves, pointlessly straightening their filthy clothes.

Then Ellwood pushed open the door and they began to walk.

34

It didn't start well.

At the swish of the doors, a couple of faces from the group turned, and even though Preston had sworn he wouldn't make eye contact, he found himself turning his head their way – three or four anonymous faces looking across the hall at them. Preston walked, staring at Mace's back. But looking casual was impossible; his limbs had gone all rusty and angular and he felt like he was marching. He actually managed to trip at one point, though how he couldn't tell.

Halfway across now. Preston realized with a sense of clinging dread that the talk from the group had dried up to nothing; they'd fallen silent. That could mean only one thing – they were watching the little procession of grubby kids. Preston daren't look to confirm this. *Stay calm. Walk.*

The double doors seemed possible now. *Ten metres away. Maybe only seven.* Someone from the group had stood up.

Then a voice, upraised, said, 'Excuse me.' Preston closed his eyes, tried to keep going. Someone ahead slowed and Preston found himself bundling awkwardly into Mace. They ground to a halt. 'Excuse me!' This time the voice was sharper. Preston could hear footsteps on soft carpet. Someone was coming. *Dammit.*

Then it got immeasurably worse.

The double doors ahead of them opened.

Security were there. Three armed guys in black padded jackets and heavy boots. And with them, Armstrong's assistant, the one who'd discovered them back at M.I.S.T., hiding in the stockroom. Ellwood stopped then, and the line drew to a halt. Two of the security guys had guns. Actual proper guns.

The man in front held a radio to his face and spoke. 'We have them apprehended, sir,' he said, giving a nod to one of his accomplices, a squat figure with a squashed face and a broad flat nose, who responded by lowering his weapon and making his way carefully around them. Armstrong's sidekick regarded them with steely disdain. Security were surrounding them now, three guys each at the point of a silent triangle, looking all SAS at them, cold, hard eyes, square jaws. Armstrong's assistant spoke, and his gaze never left Preston's. 'These are the kids who've been hiding in the toilets.'

The delegates from the meeting had backed away now, white-faced. Preston closed his eyes.

'We are in so much trouble,' said Mace. 'My dad's going to kill me.' He was at the door of the office where they'd been held, craning to get a view of the guard outside. They'd been frog-marched through the exhibition halls and out towards the rear of the centre where they wouldn't be seen. There, in a collection of workspaces and meeting rooms, an airless little cell had been cleared and they'd been locked up. Mace completed his assessment of the guards outside. 'There'll be black helicopters on the roof,' he said mysteriously.

'What's he on about?' said Ryan, scowling over his shoulder as he peered upwards at the hung ceiling of their prison. There were no gaps, pipes or vents. Just an air-con system. When the guys with guns had locked them in here, they'd chosen carefully. Now there was one of them stationed outside, and Armstrong's assistant had gone, Preston guessed, to let Armstrong know the threat had been neutralized.

Preston sighed. 'Mace is always like this,' he said. 'Go on. Tell us how this is all linked to a secret society.'

Mace threw up his hands. 'I am one hundred and ninety-five per cent serious, brotherman,' he said, stabbing the air with an extended finger. 'Black helicopters are the emergency vehicles of some sinister military order. There'll be a whole fleet of them on the roof right above us, I bet. I read about it on the net.'

'Yeah,' said Ryan. 'On a website with a black background and fifteen different fonts.'

'What's wrong with that?' spluttered Mace, aghast.

'Can we stop this?' Ellwood said. She was straight-backed and pensive, chewing her lower lip and checking her watch with twitchy regularity. 'We need a plan.'

There was a frustrated silence. Ryan pulled a chair from under the table and sat, tipping himself back on his long legs. 'Chloe. Your last plan was *let's just walk through*. I don't think we'll be trusting you to dream up a classic. Why not ask your new boyfriend?'

Preston bit his lip at this and prayed he didn't blush. But he felt the heat in his neck and cheeks all the same. Ryan could be a prick sometimes.

Ellwood gave him the finger. 'Screw you.'

Ryan laughed bitterly, waving her away. 'There's no way out of here,' he said. He glanced at his phone. 'And in five minutes, Armstrong starts. They'll keep us here until he's made his speech – make sure we don't rain on his beautiful parade. Then it'll be the cops.'

'Or worse,' said Mace. Preston nodded. When he found out, Armstrong wouldn't be letting them go. He'd be arranging a number of unfortunate accidents.

Mace had his phone out again. 'A claustrophobic office space is our prison,' he muttered darkly. 'Low ceilings, no windows. An elongated table with six chairs. An armed guard outside and – I'm guessing – a fleet of black helicopters on the foyer roof.' Mace's hysteria had no place here, Preston thought, making fists with his hands. He was about to shout him into silence when the door opened.

It was sudden and unexpected. It was Armstrong.

Elliot Mason was so shocked he dropped his phone and it bounced once, tumbling under the table.

Armstrong was dressed in a chalk-stripe grey suit, white shirt and blue tie. His eyes were the coldest things Preston had ever seen; his jaw was tight and his lips were thin and bloodless. He stared at the assembled group.

The worst thing, Preston realized suddenly, was this: when he saw Chloe Ellwood, his face betrayed nothing. Not a flicker of recognition for the daughter of the man he'd murdered. The girl back from the dead.

Ellwood, though – she was giving it everything she had just to stay upright. Preston watched her as she struggled to keep hold of herself. She'd grabbed the back of a chair and her arms, bare below her rolled-up shirtsleeves, had come up in goosebumps. Her eyes had filled up and she had to blink them clear of tears.

Armstrong's icy gaze took each of them in. Beneath his eyes, grey skin gathered in bags, and when he blinked they quivered. He held a hand out stiffly. 'Phones,' he said.

There was immediate compliance. Ryan, white-faced, handed his over. Preston gave his up; Mace turned to collect his from the floor, but terror got the better of him, and he froze in his standing position, trying not to tremble. 'I only have a moment,' said Armstrong, pocketing the devices. He seemed frighteningly calm. Preston had never been so scared of anybody in his life. He'd read about psychopaths before – people without any empathy or remorse – and he knew then, as he watched Armstrong's emotionless dismissal of Ellwood's presence, that he was listening to one. The man spoke with a finger upraised. His cufflinks were gold. 'Let me make this very clear,' Armstrong said. He blinked his grey eyes once and began his list, counting on his fingers. 'You will not speak to anyone about what you have seen. You will not communicate anything of your visit to Axle Six. You will not discuss or describe the work of the Manchester Institute of Science and Technology. You will have no further contact with Mr Jonathan Shade or Miss Esther Klein.' He looked at each of them again. Ellwood looked back at him. She'd found some strength somewhere, mustered something close to defiance. Ryan, though – he seemed to have shrunk. And by the look of him, it was all Mace could do to stay on his feet and breathe. Armstrong carried on, his voice chilly and measured. 'And let me be equally clear of the consequences of disobedience,' he said. The word *disobedience* sounded horrific the way Armstrong said it – as if it would be the most sickening mistake in the world. He checked his watch – it was heavy and glistened – and continued. 'Your liberty,' he said, 'is at stake.' It took a moment's silence for that to truly sink in. Mace was biting back tears, his shoulders jumping the way they do when you're on the edge of crying. Armstrong smiled, and it looked reptilian. 'If any of you here were to go missing again, your families would be devastated. And, of course, if you went missing this time, it wouldn't be alongside others. You would be missing *and alone.*' He rubbed his dry palms together. Preston thought of being the only person alive BTV. Him and Robinson Crusoe. 'It would be a desperate and sad way to spend your final days,' said Armstrong. 'Wouldn't it?' He made for the door, then turned. 'I have a speech to give,' he said. 'We will talk again afterwards.'

The door clicked softly shut behind him.

Mace fell against the table like a stringless puppet.

The idea of being forced back through the valve – of having to relive that journey, arrive alone at that place, was like a bullet in the gut. Nobody spoke as they contemplated it. Mace made it to a chair, then folded his arms, dropped his head against the table, and trembled. Ryan stared at the wall unblinking.

Preston thought about Shade. Of all the things Armstrong had warned them against, that one stood out. He'd named the nightwardens. That meant they presented a threat to him, even now. What had he said to Esther once? *The only way is forward.* They had to expose Armstrong, and they had to do it tonight. Or they'd be heading back BTV. Shade would arrive. He'd said nine. Even now, he might be crossing the city.

'What time is it?' Preston said, his voice a broken croak.

Ellwood checked. 'Nine eleven p.m.' She was thinking the same thing as he was. Armstrong would be on stage now. They needed to be out and through the halls towards the other side of the building; they needed to be running for the Exchange Auditorium.

This was close to all over.

Ellwood hammered the table with her fist and yelled her rage and frustration. She swore and ranted. Mace looked nervously at Preston. They backed off, gave her some space to mourn. Ryan watched impassively.

After Ellwood's rage had burnt itself out, Preston couldn't help but pace. He asked the time twice: 9.16 p.m. came the answer, then 9.25 p.m. *Where was Shade?* He squinted out of the office window at the guard. Mace went searching for his phone under the table.

And Ellwood sat nursing her hands, her knees up against her chest, her face distant and defeated.

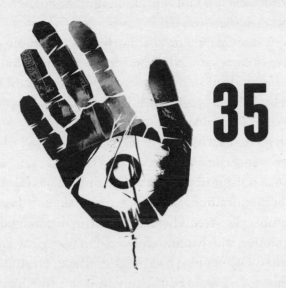

35

It was 9:40 p.m. when it happened.

Mace gave a high-pitched yell. Ryan nearly fell off his chair. Ellwood scrambled to her feet. The door had just buckled inwards – a huge pounding blow had struck it. Someone outside had tried to kick it in. It had held tight.

'Bloody hell', Ryan managed.

Then came another.

The door folded inwards at the second blow and a scrum of bodies fell into the room, a chaotic tangle of limbs. There was a figure framed in the doorway then: a slight grinning kid with dark skin and a mop of black hair.

It was Chowdhury. *It was bloody Chowdhury.* He raised an awkward hand. 'Greetings,' he said. 'All is revealed.'

Preston felt his jaw drop open. *Shade had made it.*

On the floor, Gedge was fighting his way to standing. There was another of Ellwood's crew too, looking stunned by the crush, lying on his back, blinking at the ceiling.

And then there was Alice.

She was on her knees, rubbing her shoulder and grinning. Her eyes were wide and bright, her hair all knotted and filthy, her skin smudged in the chalky grit of Axle Six. She looked fabulous. Preston laughed out loud, a surge of happiness and pride climbing inside.

'Oh my actual God,' Mace managed. Ryan gave a big shout and jumped across the table to her. They held each other for a second, Ryan crushing Alice with relief. He was laughing too.

'Gedge . . .' Alice said through his hair, '. . . is a pretty formidable guy.' Gedge grinned at them, brushing down his filthy clothes with his big left hand. On his right was a night-warden's glove. Ellwood slapped him on the shoulder and they hugged. 'Evening,' Gedge said in his soft Irish accent. He looked embarrassed, dominating the room almost apologetically, holding up a gloved hand.

Preston waited his turn, and when Ryan had put her down, he stood next to Alice. They were as near to each other in that small room as they had been in ages. She raised her eyebrows and shrugged, a greeting of sorts.

'Glad you made it,' Preston croaked.

Alice nodded. 'Nice to be home. Well . . . nearly.' She laughed.

Gedge said, 'You'll never guess what happened on the other side.'

'A nightwarden showed up to save you all?' Preston said, imagining what the last few hours must have been like for Shade. He'd have driven out across the swiftly darkening moor with a van full of databands. He'd have gone through up at the abandoned valve up there, then once BTV, he'd have had to find Alice, find Chowdhury, swerve the Longsight lads, and lead everyone back. Then, somehow, he'd got them across Manchester. Some of them, at least.

Chowdhury frowned. 'Yes,' he said. 'Pretty much exactly that.'

'Is he here?' Preston asked, heart thumping, half hopeful for once. *What time was it? Was there still time?*

Chowdhury gave a half-shrug. 'He said he'd try to be.'

Gedge said, 'So listen. That Shade guy said something about hijacking some sort of speech?'

'It's Armstrong,' Ellwood put in.

Gedge nodded. 'Yeah. Got it. Well, we better get moving. Your security guard said the speeches are nearly finished.' Gedge grinned and raised a gloved hand. 'Before I shook hands with him, that is. Magic stuff, this,' he said.

The Sleeptight. 'It'll wear off quicker than you expect,' said Preston remembering suddenly the morning that started all this; the one where he'd woken in his clothes in his room with a punctured palm and a thumping head.

Ryan made his way forward, Alice with him. They were holding hands now. 'We'd better get moving,' he said. 'We've got maybe ten minutes.'

Mace cleared his throat and everybody stopped. He had his hand raised, like a kid in class. 'Listen,' he said, lowering it self-consciously. 'How do we get back there, exactly?'

'What do you mean?' said Chowdhury.

'I mean,' said Mace, 'There's security out there. Lots of them. And some have got guns. What are we doing? Just running at them?'

Ellwood ran a hand through her hair and let out a long breath. 'Guess so,' she said. 'Anyone got anything better?'

No one spoke.

Mace shook his head. 'This is nuts,' he said. 'Let's just say we do get as far as the speeches. What then? Do we just burst in yelling hellfire?'

Preston had been working on this bit as he'd paced. 'We go in ranks,' he said. 'And we go in silent. We get as far as we can. Ellwood, you need to be up front. All these delegates and politicians, they'll have known your dad, right? They'll recognize you. It'll be a missing-kid-comes-back-from-the-dead moment. We stand there silently.' *We'll be like ghosts*, Preston thought, improvising.

Ellwood looked stunned. She licked her lips. 'Sounds like a plan,' she said. This was their last chance. No time for subtlety.

Outside there were even more kids. Close to thirty of them, all standing shoulder to shoulder in the corridor, kids in torn clothes, some with hollow cheeks, faces lined with fear and fatigue; escapees with nervous glances, some with wild grins; kids who smelt bad, looked ill. Preston didn't recognize most of them. But he did see Fox. His eyes were black and swollen. At the feet of the boys on the front row of the group was the security guard, balled up and dreaming.

This is the stupidest plan ever, Preston thought. Once out into the exhibition space there'd be nowhere to hide. It'd just be a gang of prisoners sprinting through a conference centre looking for a speech to disrupt. Surely their luck was going to run out. 'What time is it?' he croaked.

Ellwood was next to him. Their arms were touching. She shook off her father's watch – the one that was three links too big for her. 'Borrow this,' she said.

Preston blushed. He took it. 'Yeah,' he said. It was 9.54 p.m. Somewhere in an auditorium at the other side of the centre, Armstrong was probably pacing the stage and making his bid for leadership. Maybe he was already accepting the applause. Maybe he'd already contained them long enough to make his great speech and sweep away the secrets of Axle Six and the Kepler valve experiment for ever.

Ryan had no map to check any more – Armstrong had taken his phone – but he'd got the measure of the place. He knew which direction to run in, and that was all they'd need. They had maybe seven minutes. 'This is suicide,' he said as they all lined up. 'Whatever happens, keep running.'

Then they ran out into the light-flooded spaces.

They ran with all the energy they had left; they ran hard, in a pack, Ellwood in the lead, Chowdhury and Gedge and Preston just behind, Mace and Ryan with Alice somewhere off to his left. They coursed across the polished parquet flooring of the main hall under the big arc of the glass roof. It was coming towards changeover for some of the smaller events; workshops and debates were closing and delegates were beginning to come out of smaller rooms into the conference spaces, and as they passed, there were cries and shouts.

They kept running. They made it out across the exhibition hall, their footsteps hammered out and echoing. Thirty kids were sprinting in a pack, thirty-odd wild-eyed children who weren't stopping for anything or anyone.

The crowds thickened, and it stopped being easy to run. Instead, it became like sprinting through a railway station at rush hour; it turned into ducking and weaving, into dodging or shoulder-barging. The pace slowed. Someone's papers scattered. A tray of drinks tipped and shattered; someone slipped and fell. There were furious faces, angry exclamations. A burly grey-haired guy tried to hold Gedge back but the boy shrugged him off and he clattered backwards into a nest of chairs and tables.

They ran on and the thickening crowds started parting as the cry went up.

Cops. There were five or six officers with batons and a couple who looked like an armed-response team, holsters and guns, heading across the open space towards them. Preston caught a commotion off to his right and realized a group of kids had split from the main pack – it looked to be five or six, and one of them was Fox – and were heading for the main foyer and for the freedom of the night. Bad move, he knew. Security were closing in. With the group split, it became harder to track them, but those armed officers were quick and clever. Guns were out.

They were doing well – through the main hall and into the area near the gallery, running through the shouts and exclamations, running past groups of startled delegates, pushing, shoving.

Then the whole vase thing happened and it all went crazy.

A pair of ornate vases, white and purple, had gone over ahead of them, Preston saw. Maybe it had been Chowdhury, over-keen as he wove between tables, heading for the Gallery and the Exchange Hall beyond. Whatever, there was a crash, and shattered porcelain spun in a silver sheet of water sluicing across the floor; big floral displays tumbled. The spaces ahead were plushly carpeted, but the main hall's floor was shiny hardwood. Preston felt his feet go from under him in the wet, and before he could adjust his footing he was down on one hip, skidding and pedalling madly, one hand in the water, trying to push himself up. Someone clattered into him and he heard a couple of other kids go down and then there was a scrum of slipping legs and pushing arms.

Preston could see Chowdhury and Ryan were up ahead, still running, but he was aware of Mace losing his footing somewhere to his left. There was a lot of shouting. Preston was on his back in a pool of icy water. Was Ellwood caught or still free? He didn't know.

He made it to his feet eventually, clothes clinging to him and dripping, but there was already a mob of cops or security by then: angry faces, shouting, radios. They were standing well clear, Preston saw. It was a crooked kind of compliment in a way, the cops making a circle five metres away from them. *Don't try anything crazy*, it said. Mace was at his shoulder, checking his pockets. Making sure his phone was dry, Preston realized, which seemed a pretty screwed-up priority, given they were about to get arrested.

Alice was with them too.

Preston checked Ellwood's watch.

It was one minute to ten.

36

Preston felt too tired to breathe. He looked at the floor, and the smudged puddles of water seemed to pulse. He blinked and tried to focus. To his left, Alice was staring at him, pale and drawn; around him, other exhausted and frightened faces.

Somewhere beyond the edges of the web of cops, Chowdhury and Gedge were being led back, their hands on their heads. They were all caught – all rounded up now. Guns were up and guys were shouting instructions. *Stand still; don't move. Do. Not. Move.* All that stuff.

Then Ryan and Gedge and – *there she was* – Ellwood were pushed into the ring and the Axle Six gang were all trapped together, breathing hard, wiping sweat and water from their faces, eyeing each other warily, part-triumphant for having tried, mostly knackered and defeated.

Preston noticed, as he looked around, the other kids were

all looking at him for something. Alice was imploring him silently. Ryan too.

Weirdly, his memory chose that moment to kindle a little flame.

He remembered what Alice had told him – way back before the madness, right at the start of it all. *Lift your eyes*.

So he looked up. Big iron beams spanned the space above them, and further beyond them was that curved roof – iron and steel inlaid with glass.

Ellwood was next to him now. She was breathing hard from the run. She licked her lips and looked up, following his gaze. 'What?' she whispered. Preston was looking at the clouds underlit by city lights through the grid of fogged ceiling windows. It was dark and shifting up there, amorphous black and sodium yellow.

There was nothing to see except the rain, hammering against the panes, streaking in downward lines of grey diamond. Out there it'd be sending people running, Preston thought – running from bars to cabs home, running to restaurants or running for shelter.

Ellwood rubbed her neck and looked at him. 'Faulkner,' she whispered. 'We're gonna get arrested. Why are we watching the rain?'

Preston stared upwards so hard his neck cricked.

If it could rain inside, he thought, he could get everyone's attention. Get them running. It'd be like cleaning everything up . . .

The stupid joy of the idea must have been painted across his face because Ellwood, looking half worried, half fascinated whispered, 'Why are you smiling?'

Preston checked the white walls of the space – eyes darting

quickly, thinking, searching.

There was one. Of course there was. But it was suicide to go for it. There were guns with live ammo. This was for real. They'd shoot him.

Ellwood nudged him, eyes urgent and blazing, above a big wide smile.

She'd figured it out too.

'I'm going for it,' she said slowly, mouthing the words so he could read her lips. One of the guards in the circle around them was barking orders now. They were closing in. Time was running out.

Preston widened his eyes, imploring her. Crazy talk. 'No way,' he mouthed back.

She held his gaze, fierce and totally crazy. Then she moved, sudden and quick – spun away from him and started running.

It took a moment for him to react. She was really doing it. She was going to get Armstrong or die trying.

Slipping and sliding, turning back into the group, shouldering her way at first, then she started running as hard as she could. The kids from Axle Six parted ahead of her, mostly in fear and shock. Preston took a breath. Then he followed. Ryan sloshed backwards as they pushed their way past, but then Preston heard Ryan's steps as he followed. Now there were three of them. Then Alice gave a high 'Hey!' and joined them too.

Someone was shouting commands; the net of guards was breaking and shifting. 'Stop!' someone yelled, all brutal and hard and frightening. 'Stand still now!' bawled another. 'Now!'

Ahead, Ellwood was flying. She was lithe and strong and

fast, a gazelle. Preston reached the dry flooring beyond the spill, and like Ellwood a moment earlier, felt his feet grip at last. Ellwood was running for the pale grey of the wall, and he followed, his heart like an exploding drum. He was aware as they broke from the group that there were figures converging on them. But Ellwood was out in the open now. Somewhere off to his left, he was aware of noise and lights too. A film crew were shouldering their way in. Someone's camera was rapid-fire clicking and flashing.

He could see a couple of the security guys planting their feet wide, holding up weapons, steadying themselves. This was a colossal gamble. These people wouldn't shoot an unarmed girl, right? Especially an unarmed girl who looked as if she was heading nowhere – running towards a wall. Not with TV news and journalists massing. Instead, Preston guessed, they'd go for some sort of hyper-painful takedown, piling into her like twenty-stone quarterbacks, breaking her bones, pounding her flat.

He just needed her to reach the fire alarm first.

He ran hard, lungs tight and needling, eyes on the girl ahead, and beyond, the little button in the glass-fronted box – shoulder height, slightly recessed, darker against the pale wall. Everything else was peripheral – a streak and a blur. But there were security at a sprint now, weapons down – *thank God* – but closing in, cutting her off, hammering hard and shouting as they went. They were converging on the same point. Ellwood was closer to the target by the look of it, but these guys either side of her, pincering in, were sprinting faster and stronger. She wasn't going to make it.

'Stop!' someone roared again but Ellwood didn't. More camera flashes. From somewhere behind them, it sounded like a cheer was going up.

The guards reached Ellwood. She was clattered down hard, two guys bundling her over into a sliding scrum.

But that left him free. Preston hit the wall so hard he nearly struck himself senseless. He punched the glass of the alarm with a closed fist and his knuckles stung but the glass didn't shift. It smashed on his second attempt and then a figure to his right made contact and he was bundled down in some hard-ass approximation of a rugby tackle and he hit his head on the wall, then he was sprawling on his back on the floor near Ellwood. The breath was forced out of him and he was crushed under some wide-shouldered guy. He couldn't breathe.

For a second, it seemed like nothing had happened. Then he realized he couldn't hear because his head was ringing. Must have been concussion or something; his vision had started shuddering with stars and his ears were full of a high whine. Maybe the fire alarm was going, maybe it wasn't.

The reason he knew it was, in the end, was the water on his face. High up on those beams, the sprinklers were sending great wide fans of rain out in all directions and they were breaking up and falling, misting the huge exhibition space as they fell, beading on the lenses of his goggles, soaking eager journalists and camera crews.

The guard on top of him had him up now, grunting with the exertion of it, yelling something in his face, hauling him up to standing, and Preston could see Ellwood next to him, swatting an arm at a guy dragging her by the hair, shouting. Ryan and Alice had reached them too, and Mace was still running.

And behind Mace, the Axle Six gang. It was like seeing

what prison had done to them for the first time. Together, they looked phenomenally frightening. They'd all put on their goggles: gaunt, skeletal kids with sharp cheekbones, washed-out expressions and big glittering fly-eyes. They were standing shoulder to shoulder, dressed in the wringing-wet clothes they'd been bundled BTV in, all dirty, untucked and tired. The sprinklers were pouring down over them and their hair was flattening and their torn clothes were darkening. And they were all illuminated in stuttering flashes of camera light.

Security were swarming now and men and women with cameras and microphones were being pushed back. Someone was shouting in his ear, gripping his wrists, but all he could hear was high feedback.

Then a journalist with a camera was through security and suddenly close to Ellwood, stuttering off a rapid-fire sequence of shots, and Ellwood's guard was screaming, 'Put that down. No pictures! No pictures!'

Then came the rest of the madness.

Delegates began flooding the hall from the adjoining meeting rooms and auditoria, all running, hunched, from the sprinklers. There were umbrellas up out at the edge of his eyeline, Preston realized. There were queues of suits, groups breaking away and hurrying to the foyer.

The crowds of delegates were caught in a perfect storm as they emerged. The explosions of camera flashes and shoulder-held video cameras bobbing were one thing; the ruck of security guards fighting back journalists and kids was another. But the thing those people would never forget was the sight of the emaciated prisoners in horrible goggles; kids who looked like soaked and starving chimney sweeps, silent in rags all gathered in a gang in the rain.

And at the front now, dragged by a stone-faced security guard, goggles up on her forehead, was a black girl with torn clothes and a face they recognized from the papers.

Then Armstrong emerged from the crowd in a chalk-stripe suit with a blue tie, laughing with a colleague, making light of it all. Until he saw the children. Preston had, just for a second, the sweet sight of the politician's face draining as he saw who'd come back.

Ellwood saw him first and turned.

Whoever had been gripping Preston by the wrists had suddenly let him go, but he couldn't move. All around him it was crazy – cameras, microphones, questions. Eventually Mace looped an arm under his and the two friends began half carrying each other. Preston pushed his goggles up, blinking through the water. There was a mighty ruck of press pushing into the foyer, microphones held up, cameras rolling, heading for Ellwood.

And Shade was there too.

He was giving an interview – passionate, wild-eyed, a kind of ranting spokesman for the prisoners just in shot behind him. What Preston hadn't dared believe was possible looked as if it was true.

The news was out.

It didn't matter a damn what Armstrong had said in his speech earlier. This was going to be the front-page story in the papers tomorrow.

37

A month had passed since the events at Manchester Central during conference season. Preston had been in police custody at first – his dad waiting awkwardly out in the offices or taking extra shifts to avoid the tension – and of course the cops had kept the Axle Six lot apart and they'd collapsed, shattered in separate interview rooms and told their stories over and over again. Weeks had passed like that: hour after hour in stuffy rooms, nights on hard bunks in spartan cells. When Preston's mum heard, she came back up to Manchester and stayed at the flat for a week, and she cried a lot when he told her the story. Once, Mum persuaded Dad to come too and they sat together in an interview room drinking vending-machine coffee – it felt very strange, seeing the two of them like that – and when he told them both again they exchanged glances. Preston knew what those looks meant: they were unspoken conversations with unspoken words in them like *breakdown* or *psychosis* or *therapy*.

Three weeks in to the investigation, the cops lifted Mace's voice memos from his phone and had them analysed. Forensic audio experts had the sound stretched and boosted and flattened and whatever else. They were particularly interested in a conversation that seemed to have been recorded at some distance – it turned out to be from beneath a table – that clearly featured the voice of a certain Christopher Armstrong, MP, saying, 'If any of you here were to go missing again, your families would be devastated. And, of course, if you went missing this time . . . You would be missing and alone.' After that, things went suddenly silent. The next day, the journalists vanished; questions stopped being asked, interviews were concluded.

After that phase came another: the one where Preston was sent back to school. For the first week he only had to go part-time. They'd given Alice separate days so the two of them couldn't talk. It was something about normalizing, whatever that meant; they didn't realize that he couldn't talk to her any more anyway – that he'd broken the friendship the evening the whole night-walking thing had started.

Classes seemed pretty safe and normal, and very dull without Mace – his mum and dad had sent him to another school to give him a fresh start. *A clean break* was the phrase Mace had used, rolling his eyes on the bus home once. They'd bought him a tablet as compensation. He was putting together a dossier on Opus Dei.

Once that term, Preston had met Ryan. It was November. There was a World War One fundraising thing going on in the canteen and the year groups got mixed up for a session on sacrifice which Preston had dreamt his way through.

'Faulkner.' He was queuing for coffee. The bell had just gone for break. Mock exams were coming up so there were a bunch of Year Elevens shuffling cue cards, pissing about with gel pens. Some Sixth Formers were watching YouTube videos on a shared phone. Conversation with Ryan was difficult. They talked about Alice a bit – she and Ryan were going out together again – they had a stilted exchange about the Jupiter Hand. Ryan was all twitchy and distracted.

In the end he said, 'Ever think about Axle Six?'

Preston tried a smile. *All the damn time.* But he shook his head.

Ryan sipped his coffee. 'I do,' he said. He pushed his hair back. 'All the damn time.' Preston knew him well enough now to guess what was happening. He needed to get beyond those glass doors in the foyer and out into the rainswept night to explore the shore of that black sea beyond.

The funerals were later that month.

There was only a small crowd gathered at the cemetery. It was a private thing, so the gates were closed as soon as the cars pulled in. There was a thin frost on the gravestones. The trees were empty cages and the last of their leaves spun in idle circles on the paths between the graves.

His dad kept a respectful distance so Preston could catch up with his friends. There were six graves, one for each of the boys who'd died coming through the valves. The holes were fringed with what looked like green baize: a frame around six dark mouths like trapdoors dropping down into the dark. When Macc, Alice and Preston converged at the graveside, it felt all weird and dislocated. Preston swallowed a couple of times, struggling for words.

Mace talked secret societies for a few minutes, filling space.

Then Alice gave Preston a half-hearted smile. 'How was it with Chloe?' she asked.

Difficult. He'd seen her once before she went back to London just after the last of the police interviews, in the foyer of the station.

She'd been in a weird mood, waiting in reception, her mum out in the car. 'I'm going home,' she'd said by way of explanation. 'Couldn't leave Manchester without saying a final goodbye to my wingman.' He'd tried to brush the comment off with a grin, but it crushed him. She'd smiled conspiratorially, said something like, 'Don't we get prison tattoos now? Like lifers have? Spiderwebs.'

Preston hadn't known what to say. 'Can I maybe give you a call?' he'd stammered.

Ellwood had raised an eyebrow. She was wearing a cashmere sweater, dark jeans, high-tops. She had little silver studs in her ears. It made him ache. 'Sure,' she said. It seemed like a way forward for a second, but when she'd handed the number over, she'd added, 'Journalists keep getting hold of it. I change it a lot. If there's no answer, you'll know why.'

He memorized it; called her three days later, hands jumping stupidly as he punched in the digits.

There'd been no answer.

'Fine, I think,' Preston said.

After that, Mace held the newspaper between them and they read silently about Armstrong's trial. Sentencing wasn't expected until the new year. Special arrangements had been made so witnesses could testify by video link. All of that was to come.

*

At the gravesides, each of them paid their respects. Holes like the mouths of valves, doorways into darkness. Alice had brought flowers. They started with the boy from the Castlefield valve, the poor kid whom Esther Klein had carried into the warehouse the night shutdown started. No one knew his name and they didn't want to ask. They didn't visit the others. This one boy would stand for all of them.

The sky was dark-grey like iron. Alice had a taxi waiting for her. 'I have to go,' she said eventually. 'We should meet up some time.'

Press smiled. Mace nodded. Both knew it wasn't going to happen. Just as she turned to go, Preston said, 'Alice.' She turned. She didn't look young any more. 'I'm sorry,' he said.

She nodded, slowly.

Then she walked across the frosted grass to the waiting taxi.

38

Ryan pushed his way through the hatch and hauled himself up into the silent white corridor.

Ahead was the door that would take him back through to Axle Six. Beyond, he could hear the dark sea thunder. He leant back through the hatch to give Chowdhury a hand, lifting him until they collapsed against the corridor wall together. Below, he could hear Shade grunting with exertion. Soon, the nightwarden's face appeared, his forehead beaded in sweat.

The three of them spent a couple of seconds gathering themselves, wiping plaster dust from their hands and steadying their breathing. Ryan waited, hands on knees, then, when the others were ready, gave a nod. They headed for the door.

Beyond, the escalators freewheeled pointlessly, creaking and hissing in the generator light. There was no talk. There was nothing to say. They rode them upwards.

At the top, Ryan crossed the lobby and cupped his hands against his temples, leaning into the blackness of the glass doors. He watched the never-ending storm rage in silence on the other side, listening to the heartbeat thud of water on rock.

Next to him, Chowdhury whispered, 'This is where he lives.'

'How do you know?' the nightwarden asked.

Chowdhury stood back from the glass and cocked his head. He fanned his hands as usual and intoned slowly, 'I saw it all in a vision.'

Shade looked at Ryan, his face saying, *Is this kid for real?*

Ryan gave an apologetic shrug. 'Jesus, Chowdhury,' he said.

Shade said, 'But you're certain, right?'

'As certain as I've ever been about anything,' said Chowdhury dreamily, his nose against the glass. 'This is where he lives.'

'An old guy. With a beard. Out here on this side of the valve.' Shade waited for confirmation, biting his lip.

Chowdhury nodded, forehead pressed to the glass as he did so. There was a long and tetchy silence.

Eventually it happened. Something out there in the darkness moved. And it wasn't the bobbing of plants and trees in the teeth of the wind. It was a service hatch.

Ryan hadn't noticed it before. Out beyond the glistening helipad, off to the left near the high chain-link fence, beyond the valves where Hoyle had vanished, there was a circular lid – the plug of a manhole. And as Ryan and Shade and Chowdhury watched, the trapdoor shifted. It was being pushed from below, lifted. A figure emerged, moving with swift confidence. Something in his actions suggested a routine, practised and repeated.

It was an old man. He had very thin arms – Ryan could see the struts and ribs of bone, the knobs and knuckles of his elbows and fingers beneath the rags he wore. His muscles, though – they were sinewy and strong. He had a stoop, and a long beard, just like Chowdhury had said, matted and tangled with wild grey hair. He pulled himself out of the service hatch and stayed in a crouch while he shifted the lid back. He had a shoulder bag which he shrugged free, and from it, he pulled what looked like some sort of torch and headed for the cliff edge, one arm sheltering his eyes against the wind and rain.

Shade was stock-still and silent, standing in the way a man does when he's holding his breath. He shifted position, cupped his hands tighter to block out the fluorescents, and squinted into the ink, watching the bony figure in rags at the edge of the compound, battered by the wind. He had a familiar look.

He was holding up his torch and flashing it out across the grey foam-topped breakers. He was signalling. Was there someone else out there? A boat riding the mad black water? Or had the poor guy been sending out that hopeless sequence for ever?

'You've got to be kidding me,' Ryan whispered.

He lost track of time just watching. He didn't know how long the man was out there. But as the long minutes went by, the torch faded and eventually the guy gave up.

Ryan twitched nervously. Something made him want to hide. If the guy turned, he'd surely see three unmistakable silhouettes thrown into relief by the blood-red generator lights. Sure enough, as the old man began picking his way back to the dark circle of the trapdoor, he caught sight of the figures watching him.

The man didn't seem shocked. He stood stock-still, ignoring the swirl of the rain. It was hard to see what expression that deeply-lined face wore, but it wasn't anger, Ryan figured, or surprise. Mostly, he guessed, it was a kind of weary sadness.

Shade put his hand across his mouth and seemed to splutter. He looked close to crying.

'Mister,' said Chowdhury. 'You OK?' The nightwarden managed a nod in response. 'Robinson Crusoe,' Chowdhury said with a grin. 'I told you. It's Robinson Crusoe.'

Shade put his forehead against the glass. His breath made an inverted moon. 'It's not Robinson Crusoe,' he said. 'It's my brother.'

Out in the darkness on the other side of the glass, Robinson Crusoe raised a hand and held it up, open in greeting.

Shade did the same, uncertain at first, then with a grim determination. He splayed his palm against the glass, making a web in the mist of his breath, pressing hard, holding it there.

For a second or two, nobody moved.

Then, the other man lifted the lid of the hatch and dropped back down into his prison.

Author's Note: Manchester, Darkly

Lifers is set in a place called Dark Manchester – a kind of spooked-out-cousin of real Manchester. The two cities share similarities. For instance, if you happen to live in Dark Manchester, you can still walk from the Beetham Tower to the Cathedral in a long straight line. You can still watch the footy in The Moon Under Water or borrow a book from the Central Library on St Peter's Square. You can still get lost in the Northern Quarter trying to find that bootleg burger bar that turns out to have been burnt down the fortnight before.

Such are the similarities, in fact, that residents of Dark Manchester actually think they live in real Manchester. Only you and I know differently. Because there are differences: Dark Manchester is a city of cranes and – as Elliot Mason points out – new blocks and towers net spare squares of sky every day, which makes it a good place for urban explorers. There are more alleys in Dark Manchester, a whole tangle of cunning corner-cutting passageways and boltholes. And in Dark Manchester, very weird stuff happens at night.

Smaller stuff is different too. In Dark Manchester, you can cycle between the Civil Justice Centre and St Ann's Square using only backstreets. The roof of the convention centre is made of glass so that Preston Faulkner can look up through it to the storm-clouds above. Buses run at different times and cops work different shifts – almost as if they're conjured up to serve the purposes of a plot.

I point all this out in case residents of real Manchester take issue with the positions, directions, aspects or characteristics of any streets, squares, parks, gardens or tower blocks in this story.

Or in case some of the braver ones find Back Half Moon Street and follow it into the dark, looking for a left-hand turn.

ACKNOWLEDGEMENTS

I owe a debt of gratitude to so many people who helped me during the writing of this book. First, to Imogen Cooper. A lesser editor might have despaired as I found more and more intricate ways to mess up the middle of this story. Imogen didn't. Her patience and intelligence are superhuman. Golden Egg Academy members – you have yourself a 24-carat legend. To Barry Cunningham, who somehow seemed to know it would come out right in the end and whose encouragement, insight and calm advice was invaluable. To Kesia Lupo, who seemed to know instinctively and precisely which scenes were destined for the cutting-room floor, and Laura Myers for her expertise, feedback and support. A round of raucous applause for everyone at Chicken House. Thanks to Ben for his thoughtful guidance, energy and cheerful good humour. And of course to Jo, for everything.

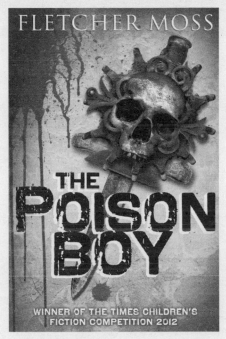

THE POISON BOY by FLETCHER MOSS

Orphan Dalton Fly, food taster to the rich, has a lucky escape after discovering poisoned wine. But his mate dies horribly, and Dalton wants justice.

Together with Scarlet Dropmore, the high-born girl whose life he saved, he sets out to find the murderers.

'The author knows just where to leave his story, with readers satisfied yet panting for more. Bravo.'
THE TIMES

Paperback, ISBN 978-1-908435-44-6, £6.99

THE MAZE RUNNER by JAMES DASHNER

When the doors of the lift crank open, the only thing Thomas can remember is his first name. But he's not alone. He's surrounded by boys who welcome him to the Glade, an encampment at the centre of a bizarre maze.

Like Thomas, the Gladers don't know why or how they came to be there, or what's happened to the world outside. All they know is that every morning when the walls slide back, they will risk everything to find out . . .

'A dark and gripping tale of survival set in a world where teenagers fight for their lives on a daily basis.'
PUBLISHERS WEEKLY

Paperback, ISBN 978-1-909489-40-0, £7.99 • ebook, ISBN 978 1 908435-48-4, £7.99

ALSO AVAILABLE:

THE SCORCH TRIALS

Paperback, ISBN 978-1-909489-41-7, £7.99 • ebook, ISBN 978-1-908435-49-1, £7.99

THE DEATH CURE

Paperback, ISBN 978-1-909489-42-4, £7.99 • ebook, ISBN 978-1-908435-35-4, £7.99

THE KILL ORDER

Paperback, ISBN 978-1-909489-43-1, £7.99 • ebook, ISBN 978-1-908435-69-9, £7.99

IF YOU WERE ME by SAM HEPBURN

Not long after Aliya's family escapes Afghanistan for Britain, her brother is accused of a bomb attack. Aliya is sure of his innocence, but when plumber's son Dan finds a gun in their bathroom, what's she to think?

Dan has his own reasons for staying silent: he's worried the gun might have something to do with his dad. Thrown together by chance, the two of them set out to uncover a tangled and twisted truth.

'A tense and gripping thriller . . .'
SCOTTISH BOOKTRUST

Paperback, ISBN 978-1-909489-80-6, £6.99 • ebook, ISBN 978-1-910002-42-1, £6.99